PIED PIPER: A DEMMONICA DARK ROMANCE

Grim and Sinister Delight #6

EMMA JAYE

CONTENTS

Editing Team:
SublimeNovels.com
Cover Design
Miblart

Follow Emma Jaye via the following platforms for

exclusive teasers, giveaways, and more:

FACEBOOK

FACEBOOK GROUP

NEWSLETTER

emmajayeauthor.com

GOODREADS

WARNING

These books are for adult readers who enjoy stories where the lines between right and wrong are blurred. High heat, twisted and tantalizing, these are not for the faint of heart.

SILENCE IS GOLDEN WHEN WORDS CAN KILL.

The best thing the only male siren can do is die, without ever saying another word. One more night of life proves one too many. His mother's family wants Domino alive until he's fulfilled the prophecy of fathering the most powerful siren ever to exist. Then his bones will become commodities on a mage's shelf.

Goading his captors into ending his miserable, guilt-ridden existence fails thanks to a new, irritating, and cheerful abductor who claims to be saving his life but lies through his teeth.

Silent sarcastic sirens with a death wish aren't Jude's typical bounty. But the job to return a runaway to his mage father sounds like easy money for the leopard shifter. Money that will help fund Jude's only goal in life, ending the rats who murdered his family.

Not getting involved with his bounties is a life rule Jude never breaks, but there is something about this kid, besides having a voice that could wipe out every rat in existence with a word.

Bone amulets, prophecies, and shifters bind this dark web of secrets that could cost not only their lives but the world.

Pied Piper is a dark paranormal romance set in the same DeMMonica world as Emma Jaye's Incubus series.

Grim and Sinister Delights is a dark romance series based on classic fairy tales and stories. You will find standalone tales of gay romance

that range in darkness and kinks. If you dare to take the challenge, read them all to find yourself lost in a classic that you think you know. These stories are for adult readers and may contain morally ambiguous themes.

CHAPTER ONE

Watching the rising sun glint on the water, Domino could almost believe he was at home, except for the lack of waves. As he honed his left thumb talon, the familiar rhythmic scrape of the nail file reminded him of the hiss of the surf.

The couple walking on the other side of the river didn't even stare as he sat with his sweats pulled up and his bare feet in the rising water. They should be staring; the temperature was barely above freezing.

The inescapable, depressing conclusion was that the locals had grown used to him and his peculiar ways. A month ago, he would have moved when he saw the couple coming, would have hidden, would have cared. Complacency. An elegant word for an ugly, depressing descent into oblivion.

Death might be closer to him than for the humans he hid amongst. Only six months ago, he would have sworn he'd be damned if he'd go quietly. He'd spent his entire life hiding and intended to experience what life had to offer before he bowed out. He'd done most of the things any dedicated hedonist craved, but here, in the quiet of the dawn, it wasn't enough. It'd never be enough.

He'd never experience the high of getting something he'd worked for years to achieve. There would be no academic or work accolades, no partner he knew better than himself to welcome him home.

He huffed, breath visible in the chilly air. His life's greatest achievement would be not achieving his so-called destiny. Even his ultimate positive was a negative. Not being born at all would have been better for the world.

A car driving past broke his thoughts. He wondered where the driver was going, their plans for today. Anyone his age would be headed home after a night out, or be preparing for work, college, their future.

Tonight's agenda would be the same as last night, the same as every other night —oblivion and pleasure, because he had nothing else. It beat the alternative, for now anyway. Dancing, sex, and alcohol, or maybe he'd just watch others experience and enjoy things they shouldn't, just for the hell of it.

Domino could get all of that right here in this odd inland port. Finding somewhere else as safe as this would take time, but he'd already been here two months. He had zero enthusiasm for moving on, but he didn't want to stay in this limbo either. That the net must be closing in again was the only factor that got him moving away from the water rather than jumping in and riding the freshwater flow to the sea.

If any siren sorority caught him, he'd probably spend the rest of his days chained to a rock in an ocean cave. Touching the ocean again would almost be worth it. He bet all the siren sororities knew about him by now. There would be spies in every port and seaside town on the planet, watching, waiting. A shiver that had nothing to do with the temperature stormed up his spine.

With his lack of enthusiasm for running again, maybe the time had come to head further inland. Even when dead, his family would find a use for him, if they found his bones. When the end sprinted toward him, rather than its current stroll, he'd head as far from the sea as possible.

He already had a van kitted out for his final journey. The tank full of brackish water from the river would hopefully get him further than his kin could track. Once in the middle of nowhere, he'd simply start walking, dig himself a hole, and inject the syringe of heroin he'd prepared months ago. However much dirt he'd be able to pile over himself before the drug took him would have to be enough to hide his body.

On a whim, he took a coin from his pocket. Tails he'd go now. He flipped it, watching as the silver surface reflected the rays of the rising sun. He caught it, slapped it on the back of his hand, numb as to the outcome. He lifted his hand.

Heads.

Domino put the coin and his nail file away, got up, automatically pulling his broad-brimmed hat down. He'd flip the coin again tomorrow; it was as good a plan as any.

TOO LATE, TOO DAMN LATE.

Domino nodded his acknowledgment to the black-haired man who'd been scanning the club ever since he entered. Dimly lit, full of anonymous sweaty, horny bodies, Blaze was as close as Domino got to feeling safe.

At first, Domino assumed "leather jacket guy" was just

trying to hook up like everyone else, but he had a presence, an aura, the humans didn't. Shifter, demon, or something new, Domino didn't care, but the guy could see him in the dark from across the club. Even with his mask and every inch of skin covered, he'd been identified.

The way the man stiffened, shocked that Domino had spotted him, gave a shot of pleasure. The hunter underestimated his prey. Domino hoped to shock him a few more times before the game ended. That the contest would end in his death, Domino didn't doubt. Where that death occurred, and how much it cost the hunter, would be the prize.

Domino had left his van parked just beyond the entrance to the alley behind the club. Maybe with a head start, he could still execute his plan, but he needed a distraction.

A familiar figure swerved through the crowd, touching, teasing. Even though the costume hid Rory's features, the way he moved and interacted with his fellow clubbers singled him out.

Rory stopped in front of Domino, tilted his head, mimed panting with his hands raised. Over the last few weeks, he and Rory had become something of an item. Using Rory's sweet submissive side for his own purposes was unforgivable, but if it worked, Domino wouldn't be here to forgive. Stroking down the shorter, broader man's latex covered butt, he squeezed. The man in the pup costume shivered at the flash of erotic pain and looked up at him. Domino indicated the hunter with his chin, setting the game in motion.

The door to the club opened. Domino cursed. The man sweating in the leather jacket might be a new mysterious foe, but the three canine shifters were familiar; they and the other member of their four-strong pack had been on his tail for months. He'd last seen them lurking around the day before boarding the flight that dumped him here.

Why the fuck didn't I listen to that inner alarm bell this morning?

Because, deep down, he'd wanted to connect with another living being one more time. Tonight, Rory wore a full costume to hide the marks of passion Domino had left on his body the night before. Although Rory liked pain, Domino preferred to bite and suck on his pale skin, rather than hitting him. The livid red marks would fade in time, but seeing them gave Domino a sense of being present in the world.

As always, Rory understood what Domino wanted without him saying a word. A pointed glance, a gesture, and Rory obeyed. Maybe his kink of playing at being an animal helped him understand non-verbal communication. Out of role, Rory couldn't stop talking and often took on the chore of communicating Domino's wishes to others.

Domino would miss his company, in and out of the bedroom, but perhaps this way was best. Rory would be sad, confused, and likely hurt, but he'd cope with being abandoned. The man was a butterfly, flitting from one partner to the next. Hopefully, the next man in line would ask who had left the marks on Rory's body, but now it was time to go.

Cold hit Domino as he forced his way out of the emergency exit, breath steaming. His outfit was designed to cover skin, not keep it warm, but he didn't intend to be outside long enough to freeze.

Domino got halfway down the rubbish and condom-strewn alley before he knew he'd fucked up. Adrenaline rushed faster when a familiar blue van, his van, pulled across the alley entrance, blocking it, tires squealing. The side door slid open. Another heavily built shifter hopped out, holding a ball gag and cuffs.

Inside Blaze, his pursuers probably wouldn't have tried anything too drastic with a club full of human witnesses. The edict from the Supernatural Council, to conceal knowledge of supernaturals from humanity might have provided some protection.

Domino spun to face the more significant threat, the three shifters exiting the club. As one, all three men pulled identical silver chains with bone pendants out of their shirts. *Protection amulets.*

Jaw clenching at the insult to his word, Domino knew who had sent them. Only the bone of a relative could protect the wearer from a siren's song. His family were trying to reclaim him before the end. They could go fuck themselves. Being taken alive wouldn't happen.

He'd been sharpening his thumb talon for exactly this scenario, but if he could get somewhere where they couldn't recover his body, he'd take that option first. Ending up as a hundred amulets or as powder on a witch's shelf was almost his ultimate horror.

The amulets meant his family assumed he'd go back on his vow of silence when things got tough. It proved how little they knew him. He wouldn't use his voice, not even to save his life, when innocents were within earshot. He might not have many morals, but humans didn't deserve to die as collateral damage in a supernatural dispute.

Hungry smiles, wide stances. These dogs expected, yearned, for him to fight, provide a little entertainment, before they delivered him back to his family. Between the van and the alley walls, they had him boxed in, but if they wanted a fight, they'd get one. Siren song wasn't the only weapon Domino possessed.

His cousins could find another way to bolster their sorority. Even if they were the last holes on Earth, Domino wouldn't be shoving his dick in any of them.

There hadn't been a male siren for a thousand years, but somehow, fate had kicked out an impossible random turd, him. If he'd had a shred of decency, of courage, he would've killed himself as soon as he'd found out about the prophecy. And yet, he'd spent the last five years drinking and fucking his way towards his supposed expiration date with grim determination. The alcohol and sex with strangers didn't even do it for him that much anymore, but the atmosphere, the sheer raw hedonism of Blaze, drew him like a fish on a line. And he'd been well and truly caught.

"Easy now, boy, come quietly," the curly-haired shifter on the right said. All three had similar features, broad noses and red hair. The one speaking was bigger than the others, the alpha. He would still bleed.

With a wave, the alpha gestured his two betas forward. The one yellow bulb above the exit made their shadows reach for Domino like giants, but sometimes the little guy got lucky.

Domino feinted right. The smaller beta, clearly the youngest, grabbed for his arm. Domino flicked his thumb, opening a slice in the man's bicep.

The beta hissed, hand going to the heavily bleeding wound as he dropped back. The alpha and the other beta growled, spreading out. Another enemy lurked behind, but Domino couldn't risk turning his back on these three.

"That was uncalled for; he wasn't trying to hurt you," the big beta growled. Lines creased the skin beside his eyes as he concentrated on Domino. This one had experience, maybe more than the alpha.

The big beta carried on talking, inching forward. "Our

contract is to take you home. It says nothing about your condition, except they'll pay more if you're breathing and with your cock and balls intact."

A voice came from behind. "I can't understand why he's fighting at all. Living in luxury, fucking willing sirens? Not a bad life, even if it is short."

That they knew about his impending death didn't surprise Domino; his family would have given the information to speed his capture.

Putting his back to the wall let Domino see all four attackers. The biggest beta grabbed for his wrists as the other had done. Domino crouched, thrusting up with his sharpened talon, trying to keep his opponent at bay, to give some time for help to arrive. Rory would have seen what had happened, would be getting help.

Once, twice, he thrust, the beta lunged. His talon stabbed into the beta's throat. Hot fluid burst over Domino's hand, he pulled back in shocked disgust.

In silence, the beta went to his knees, hands grabbing at his neck.

Domino froze, stared, hand dripping with hot blood, not quite believing what he'd done.

A meaty fist cracked against Domino's cheek. His shoulder hit the filthy, freezing concrete before he realized he'd been punched. His mask spun from his face. Blinking, he fought for consciousness. Hands seized his wrists, pulled them behind his back. At the same time, a hand that stank of burgers forced a huge ball gag between his lips, almost taking a few teeth with it.

"Ulrike, do something." The panic in the younger shifter's voice curled around Domino but didn't sink in as he hung onto consciousness with his fingertips.

"Let's get out of here," a deeper voice replied.

Going from horizontal to vertical, an arm under his shoulder, had Domino's head spinning even faster. He tried to step forward, but his legs refused to hold him. His knees buckled. The alpha dragged him forward, one arm under his armpit. Domino found himself on his side, face squashed against the water tank in his van. The vehicle rocked as a dead weight landed next to him.

"Hey, let him go!"

Domino didn't recognize the voice, but the sound was cut off by the engine roaring, and the van took off.

"What do we do? I've tried licking it; it's not working!" A frantic voice beside him contrasted with gut-churning gurgling noises.

"Out of the way, let me see." Bodies moved around him. "Aw shit. Ran, Ranulfo, listen to me, listen to your alpha." The hard voice didn't stop the gurgling noise. "You get the honor of representing the pack in the afterlife, guard our way, carve us a place, understand?"

"No, no, he can't be. Ran, please, don't die." Through the frantic voice, and the engine, Domino wasn't quite sure of the moment when the gurgling stopped, when the man he'd killed died.

His own heart stuttered. *Again, I did it again.*

"Kill him, Ulrike, or I will. I demand vengeance for our brother." Cold anger dripped from the voice of the driver.

"Think for once, Tunstall. He wouldn't want to have died in vain; the siren is worth three times as much alive. I know this is hard, but we can get something for Ran too with the dead or alive bounty."

"You're going to sell his body?" the other shifter, the one who had been panicking, didn't sound as though he believed his ears.

"It's what he'd want, Rollin. He doesn't need it

anymore. I've still got contacts that'll hand him over for a cut. With the bounties on Ran and the siren, we'll be able to start afresh somewhere else. The pack is all that counts, my brothers, you know that."

Given his own kind's attitude to a person's remains, Domino shouldn't have been shocked, but the hot blood of the man he'd killed still soaked into his shirt. Would his family wait until he stopped breathing before carving up his body? He pictured a line that stretched into the distance of sirens, mages, and witches all eagerly waiting for their portion.

"Now let's make sure our meal ticket stays quiet, shall we? He might not be able to influence us because of the amulets, but he can still control everyone else within earshot. I've no wish to be attacked by a crowd of brain-washed humans."

A weight landed on his legs as he lay on his front. He couldn't move his arms. Sometime in the scuffle the cuffs he'd seen must have been put on him. Twisting and struggling didn't dislodge the heavy body riding him.

"You sure this'll work? It doesn't work on demons," the shifter sitting on him growled out. Domino couldn't see anything except the green metal tank he'd filled with water from the tidal river.

The plan had been to open the tap, run the water he needed over whatever exposed skin he could. A bucket would catch the remains so he could use the same water over again until he depleted its life force.

"He's a siren, not a demon, and the human said he likes smoking weed. He wouldn't do that if human drugs didn't affect him. Speaking of which..." the driver, Tunstall, said.

The van slowed. The door opened and shut before it took off again.

"No, not in his butt, a vein, it needs to go in a vein to work quickly. Here, I'll do it."

Domino stilled at Rory's voice. *He's in on it?* He'd felt betrayed by his family, but they'd never really pretended to love or even like him, but Rory? He'd thought they had something, at least mutual affection, friendship. Something tugged at his sleeve. The cloth ripped. A needle pierced the inside of his elbow.

Automatically, he started counting. *Five, six, seven–* The drug hit, he relaxed. Nothing mattered, nothing at all.

Strong hands rolled him over, and he stared up at the battered ceiling of the van. Three faces peered down at him, two with ginger hair; two twisted with hatred and lust. Rory's eyes sparkled with excitement.

"Fuck, that mark's ugly; no wonder he..."

Their words faded as lassitude stole over his limbs. His eyes fluttered closed as a last coherent thought swirled. If they'd used the syringe he'd prepped, he wouldn't wake up.

His family would be furious.

CHAPTER TWO

"Touch my ass again and I'll break your fingers," Jude smiled cheerfully at the handsy guy behind him in the queue. It was bad enough having to wait outside this dive to get in without being groped too.

"Jeez, just trying to say hi," the man murmured.

After getting a nod from the doorman who looked as if his prime strategy for subduing miscreants would be to sit on them, Jude took a last breath of relatively clean air and stepped inside.

Smoke, of all kinds, hot bodies sweating out alcohol, overpowering artificial scents and music vibrated through his feet. *Hell on Earth.* But in this game, he often needed to get dirty to make real money.

Why didn't his targets ever think hiding out in the woods was a good idea? Outdoors, most wouldn't have a hope of avoiding him. In here, the playing field was leveled by the throng of humanity. He'd wanted an easier target this time, but he'd almost prefer another fight with a demon.

A month ago, Jude delivered his previous bounty, a vampire wanted for killing humans, to the supernatural prison. After making sure his bounty had been transferred into his account, Jude walked out into the frigid air of the high Himalayas. For the sake of convenience, and its remote location, the prison lay at least half a mile beneath the council chambers. No one got in or out without sanctioned magical assistance. Most visitors didn't see the light of day for decades, even centuries, when they came here. For Jude, half an hour was enough.

The vampire had pleaded, promised huge sums for him to look the other way. Jude could be bought, he had been many times, but his integrity wasn't for sale. Especially after the fucker bit him. Jude rolled his shoulders and winced as he stood under the overhang where the prison portal magic deposited him. The spot where the vamp had taken a nibble still smarted.

"Where to?" the pale blue air elemental said as it popped in beside him. It sounded bored, and it probably had a right to be. Being contracted to the Supernatural Council sounded exciting, but the reality, like every other job, probably sucked.

Having delivered a bounty, the being would take him anywhere in the world he requested. The offered transport wasn't only a kindness; having people tramping down, but not up, a mountain might draw unwanted human attention. The transport perk added an incentive to council work, even if other jobs paid more.

He gave the being a smile. They all looked the same to him, blue skin, skeletal, pale flowing hair, and wearing a wispy shift from neck to knee.

"Hang on a moment, and I'll find out." Smiles and banter were some of his favorite weapons. The air elemental was a tool, pissing it off for the sake of a little conversation could bite him in the ass big time when he needed hauling out of a dangerous situation.

Jude pulled out his phone, scrolled through the latest list of bounties. As always, he checked the dead or alive listings. The remaining two rat shifters from the Scibetta clan were still there, as they had been for the last three years since he'd last whittled down their numbers. That two still lived used to make him burn, now he just felt cold satisfaction that while he roamed the world, they hid in a hole and feared him.

He carried on down the list. He didn't feel like tackling another possible wet work case right now, but he liked to keep up to date with what went on in the trade.

Tiger shifter – shifter murder $550K
Blood demon – human murder $600K
Avarice demon –human murder $400K
Karnak pack – human abuse/murder $500K each.

Jude clicked the last one. *Huh.* The Karnak brothers had gone rogue. The splinter canine shifter pack had always been a thorn in his side, stealing bounties from under his nose. That they'd gone one step too far and killed one or more humans didn't surprise him.

He toyed with taking the contract for a few seconds. Yes, bringing the Karnaks in would be satisfying, but he'd have to do it one at a time. The brothers knew their advantage lay in numbers, and taking them out would be difficult, even if he was on top form. Tackling all four at once would be suicide, even without his current exhaustion and healing shoulder wound.

Many more hunters had access to the non-council bounty list, but it often threw up easier cases. Right now,

Jude could do with a little "easy". After tapping in his passcode, he scrolled through the mostly human bounties and runaways. Humans were easier to catch, but without access to the council air elementals, he'd be left sorting out his own transport. The thought of hours, even days, stuck with a whining bounty for a few thousand dollars, almost had him going back to the council list.

The next entries caught his eye, and not only for the huge sums involved for non-wet work.

Siren – missing person. $1 million.
Siren – missing person. $500K plus spell of your choice.

Sirens were one of the less common supernatural species. He'd never gone after one before, hadn't even met one as far as he knew. These had to be the same target. The challenge of hunting someone who could control you with a word piqued his interest, as did the fact that two people wanted to play tug of war with this one.

He clicked on the second entry. Having an I.O.U. from a powerful magic user could be worth far more than cash in the long run.

He contacted the client, Orcus, and the air elemental deposited him outside the mage's whitewashed mansion in Washington state and blinked back out. Looking up at the building, Jude decided magic paid a hell of a lot more than bounty hunting.

"Can I help you?"

Jude turned to see a young guy, barely into his twenties with spiked dark hair. The man wiped his sweating forehead on his red plaid shirt-sleeve. He'd been turning the dirt in a flowerbed on the opposite side of the wide gravel forecourt.

"Beautiful day, isn't it?"

"Yeah, if you like the temperature around freezing. Name's Moreno. I'm here to see Orcus?"

The guy nodded, smiled. The smile turned him from ordinary to attractive. *It's been too damn long since I got laid.*

"He's inside. He feels the cold, not surprising as he's over eighty. I'll take you in. I'm Horace, but if you call me that I'll have to kill you. Call me Ace or Hor, your choice."

Jude blinked at the blatant flirtation. The guy stuck his fork in the dirt and jogged over, past Jude and up the wide stairs in front of the imposing wooden door. The door creaked open and Ace, Jude refused to think of him as Hor, went inside.

"Hey, Uncle, someone to see you," Ace's voice rang out, then he popped his head back out the door. "He'll be down in a minute. It takes his old bones time to get moving." The door shut again, leaving Jude out in the cold. *Rude.*

Jude's phone pinged, and he opened his notifications. The other bounty on the target's head had disappeared from the app.

Jude turned around intending to leave. That could mean the bounty had been claimed, or that sufficient hunters had been contacted. The door to the mansion creaked open, and an elderly human in a three-piece suit emerged.

"You're Moreno?" The human looked him over, his nose wrinkling a little. "I thought you'd be bigger." Politeness didn't run in this family.

"Yep, that's me, but I seem to have wasted your time. Looks like the other party has already paid out. Goodbye."

"No, it hasn't been claimed. I'd know if he'd been found."

He? Now that piqued Jude's interest. As far as he knew, all sirens were female, but it wasn't enough to butt heads with other bounty hunters.

"Sorry, not interested. Even if the bounty hasn't been claimed, I bet there are at least four hunters going after it. I don't like one in five odds of getting paid."

"Not as good as your reputation then? What are you, a man or a mouse? Perhaps a rat?"

Jude's jaw clenched at being compared to a rodent. It appeared he wasn't the only one who could do research.

Plastering a smile on his face, he said, "I'm a professional which you'll know from your research. I wish you luck with finding your siren." Jude turned and started down the drive with his small pack still on his shoulder.

"I'm sorry for my rudeness, that was uncalled for. And I'll pay a retainer for as long as you're on the case. A thousand a day. He's my son, and he's dying. His mother's people put the other contract out on him. It's them he's running from. He doesn't know I exist."

Jude turned back around. Money talked. "I thought all sirens were female?" The competition didn't bother him. A race added incentive, and Jude intended to collect the entire prize.

Without other information, Jude's hunt began by researching his target's species from the mage's mansion. Sirens needed contact with the ocean in the same way shifter species needed mundane food, fae required information, and sex demons fed on lust.

That fact confined Jude's hunt, and probably that of any other interested parties, to coastal areas. At first, the contract seemed like easy money, especially with the prospect of a little action with the flirty nephew.

As the days progressed, he had to admit that nothing

here was as easy as it had first appeared, not the case, not Ace. He saw Ace a few times, but he always seemed to be leaving as Jude was coming in. It was a shame the guy wasn't as into him as he'd first seemed, but Jude could take a hint. Perhaps the guy had something against supernaturals.

Jude also concluded that his bounty possessed significant cunning. Barely into his twenties, and he'd eluded both his mother's people and his father for five years, and by the sound of it several bounty hunters, including himself, for ten days.

The clang of the brass doorbell came again. Jude ground his teeth after checking the time, nine p.m. The three members of Orcus' staff went home at eight p.m. Ace had returned to school, or so Orcus claimed when Jude asked where he was. It left Orcus, moving with the speed of an arthritic tortoise, and Jude in the house. A break would be very welcome.

Closing his laptop on another day of watching CCTV, Jude padded down the broad wooden staircase shirtless and barefoot. The added connection bare skin provided to his environment always settled him, or perhaps it was being one step nearer to shifting without pesky clothes and shoes.

The doorbell rang again, so did Jude's phone with a text message.

Let him in. I'll be available around midnight.

Annoyance at being treated as a butler drained as soon as he opened the door.

"Well, hello. Orcus has definitely upgraded the staff since last year," The copper-skinned man said with a smile. Jude's groin twitched.

"Incubus?" Jude said, but it wasn't really a question. The guy couldn't be anything else. He was too perfect. Not too big, not too small, and with a slim, athletic build that would appeal to the widest possible range of feeders.

"Yep, name's Lambert, and you gorgeous, are a–" Merry hazel eyes ran over Jude from head to foot, but remained on Jude's groin for far longer than was polite.

"A really horny shifter. Canine?"

"Cat," Jude replied. "He won't be free until midnight." Jude opened the door wider and automatically checked the grounds behind the demon. Empty. "Fancy a proper meal before you see the old man?"

"I thought you'd never ask. Lead the way."

Once in Jude's room, both supernaturals stripped. "It's so damn relaxing to get a meal without having to muck about seducing it first."

"Hands and knees on the bed," Jude ordered, then admired the flawless skin and fluid movements as the demon complied. He'd never met a sex demon who didn't possess natural grace, and he'd been with quite a few. Sex with incubi was satisfying, uncomplicated, an itch scratched for him and a meal for the demon.

"No territory?" Jude asked as he palmed the perfect smooth rounded butt raised for him.

"Who wants to be bothered with all that paperwork and record-keeping? I've got a nice, profitable route along the entire Canadian border. This is one of my more lucrative stops. You're a bit of a bonus though."

"Thanks," Jude murmured, but he was more interested in the hole that had just fluttered for him, glistening and ready.

Sex demons had to be careful about how frequently they fed on individual humans to avoid addicting them. Traveling between hook-ups had become a lifestyle for many of them. In these modern times, addicting human feeders attracted harsh sentences.

Jude couldn't imagine anything worse than having a group of horny, needy humans dogging his every step. But there were already a handful of sex demons in the prison for such offenses, along with the poor fucks they'd addicted.

"You ever had a cat?" he asked.

"Probably. Like I said, I don't keep records."

Jude smiled to himself. Even without paperwork, he bet the incubus would have remembered taking a male of his kind.

He pushed into the slick, wet heat, groaning as the demon's muscles clenched around him. He held still, enjoying the sensation, knowing it might end prematurely. He'd never had an incubus end sex without receiving the payload, then again, he did usually let them see what they were getting themselves into first.

Jude pulled his hips back.

The demon stiffened, hissed. "Ah, fuck, warn a guy, will you? What the fuck's up with your dick?"

"Cat shifter. I told you that." Jude held Lambert's hips a little tighter. He wouldn't force the demon to stay put, he might not be able to anyway, but unnecessary movement would cause additional pain.

"Fuck, you're intense, give me a second to adjust. Why don't you wear a fucking bell or something to warn people? At least the last weirdo I found gave out warning vibes before I tried anything."

Jude stopped mid-thrust. "Weirdo? Not a vamp was it? You know what happened to Erotes, right?"

"I'm not that stupid, and I have my route lodged with the Sex Demon Council. Alarm bells will ring if I go missing. But as soon as I walked into that club, I could feel there was something different in there, not a demon, not a shifter either. One of these guys is not like the others, you know? Bit like your cock. Now are you gonna serve dinner or not?"

Lambert wasn't a spectacular fuck, but at least he took Jude, which not many non-incubi did. Jude filed Lambert's odd comment in the back of his mind, as the incubus slipped out of his room to see his paying client. Jude was damn glad he'd got to Lambert first. There was no way he would have gone after Orcus.

The hunt for his elusive quarry stretched into a month without a firm lead. Throwing in the towel looked more likely with every passing day. Living in the mansion with Orcus and his equally creepy, jasmine and mothball smelling visitors was getting old real fast. The only exception to the monotony had been Lambert. Even the weather conspired against him. It had been raining or sleeting almost non-stop since he got here. Jude hated going out in the cold and damp only a little less than being in the house.

The virtual search had taken him from coast to coast. It didn't help that his client had no description, apart from the target's species, racial profile, and approximate age. Siren, Caucasian, male, twenty-three, and about to be living on borrowed time. That the kid had an expiration date lent urgency and a hefty price tag to the case. Oh, and the youngster would have a probably extensive birthmark somewhere on his body. As the target needed to be immersed in seawater regularly, Jude was scrolling through CCTV footage of beaches looking for a needle in a haystack.

Orcus seemed convinced his son had traveled from his birthplace on a remote Scottish island to America, but couldn't provide any evidence other than his son felt "closer". Jude hoped his prey hadn't managed to get back to

Europe, if he'd ever left, but it would explain his lack of success.

Frustrated and bored after yet another fruitless day, and having exhausted all his US contacts, Jude called an old colleague. Milo, a terrier-type shifter, worked Europe, mostly the UK, or he had done before hooking up with the famous incubus Ezra Erotes and his human lust battery. The incubus had gone from a dirt-poor pity case to the most wanted incubus on the planet thanks to stumbling across the first vascellum in several hundred years. Some people had all the fucking luck.

Jude explained his issue to Milo without any unnecessary pleasantries. It might be late here, but it was pre-breakfast time in Europe, and he bet Milo had a full day ahead.

"Have you tried places with tidal bores?" Milo asked.

"The what?"

"Google it. Start with the Severn Estuary in Wales. My pack lands are near there." Jude heard murmuring in the background, a male voice that didn't sound happy.

"Everything alright?" Jude asked, although what he could do from several thousand miles away, he didn't know.

"Yeah, we've got an issue with Finn right now."

Jude frowned. "The vascellum? What's the problem?" He'd met the scarily young human when he'd taken a vacation on the Mediterranean island where the group lived a few months ago. Ezra had been a hell of a lot better in bed than Lambert. He'd considered Jude's cock a challenge, not a problem.

"He's developed a new masochistic kick that Ezra doesn't share, thanks to those fucking vamps. Give me a shout if you need any more help, and I expect a share of the bounty if my idea produces a lead." The line went dead.

After doing a little googling, Jude found himself staring at the name of the town Lambert mentioned.

Fourteen hours later, with a locator charm inscribed on the back of his hand, Jude was inside the kink club hunting for the "weird" that had scared off the incubus.

Garish, loud, and shadowed, Blaze drew the desperate, the addicted, and those after easy lays. A revolting pit filled with the lowest of the low and those who didn't want to be found.

Not lifting his lip in disgust as the tacky floor attempted to hold onto his boots took control, but blending in was the name of the game. Jude was on the big side for a human, but not outlandishly so.

Without first braving the throng at the bar, Jude propped himself up against a spare patch of wall. He prayed the peeling paint, in an amateur looking flame motif, wouldn't stain his black leather jacket.

Maybe because of the freezing temperature outside, or the lack of clothing inside, the club manager kept the heating cranked up. Sweat already stuck Jude's shirt to his back, but he'd refused to leave the jacket with the coat-check guy. He'd rather be uncomfortable than risk losing his father's bequest.

The clothing of the clubbers varied from his own casual jeans and shirt to lingerie, leather harnesses, animal costumes, and nothing but shorts and collars. Most patrons were male, but there were a scattering of females and several whose gender remained their own business. People gyrated, posed, strutted, and mingled on the dance floor and in discreet booths. If his client's offspring hung out here regularly, Jude didn't hold out much hope for a happy family reunion. He couldn't imagine Orcus understanding anyone in their right mind wanting to spend time here.

Here at Blaze, private bathrooms with plastic covered couches were rentable in time increments of ten minutes. Jude didn't get laid as much as he'd like but in this place? Even if he found someone willing, hell, no. He'd felt contaminated merely by walking past the place earlier to scope it out. As the music pounded, sly glances came his way from horny guys trying to make him tonight's hook-up.

Jude kept the nearest ones at bay with arms crossed over his muscular chest and a permanent scowl. Although, by the look of some of their expressions, it just made him more attractive.

The music throbbed, dulling Jude's sense of smell and his hearing. The darkness didn't bother him in the least, like all his kind, he preferred the dark.

A siren wouldn't be as strong here, thirty miles from the open ocean, but he bet one could survive with a twice-daily influx of seawater from the nearby tidal river. If tonight didn't throw up a lead, Jude would be stalking the riverbank at high tide tomorrow morning.

A tightly muscled short man wearing a black and white skin-tight jumpsuit and a full, matching pup mask made his way through the crowd. It wasn't the most outlandish costume Jude could see, but most outfits exposed far more skin. The guy was overly muscular for his target's age, but people of any age could work out. Maybe it was a disguise. No one would expect a young siren to have a bodybuilder's physique.

The vague "he'll have a birthmark" from Orcus had stimulated Jude's early research. Siren hierarchy depended on the power of their voices, and magical ability in the species had a physical manifestation. The most formidable sirens usually wore little clothing to display their purple birthmarks, wherever they were on their bodies. The traditional lack of clothing certainly didn't hurt them when the females went looking for a sperm donor.

For sirens, prominence, size, and darkness of the power marks meant better. Male sirens were rarer than vascelli and rumors said they were far more powerful than the females. His prey would have a tell-tale purple mark, or marks, somewhere on his body; blotches he would hide if possible.

Ingratiating himself into a group, making small talk, was often part of hunting, but it'd be the last resort in this kink club. Jude's strategy would be observation then ambush before the prey even knew he was being hunted.

The technique would be essential here, as his quarry could stop an unwary hunter with a word. The kid would be going to meet his father wearing a gag, whether he liked it or not. Jude's contract paid out when father and son met face to face; what the pair did after that didn't concern him.

If he couldn't identify his target by observation in the next couple of days, Jude's next move would be pumping a sociable local for information. Some guys got really talkative with a cock in their ass, especially one like his.

Jude's gaze returned to the guy in the dog costume. Even if he wasn't the siren, he bet anyone who pranced around in a ridiculous pup outfit would sing under him in no time at all, and that ass looked delicious, round and hard.

The costume emphasized a stocky body without an ounce of fat. At first, because of his build, Jude decided the human imagined himself to be a bull terrier. He reassessed as the costumed man moved through the crowd. The guy touched everyone, mostly fleeting brushes, but he also stopped frequently to receive more intimate, longer caresses. No, not a terrier, they were focused, vermin hunters. Despite his physique, this guy was like one of those manic lap dogs, craving and debasing himself for a touch of attention.

Lambert would have made a beeline for him. A flash of light brown skin on the back of pup guy's neck was all Jude could tell about his appearance. A tanned Caucasian, or was his skin naturally darker? If it was naturally darker, he probably wasn't Jude's quarry. Orcus was pale enough to be a corpse, and he'd said the three sirens he'd fucked had all been pale skinned too. Jude still shuddered at the thought of Orcus at the center of an orgy.

Pup guy even wore matching gloves, although they weren't the "paws" he'd seen other kinky humans wear. *Please don't let this guy be the siren.* Spending any time with him would be pure torture. Orcus lived fifty solid hours of driving away, and Jude wouldn't get paid until he delivered.

The wailing woman on the next track caused Jude to squint in discomfort; at least the light level didn't hurt his eyes.

The humans were all enjoying themselves, thinking they were safe in their smutty, dirty club. Would they be excited or frightened to know they had a real predator in their midst? Judging from the humans who either couldn't take their eyes off him and those who avoided him his current shape did both.

Despite the amount of flesh on show, or maybe because of it, Jude's eyes flicked back to the black and white "pup" every few seconds. *Could he be the one?* He hadn't heard the man speak, and his lips were hidden because of the mask, but no one appeared to be rejecting his attention.

Siren compulsion, or are the humans just playing the game? Perhaps he's trying to hide by being so visible no one suspects him. It wasn't a common strategy for those on the run, but he'd come across it a time or two. It certainly took balls.

For all he knew, male sirens were all like this. The myriad of supernatural species, shifters, demons, elementals, and others, all tended to stay away from each other as well as the far more numerous humans. From the little his research revealed, sirens were ocean sprites who used their hypnotic voices to lure human mates then killed them after sex. That might have happened years ago, but now? Although Orcus was decrepit, he was definitely still alive.

Female sirens worked in groups as they weren't strong individually. Once they caught a suitable male, they all had a go. Maybe that's why Orcus looked half-dead; the sirens had fucked years out of him.

Jude hadn't found a single reference to a male siren. They seemed pretty much a myth, even to their own kind. Orcus claimed there hadn't been one for over a thousand years, and that male sirens were far stronger than females. It also stated that they burned themselves out before their twenty-fifth birthday. For Jude's kind, at twenty-five, you weren't even considered an adult.

Pup man moved to another group, who all greeted him with smiles and pats. The guy wiggled his butt, making the upward curving plastic tail attached to it wag from side to side. *Pathetic*. Still, he seemed to know a lot of people. Even if he wasn't Jude's target, he would probably have some useful information.

A slim man, wearing a close-fitting black shirt, tight leather jeans, and a grungy silver skull mask that covered his face except for his mouth and chin, approached the pup from the gloom. Collar-length dark hair, pale skin, and thick, pouty lips were all Jude could tell about him although he seemed on the young side. The man's hand landed on the pup's neck, squeezed. Jude frowned, focused a little harder; the guy's thumbnail extended at least two inches. Even from across the room, he saw the red welt it left on the pup's exposed neck. Rather than objecting to the pain, the pup leaned into his hold.

Jude fought not to roll his eyes. *A masochist. Good for fun, bad for business.* Usually, moderate pain helped loosen tongues, but not when the recipient enjoyed it.

Mr. Thumb didn't smile, his lips didn't move, but the pup quirked his head as if listening. Both men turned to Jude, and dark eyes met his gaze through the silver mask.

Jude froze. From his shadowed position on the other side of the crowded room, he would've bet his future fee that a human wouldn't be able to pick him out.

The man in the pup costume wagged his tail, then made a beeline for Jude. He lost any interest in the pup. He'd found the person who didn't fit. The man in the silver mask didn't give out any shifter or demon vibes, but picking Jude out meant he wasn't an ordinary human.

A smile quirked the masked man's cock-sucking lips as he inclined his head in acknowledgment. That his prey would run, Jude didn't doubt. All that remained to discover was how far he'd get before Jude caught him. Possessing a voice most beings couldn't refuse, Jude anticipated that his quarry lacked combat skills, but he didn't assume.

His family had assumed rat shifters didn't pose a threat either.

If things went to plan, the siren wouldn't get a chance to use his voice. The smile vanished from his quarry's face as his gaze focused on Jude's left. In the seconds it took Jude to identify the three canine shifters making their way through the crowd, his prey vanished.

Even if Jude didn't recognize the Karnaks as individuals, the three males couldn't be anything else but canine shifters. Scruffy and sniffing at the air, they screamed "dog" louder than the guy in the pup costume who now stood in front of Jude.

One of the canines pointed to a softly closing door marked "staff".

The human in the black and white costume in front of him might be hunting Jude, but the Karnak brothers were hunting Jude's quarry. It only confirmed the masked man's identity.

Taking in one or more of the wanted canine shifters, as well as the siren, would significantly up his bank balance. Small bribes hadn't forced the rats out of their holes, but with this much money?

He glared at the man in front of him, then added a growled, "Not interested." The pretend pup held his ground, put his hand on Jude's chest.

"Stay awhile, big guy, and I'll gobble you down like a good dog."

His prey, all four of them, were escaping. Jude shoved the human sideways, snarling, "Move."

The pup flailed his arms, squeaked, and fell into a group of leather-clad "bears" standing a few feet away.

The pup clutched onto the nearest one, a hairy guy with a ridiculous mustache who'd probably get out of breath climbing a flight of stairs. He outweighed Jude by around a hundred pounds, and he had friends.

"What the fuck?" the human bear growled, holding the whimpering pup against his chest.

"You ok, Rory?" A second leather man said.

Jude pushed past them, intent on the canines about to steal his prey from under his nose.

"I... I think he broke my wrist," Rory sniveled.

A heavy hand landed on Jude's bicep, spinning him around.

Leaving bruised humans in his wake, Jude barreled out the door his bounty and the Karnaks had disappeared through.

As the group bundled his quarry into the van, Jude shouted and sprinted to the end of the alley, reached into his pocket, and threw the black ball Orcus had given him at the retreating vehicle.

Instead of bouncing off like any other hard object, it stuck to the blue metal. Even in the dark, to his eyes, it was glaringly obvious; a black lump of crud near the door handle. Orcus had assured him it wouldn't be noticed, just like the circular design the mage had painted on his skin in the few minutes before he'd left the mansion.

He'd almost refused the magical help, but Orcus reminded him how slippery his prey had proven in the past. If he could get near enough to the siren, even once, the magic charm would let Jude track his prey wherever he fled.

CHAPTER THREE

So near and yet so fucking far. Jude had been within fifteen feet of half a million dollars, and it was now passed out cold in the Karnaks possession.

Tracking the van the old-fashioned way wouldn't be easy, and having some help would be welcome right now. Jude squinted at the back of his hand in the dirty yellow light from the single bulb above the back exit of Blaze. Nothing. *What am I expecting, a flashing arrow?* Jude took off towards where he'd left his hired car. Five bounties were getting away.

Cursing to himself, Jude sat at an intersection on the way out of town. Without headlights, he could see further, but he couldn't see a single taillight. The van had headed in this direction; besides, it was the main route out of town. From here, it could have gone either east or west, and there were further options in around a dozen miles. If he went the wrong way, he might never catch them. The Karnaks logical choice would be to head straight for the siren sorority house, but that meant a cross-country road trip of several days. Not good for a siren who needed daily immersion in seawater.

If they had been able to procure air elemental transport, they wouldn't have taken the van. It didn't mean they couldn't hire a plane from humans. Jude turned west towards the nearest private airfield and put his foot down, eyes on the distance, hoping to catch the red glow of the van's taillights.

The third time he scratched the back of his hand, he looked at it, hoping to see a glowing arrow. Nothing. Pulling over, he stopped for a better look. Even in the light from the half-moon, the back of his hand looked perfectly normal, except for the slightly reddened skin near his knuckles where he'd scratched it. The tickling sensation had vanished.

So much for magic. Putting the car in drive, he checked over his shoulder and pulled out. *Now, where the fuck did–*

This time, there was no mistaking the stinging line near his knuckles. Pulling over again, he got out, back to the car. Feeling like a complete idiot, he stuck his arm out in front of him and formed a mental picture of the van.

Pain radiated from the outside of his hand. The same direction as before. Thinking about the van, he rotated, the pain moved too, except where he faced the way he'd come.

The mage's words when he'd asked how the charm worked came back to him. *"Avoiding pain is always a promising idea."*

"Fuck." Seconds later, he was heading down the highway, in the opposite direction, towards the interior of the continent.

Thirteen hours later, with the sun high in the sky, having been awake for nearly thirty-six hours, Jude gave up and pulled over. Either he'd been getting less sensitive to the pain, or proximity lessened the sensation. The Karnaks would be able to change drivers, while he couldn't. Even if he caught up to them now, his exhaustion would put him at a disadvantage.

Pain pulled him out of his doze. Lifting his hand to stare at it, he hissed. It felt as if someone was drawing a knife across the area next to his thumb.

"Fucking witch. Yeah, yeah, I'm on it," he grumbled, and the pain faded. After cracking his neck from side to side, he got out to take a piss.

Mountains rose in the distance, their lower slopes wearing skirts of dark trees. Hopefully, that's where he'd catch up with his prey; the thought of a hunt through a forest almost made him smile, then a frigid blast of air made him shiver. He turned up the collar of his jacket. Here in the rain shadow of the range, the land remained flat and exposed. At least it wasn't snowing. It could be brutal at this time of year.

After checking that the road remained empty, he unzipped, pulled out his cock and aimed at the base of a stunted tree beside a barbed-wire fence. It took a few seconds and thinking warm thoughts to get the flow of urine going. *Fuck, I hate the cold.* But at least the temperature took his mind off his disheveled state.

He zipped up, checked the road again, because he knew he'd look like a dick, held his hand out, closed his eyes to concentrate on the van, and rotated. When the pain centered near his wrist with no tendrils up either side, he opened his eyes. Northwest. From his sat-nav, he knew the highway carried on due west. The siren sorority house his target fled years ago lay two thousand miles to the southwest.

Where are the Karnaks taking him? Rather than heading off immediately, as soon as Jude got back in the car, he got out his phone. Hunting smarter than his competition made him one of the most successful bounty hunters in the business.

It took twenty minutes to find the sea life center two hundred miles away and another hour of playing on the dislike of the Karnaks to arrange a lift.

As always, he jumped when the blue-tinged air elemental appeared beside him. Grabbing his chest, he hammed it up.

"Fuck, do you lot ever get fed up with giving people heart attacks?"

The elemental grinned, showing pointed teeth any predator would envy. "Never. It's a perk of the job." The smile dropped from its face. "Rumor is, you've found the Karnaks and want a lift."

Jude inclined his head. "I've got a pretty good idea where they'll be tonight, but I'd rather be there before them. Capturing all four without the element of surprise won't be easy."

Blue eyebrows drew together. "You want to bring them in alive?"

"You care?" Jude shot back.

"Yeah, I do. Dead on delivery, or you can find another lift."

"Bloodthirsty much?"

The boney shoulders shrugged. "They collected the bounty on two of my flight two years ago. Idiots got mixed up with human gangsters. Bounty specified alive. They did transport the wrong people, I'm not arguing that, but they didn't deserve..." The elemental drew in a breath. "Those earthbound fuckers wrapped them in a silver infused net, grounded them for life. They both dissipated when they realized; they didn't even make it to prison."

From the terminology, Jude assumed "dissipated" was the air elemental equivalent of suicide.

"All the dogs got was a lecture on 'safe detention'." Blue eyes focused on Jude. "They knew. Everyone who ever travels with one of us gets told about silver. It burns like acid." Jude remembered his first transport, the lecture that if he'd touched silver in the last twenty-four hours, even if he'd washed thoroughly, no air elemental would transport him. Many of their supernatural bounties wore silver to guard against unwanted transport.

The being presented an impossibly thin arm. A deeper blue inch-wide scar showed on the almost translucent flesh. "I brushed against a candlestick when I first started working for the council. I can still feel the sting."

"They didn't deserve to die like that," Jude said.

Silence stretched. "So you'll do it?"

"Kill the Karnak brothers?"

The elemental inclined its head, causing its fluffy hair to shift as if someone had held a balloon next to it.

"Transport whenever I want it for life?"

"Twenty trips," the elemental bargained.

Jude let out a bark of laughter. "You're kidding, right? I could die."

"You're more likely to die if you try to bring them in alive."

"True. Fifty years, and I promise not to abuse the privilege." He paused then added, "Scout's honor."

The blue lips twitched. "You were never a scout."

Jude grinned. "Also true. Well, do we have a deal?"

"Fifty trips, no more."

"That could take more than fifty years, I'm pretty frugal."

The elemental laughed, a surprisingly deep sound for

one who looked so frail. "Yeah, and I'm a whale shifter. But, yes, you have a deal. Grab your pack and picture where you want to be."

"Not right outside the entrance though," Jude said quickly. Appearing out of thin air in the middle of a lunchtime crowd of visitors wouldn't exactly fit his reputation for stealth.

The elemental rolled its eyes. "Give me some credit. I've been doing this a while."

Jude had never had a conversation with an air elemental, most appeared, raised an eyebrow, and he gave it a destination.

"How long?" Jude shifted in his seat to face his passenger. "How long have you been transporting people around the world?"

The blue head tilted, birdlike. "Would it make a difference if I said five centuries, five years, or five weeks?"

Jude gave it the grin that had served him well on many occasions. "Nope, I'd still think you were awesome whatever you said, but I'm curious. There's virtually no information about your kind."

The elemental's brief smile became a little strained. "And that's the way we like it."

"Come on, just tell me your name. I need to know who to moan about when you renege on our deal."

The elemental slumped, looking even frailer. "Won't happen. One of the dead was my sibling. If you need me, just say, 'Oroshi, you're awesome,' and I'll be there." It reached out a bony hand, grabbed Jude's backpack from the rear seat, then icy fingers touched his arm.

Jude's butt hit the ground, and he swallowed against the usual nausea caused by the instantaneous change of location. He and the elemental sat at the base of a pine tree. A blue steel warehouse-like structure was visible through the trees. The sound of excited children echoed in the cold air.

"Thanks, Oroshi," Jude said and stood up. "Don't worry, I'll do as you asked. To tell the truth, I probably would have done it anyway. The world will be better off without the Karnaks in it."

The blue lips pursed as the elemental examined him. "Names have power among my kind. If another terrestrial ever uses that call sign without my permission, I'll make sure no air elemental ever transports you again. Good hunting." A brief blast of wind was all the elemental left behind when it vanished.

The entire back of Jude's hand pulsed. He couldn't help glancing down, but again he couldn't see a damn thing different about his skin. He also couldn't tell which direction the pain indicated as it all seemed to hurt. Maybe that's what happened when you were almost on top of the target.

Looking up, he decided the tree almost perfectly fitted his needs, especially as the slight breeze blew from his left, from the direction of the parking lot. Hopefully, he'd see the van before its occupants scented him above the throng of humans and pine resin.

Once he removed his boots and socks, it took minimal effort to climb to a spot where he had an uninterrupted view of the parking lot. His family had teased him for forgetting to form fully human hands when he shifted sometimes, but the ability others ridiculed had come in handy more than once. Having retractile razor-sharp claws without concentrating proved a huge advantage for tree climbing and killing.

The parking lot bustled with vehicles and tourists, including two coachloads of kids. One herd of children headed towards a vehicle, all clutching merchandise, the other group were almost bouncing as the adults tried to get them walking safely towards the exhibit. All were human, none had any idea about the supernatural perched above them, or the ones in the blue van Jude spotted hidden at the very back of the lot.

No other vehicles were parked nearby, which was odd considering the packed attraction. Squinting, he peered into the gloom and got an answer. The van rocked rhythmically. Jude grimaced in disgust, hoping the siren wasn't getting it on with one of the dogs. Spending any time with a bounty who stank of dog cum would not be pleasant. Still, with the elemental on call, it might not have to be long. He wondered how many people, dead or alive, a single elemental could transport. His preferred option would be to stay in touch with all his bounties until he'd been paid, but that centered on the siren being cooperative. If he was enjoying living it up with one of the Karnaks the logistics could get tricky.

Jude stilled further as he caught sight of two of the canine shifters, Tunstall, the prime beta, and the youngest, Rollin, ambling towards the van holding takeout bags. Jude sniffed. Burgers and fries. That the canines consumed vegetation and carbs just proved their place on the predator hierarchy, several steps below the cats.

They could have been chatting about the merits of ketchup versus mustard, or what they intended to do with the siren next, but Jude couldn't hear them above the humans. Blood heating in anticipation, he knew it was time to stalk his prey. A deadly prey who knew him, one who would be on their toes. He smiled.

With two of his targets in sight, another maybe injured, and the fourth thoroughly distracted, the temptation to simply move nearer bloomed. Complacency in this game didn't lead to a long life. He hadn't confirmed the identity of the second body he'd glimpsed in the van even though he'd scented blood. The body could have been Ulrike, Ranulfo with a minor injury, the person could have been dead or someone else entirely. It didn't mean there wasn't a Karnak or two guarding the others from a distance. The dogs had been in this business for a long time too.

Jude stayed put, snug and comfortable in his tree, and waited for dark. Dogs were active hunters, always busy, flushing their prey. The correct opportunity against four, even if one were injured, could take days. They might have numbers, but Jude had three aces in his hand, the tracker, the element of surprise, and an air elemental at his beck and call.

CHAPTER FOUR

Eight hours later, Jude climbed down from his freezing perch, leaving his pack in the tree. The staff and visitors had gone home. Apart from the two shifters crouched next to the blue van, the lot was devoid of life. The Karnaks would be making their move soon.

Standing in the shadow of his temporary refuge, Jude flexed his arms and legs, warming his muscles with as little movement as possible. Canine shifters might not have his keen eyes, but they had better sight than most beings, and their noses were superior to just about anything on the planet, especially in their fur form.

Tunstall and Rollin hadn't gotten back in the van, although they spoke through an open window to Ulrike. It confirmed that Ranulfo was the injured brother. Whatever his injury, Jude hoped he'd been rendered unconscious. Out of the four, Ranulfo was the one who held the others together and tempered some of their actions. Killing Ranulfo held the least appeal, Ulrike and Tunstall, the most. Rollin had always been a blind follower. In different circumstances, the youngest member of the rogue pack might have been a decent person; now, he'd become as black as the rest.

The van rocked as someone climbed from the back to the front. The engine started, and it rolled towards the building. Jude took advantage of the covering noise to slip to the corner of the exhibit.

The engine turned off, and Ulrike got out. "Right, let's get–"

Tunstall held up a hand, cocked his head. Jude froze, not even breathing as the three shifters scented the air. The strong wet smell wafting out of the building should cover Jude's scent. Rather than giving in to the temptation to duck back and probably draw their attention, he closed his eyes to prevent any light reflecting from them.

"Anything?" Ulrike asked after thirty nerve-jangling seconds.

"No, I guess I'm just a bit jumpy."

Ulrike patted his brother's shoulder. "We will get through this, ok?"

That they cared about each other Jude didn't doubt, but they'd hurt and killed innocents, including Oroshi's kin. Jude hadn't handed down the sentence, but he trusted the council to come to the correct verdicts. By his hand or another's, the Karnaks were already dead; they just didn't know it yet.

Jude risked opening his eyes as the side door of the van rattled open. Mingled scents of death and sex wafted out. He remembered the earlier rocking, and his nose wrinkled in disgust. *Had Ulrike been fucking a corpse?* Any empathy he'd felt a moment ago vanished. They really did need putting down.

He almost breathed a sigh of relief when the van rocked as someone else climbed out. *Not fucking a corpse then.* It didn't mean Ulrike hadn't done the dirty right next to his dying or already dead brother.

If Jude had acted a little sooner, he could have spared the poor siren that experience. Plus, if this mission went to plan, he'd be spending at least some time with his primary target. If the guy stank of canine cum, Jude might not be able to control his stomach.

A male human appeared from behind the van and almost threw himself at the alpha, wrapping his arms around him like an octopus.

Well, that solves the who was being fucked issue.

Widening his eyes to capture as much light as possible, Jude concentrated on the human. Was this an innocent he needed to consider, to protect? A human with knowledge of the supernatural world caused all sorts of headaches. Including Jude having to take him along for a bloodsucker to do a memory wipe.

Brown hair, medium brown skin, stocky, short. He wore jeans and a familiar black shirt that looked long on the arms. The buttons gaped with the strain of a wider body. Jude didn't think the siren would have given up his fancy shirt without a fight. An injured "retrieve" bounty was the last thing he needed. He felt a little better knowing that the Karnaks needed the siren alive too. Their tongues could heal most superficial wounds. He suppressed a shudder. Jude would rather suffer an injury healing naturally than have a canine slobbering on him.

"Master, can I stay with you? I promise to be good and staying in there with your brother is kinda creepy."

The damn pup guy had sold the siren out. You couldn't trust humans as far as you could throw them, but at least he knew the identity of the corpse. One Karnak down, three to go.

Ulrike fisted the human's hair, tearing him away from his body. "Stop pawing me." The human stepped back, shoulders hunched, lips pouting, as the alpha continued to issue orders. "Tunstall, get the siren. Rollin, keep watch for Arioch and any stray humans."

Jude shouldn't have been surprised that the most prominent vengeance demon on the planet was mixed up with the Karnaks. Arioch changed its appearance and gender at will and fed on guilt and regret.

Maybe they'd invited the demon to feed on the human in return for future favors. The human might not know it yet, but he was in for a world of justifiable hurt. The Karnaks wouldn't keep a human around for long. Ulrike already appeared fed up with his new toy, and the human knew too much to go free.

Without a word, the big beta leaned into the van and lifted a naked, lax body to his shoulder. Even from this distance, the dark patches on the shockingly pale skin glared like a beacon. He appeared unharmed except for a rough bandage wrapped around his left thumb and his lack of consciousness.

"Rory, your job is to get him to comply when he wakes up. He likes you, right?"

"Like butter in my hands." The human smirked.

This Rory deserves a significantly painful end.

"I want his focus on you, got it?"

"You want me to make him jealous?" Rory's white teeth showed in the gloom as he grinned. "I can be so bitchy you wouldn't believe–"

Rory let out a squeak as Rollin grabbed a fistful of his shirt and shoved his back against the van, making it rock.

Face twisting, he snarled, "My mother is a bitch, and she is nothing like you. If you ever, and I mean ever–"

"Put him down, pup. If he doesn't perform, you and Tunstall can play with him later, ok?"

With a final shove to the human's chest, the youngest Karnak stepped back, growling under his breath.

The group disappeared into the building. Jude reckoned he had at least half an hour before they emerged. Arioch, if the demon turned up and was so inclined, could squash him like a bug, but Ranulfo's body was in that van, laying there like a big bag of cash, and Rollin was almost as accessible.

The youngest Karnak moved to the front of the van, staring out into the night. Shifting his fingers, Jude crept around the back of the vehicle. As his hand brushed the van, the constant painful itch on the back of his hand vanished. It seemed touching the object being tracked broke the spell. He'd just have to make sure none of the Karnaks survived to take off again.

Rollin Karnak was the first order of business.

Stepping in, Jude's hand went over his victim's mouth as he stabbed his claws into the soft skin under his chin and ripped out. Rollin thrashed in his arms, blood spraying the ground in front of them. Jude held on, muscles straining as he waited for his kill to bleed out. Twenty seconds, thirty, the body sagged then collapsed. Jude let the dead weight sink to the ground, quite impressed with himself that the only blood he had on him was on his hand. Usually, he got covered, which was why he preferred being in fur form when he killed.

A slow clap came from a few feet away. Jude crouched for the coming attack.

"Don't stress yourself, my boy. In the painless slaughter

without an artificial weapon category, that could be a winner. He hardly had time to panic, let alone regret his actions, which is a shame from my point of view." The cultured rumble came from an eight-foot-tall, black suit wearing male, with thick curling horns sprouting from his head.

Jude gaped. Yes, he'd met demons before, but he'd never seen anything like this. *Fuck, I knew I should've stripped first.* He might have had a chance of making a run for it in his cat form, but his clothes might as well have been ropes.

Arioch looked down at himself. "Dear me, I do apologize. I forgot to change out of my office attire."

Between one heartbeat and the next, a curvy dark-haired, pale-skinned woman wearing a tight, blood-red cocktail dress stood in the demon's place. A rich chuckle bubbled up. "Oh dear, no, silly me, that's for later."

The woman shimmered, to be replaced by an athletic, dark-skinned guy in a red t-shirt and black jeans. He held his hands out, palms up. "Better? Casual is so much more comfortable for a chat between friends."

Jude didn't know what to say. At least he knew who he was dealing with now. He'd met Arioch before, and he'd heard the demon now ran the supernatural prison. He couldn't believe the demon wanted to talk fashion while Jude stood, hand dripping with the blood of the man whose life he'd just taken.

"We're not going to..." He waved his bloody hand limply between them.

"Not unless you have a particular urge to fight or fuck. I'm not sure what–" he copied Jude's hand movement, "–means. Either would be quite entertaining at another time, but I'm here because Ulrike asked me to collect his brother and pay him the bounty on behalf of the council.

The demon glanced at the body on the ground. "I must say, it's not really a sustainable strategy for making a living, even if you belong to a prolific species. You'll either run out of relatives or your relatives will smell a rat sooner or later." Arioch tilted his head.

"Ah. Now I remember. Rats are a bit of a sore subject for you, aren't they? You could always engage a vengeance demon to take care of the issue; you have justifiable cause. I can assure you that I, or one of my brethren, would provide a satisfactory service."

"I'm more than capable of taking care of it on my own." Jude looked towards the door of the facility, wondering how much time he had.

Arioch's full lips pursed. "I understand the sentiment, but it might take a long time; it already has. Rats are damn good at hiding."

Jude interrupted before the demon started a conversation about the weather. "I don't want to be rude, but is there a point to this little chat?"

"Unfulfilled revenge makes my horns ache, and as you saw earlier, I'm pretty well endowed in the horn department."

Automatically, Jude's gaze dropped to Arioch's pants, then back up to the demon's smirk.

"There too, but that only aches when I feel like fucking, or when Avery is around, although those two conditions are fairly co-existent."

Jude tried for a bland expression. Yes, Avery was an incubus, but talking about fucking the head of the supernatural council sounded almost blasphemous. To Jude's joy, the smirk slipped from the demon's face.

"Right, I should have remembered how much fun you big cat shifters aren't. You should take a leaf out of the house cat book. Have you seen the number of funny cat videos on YouTube?"

Jude stared back, over the cooling body of the man he'd just killed. Arioch sighed.

"Look, my point is, without a direct plea for help, my kind can't take on a case. It doesn't mean that cases like yours don't irritate the fuck out of me. So, as you are helping me out with these naughty puppies, I'd like to assist with your little rodent issue, as well as several other cases."

"And how are you going to do that without getting involved? Because I'm sure that would compromise your job at the prison."

Arioch circled his hand. "Advice. Suggestions. Case in point, the means to draw the rats into the open is currently being dunked in a shark tank about sixty feet away. You persuade the siren to draw them out of hiding, and then you kill them. The Karnaks intend to try a similar thing."

A cold gust of wind caused the trees to sway, but Arioch didn't appear to notice. "Although you'll have to get him over his no-talking rule. Right now, he won't let out a peep, even to save himself. Damn waste of talent if you ask me. That boy is the most powerful siren there's ever been; it's why he's such hot property. Think about it." The demon gave him another bright smile and vanished.

The faint scent of sulfur dissipated, leaving Jude surrounded by the stink of death and pine. The demon's plan sparked hope of finally getting justice for his family, but to even start to explore the idea, he needed to remove his current competition.

"Oroshi, you're awesome," Jude whispered into the night.

"Did he suffer?" Even though he'd called the elemental, he still twitched at the voice coming from behind him.

"Not a lot, but you wanted dead, not tortured. Ranulfo is in the van, wasn't me who killed him though. Get going before the other two come back."

The elemental vanished, reappearing a heartbeat later crouching beside the body of Ranulfo. Keeping a hand on Ranulfo's chest, it reached a hand towards Rollin's.

"I'll make sure the money is deposited into your account." The air elemental said and touched the still-warm body. It flinched back, hissing in pain, shaking its hand. "Silver, there's silver on him somewhere."

Jude went for the most probable places first, hands and wrists. No rings, no watch. He cursed at himself. What self-respecting shifter would wear something tight that couldn't be easily removed for shifting? Wrinkling his nose at the smell of urine, Jude checked Rollin's belt buckle next. Silver color, but chrome, not precious metal. Checking his pockets would be the last resort because of the piss. Instead, Jude extended a claw and ripped open Rollin's shirt.

The chunky silver chain caught what little light came from the almost new moon. With a tug, Jude pulled it free.

"Bastard must have wanted to make sure none of your kind popped up and transported him. I bet they're all wearing them." He tossed it a few feet away.

"Wait, what's that?" The air elemental pointed to an off-white pendant that must have been hanging down Rollin's back.

Jude reached for it again. "Looks like some kind of ivory." He held it up to get a better look in the meager moonlight.

"It's a finger bone. That, my friend, is a protection talisman, probably against the siren. I'd hang onto it if I were you." The elemental touched both bodies again.

Jude was left looking at a patch of tarmac with nothing

but a dark stain to indicate where Rollin had died. He slid the metal over his neck but didn't tuck it into his shirt. He shivered at the thought of it touching his skin.

Two down, two to go. If he and the siren both survived, he'd think about what Arioch had said.

CHAPTER FIVE

Eddying, vague pain. With every passing second, Domino became a little more aware. His jaw ached, his hand stung, but he didn't want to move. Clinging on to the numbness, he drifted as sounds came and went at an unreachable distance. Voices, grunts of passion, of pain, movement, and the stink of bodily fluids.

Time passed. He dreamed about the smell of the ocean. The discomfort in his jaw, his hand, made it difficult to bask in the fantasy of lying on a rocking boat. Confusion swirled as he tried to bring his hand to his face. It didn't move.

"Dinner time, you little fucker." A rough voice above him had Domino fighting to open his eyes as he lay on his front. Chains rattled. He dropped, perhaps three feet, cool water closed over his naked body. He automatically tried to close his mouth but couldn't. Pain shot through his left hand, radiating down his arm.

Eyes shooting open, he thrashed, but none of his spread limbs moved. Metal cuffs wrapped around his wrists and ankles and bars pressed into his flesh. With his head turned to the side, he could see up through the few inches of seawater. Vague shapes loomed over him, including a dirty blue-painted roof five feet above. Below him, was a body of water, around fifteen feet deep. It called to him and he struggled to get free, not caring that skin was being rubbed off by the cuffs.

As a siren, he could go without breathing for ten to fifteen minutes, but eventually, he'd drown just like any other air-breathing animal. It gave him time to assess his situation, time to consider escape; time to die slowly.

Skin tingling, his muscles relaxed as if he'd experienced an epic orgasm moments before. Domino closed his eyes, basking as the energy of living seawater sank into his body. The water held an artificial, synthetic tinge along with the spark of life, but it was enough to feed his near starving body. Energy infused through his skin, waking, renewing every cell.

Renewing. They're taking me back.

He thrashed again, mindless, desperate to avoid the life being forced into him.

The frame shuddered and then emerged from the water. Domino gasped, blinking in the dim light. Reflections of water danced over every surface. Chains clinked, ground, accompanied by the echoing slaps and drips of disturbed water.

A canine shifter he didn't recognize worked a pulley. He guessed this was the driver, Tunstall. He wasn't as big as the alpha, or the man Domino killed, but he had the same shaggy red hair and broad nose. Expressionless, the man who wanted him dead, watched him. At least they had something in common.

The frame juddered, moved sideways away from the walkway where Tunstall stood. Turning his head, Domino looked down as the frame traveled over the huge tank.

Water rained down from his body onto the surface, obscuring the tank's contents, before slowing. A ray, perhaps three feet across, flapped its wings, flying lazily. The sharp fins of a small shark sliced through the water below it. They'd brought him to an ocean exhibit. The frame must be used to transport heavy items in and out of the tank.

The frame moved over the edge of the tank. Vertigo swirled as he inched towards the blue floor of a maintenance area at the rear of the exhibit. Below him, out of the way of the dripping water, Rory snuggled up against the alpha's side. He wore skinny jeans and... *bastard stole my favorite shirt and it doesn't even fit him.*

"I thought he would grow a tail." Rory pouted, his voice loud, almost obscene over the watery sounds.

"I told you, he's a siren, not a merman," the alpha chuckled. Domino tried to remember if he'd heard his name in those last few frantic moments in the van, but it eluded him. The name of the man he'd killed, Ranulfo, wasn't so easy to forget.

"Merman would be cooler," Rory grumbled.

"Cooler than us?" the alpha's voice hardened.

"No, no, of course not, the whole shifter thing, it's–"

Domino ignored the pathetic sucking up, angry at himself for falling for the human's act. How he'd missed the falseness that now hovered around the man he didn't know. Escaping, one way or another, before the shifters made their delivery, was his single priority.

The frame clanged, tilted upright. Dizziness swirled at the change of attitude. His weight hung on his wrists. The base of the frame bumped as it hit the ground. Pain shot through Domino's hand at the sharp movement. He looked up. The throbbing that had been there since he woke forced itself to the front of his mind.

His hands and ankles were cuffed to each corner of the frame. A blood-soaked wet bandage wrapped around his thumb, a thumb that no longer had a talon. The entire top of the joint might have been chopped off, or it might just be bleeding because it'd been cut too near the quick. He couldn't bring himself to care. A thumb for a life? He deserved, wanted, to suffer more.

"Up about four inches," the alpha said, from a few feet away, arm still around a smirking Rory. Body weight dragged on his raw wrists; he scrabbled until toes found purchase on the metal, relieving the pressure. Rory and the alpha stared at him as if he were part of the exhibit. The silver chain and the top of the discolored finger bone still nestled in the Alpha's red chest hair.

Still groggy, it took another second to put two and two together. He retched against the plastic ball gag. He'd never heard of using a living siren's bone for an amulet, but it had to be more powerful, right? He pictured the small bone sitting in a dish somewhere, maybe in a tank with a sea creature eating away the remains of his flesh.

"We would have let you paddle for longer, but this is a shark tank. I'm sure they'd be happy to have a little nibble with the way your hand is bleeding."

Domino blinked a drip of water out of his eyes. Being fully exposed, having all his birthmarks on show, was the least of his problems. It still made his flesh creep. He knew what they could see. The purple blazed against his otherwise pale skin. The lowest one started above his left knee, curled around his hip, across one buttock, and then split into a series of blotches on his chest and back. The only parts of him not marred were his extremities and the front of his neck. Although with the damn big patch across his eye and cheek, it hardly mattered.

The shifter smiled. "Nothing to say, siren? Oh, you can't, can you?"

Even over the scent of the exhibit, Domino detected sweat and damp foliage. Any other time, the masculine body odor, the dangerous vibe, the jeans and shirt covered, powerful broad body, would've piqued Domino's interest. Although even if the man had been human, Domino would only have admired from afar.

During his travels, Domino discovered that he didn't have a specific type, except he liked men with fit bodies. He appreciated attitude, far more than other characteristics, although he avoided supernaturals whenever he'd encountered one. Very few of his human partners ever saw his body or his upper face. He'd let the rumor that he had a thing for blindfolded partners, as well as being mute, run through Blaze. It led to plenty of offers from more submissive guys. Domino took what he could get before Rory almost publicly claimed him.

The masochistic bottom looked in heaven cuddled up to the Alpha like a damn limpet. Adoration oozed from him like sweat. He'd done the same to Domino many times.

The betrayal hurt, but he probably should have known that trust only ever caused pain in the long run. When even your family saw you as an asset to be used rather than a person with rights, being surprised that a guy you'd fucked several dozen times could do it too was stupid.

He'd tried to fulfill the human's needs, but Rory's demands to be hurt spiraled beyond Domino's tastes. Rory never asked, and Domino had never admitted that he fantasized about bottoming. Being on the receiving end of a dominant top haunted his fantasies and nightmares.

"News, you just fucked me, so if you hate faggots so much, how about starting by killing yourself?"

Domino swallowed down the rising bile at the memory of the last time he'd spoken aloud. *Never again.*

He didn't realize how much he'd drifted into an inner world until the alpha unbuckled the gag. He turned his head, used his tongue to push the foul object out. Pain flared as Domino tried to close his mouth when the black ball left it.

How long did I have that in? More importantly, how far from a sorority house am I?

"Is it safe to take that out? You said he controlled, killed people with his voice." Rory shifted from one foot to the other, glancing towards the exit of the exhibit.

The alpha patted Domino's face, smiling. "Oh, he can, can't you? You're one lucky human that we came along when we did, otherwise, you'd be dead too. Just like any other siren, he entices, fucks, and then kills his partners with just a word. Our dear brother is another number on his body count, although he had to use a different weapon because of the amulet."

Rory licked his lips and glanced between Domino and the shifter. "You've got a spare amulet now though, right?"

"True. What are you prepared to do for protection from this evil bastard?"

Rory gaped, then a sly smile appeared. "Anything, I'll do anything you want." Licking his lips, Rory started to sink to his knees. Domino's stomach rolled at the imagined unkempt red pubic hair where his former lover was about to bury his face with so much relish.

"Ah, ah, not that, human, not yet anyway. There's something very special you can do for me and my brothers."

Rory's eyes lit up. "At the same time? I've never done that, not with werewolves anyway."

A soft growl rumbled from the alpha's chest. "We're canine shifters, not creatures from human fantasies."

Tunstall emerged from the gloom behind the alpha. "Ulrike, we've got four hours before the staff returns." The big beta's voice reeked with cold disgust. "If you're going to play with it again, do it sooner rather than later."

Ulrike stared over Domino's shoulder. "Still the alpha here, little brother."

"I'm older than you," Tunstall ground out.

"And yet, I'm the alpha, unless you wish to challenge?"

Seconds ticked by, and Domino's mind whirled with how to take advantage of a fight breaking out.

Tunstall dropped his gaze.

"Good choice," Ulrike said. "We can't afford to fight among ourselves, but you're right about a little playtime." Cold green eyes turned to Domino.

"Come on then, siren, make the human do something; dance, or die, you pick. Personally, I'd say die; he did sell you out for five grand and a fuck, although it was a damn epic fuck even if I say so myself."

Domino held Ulrike's gaze, as Rory let out a squeak and sprinted for the exit. A door slammed.

Tunstall took a few steps forward. Side by side, the beta was a little shorter, and not quite as broad as his brother; he still loomed over Domino.

"With your permission, alpha?"

Ulrike scowled as if someone had stolen his birthday present. "Knock yourself out."

Instead of making for the door, the beta stripped off his shirt, toed off his shoes, and then shoved his jeans down. Domino got a fleeting glimpse of a hairy, tanned body, then the shifter's outline shimmered, and a giant GSD type dog with reddish fur stood in his place. The animal yipped, then took off after Rory, the amulet still around his neck.

"We tested that they stayed in place when we shifted, just in case."

Domino turned his attention to the exhibit. He'd never seen such a big tank. It seemed to be a real slice of the ocean until he looked closer. The rocks weren't real. They were artfully designed to hide the human-made pipes and equipment that kept this prison functioning.

The ray, the sharks, and groupers, were prisoners as much as Domino. He wondered if they'd always lived here, or if they remembered the open ocean. If they did, would it be easier for them to live on the memories or to never have experienced that freedom? If he didn't manage to escape, Domino would soon know the answer from personal experience.

"Nothing to say? No pleading on your pet's behalf? Tunstall will rip him apart unless I stop him; he hates anyone who isn't pack."

Domino stared at the alpha, determined not to give him anything, especially not his emotion. He was a commodity to this shifter, nothing more, and he'd be damned if he gave them a sliver of entertainment. One request would lead to another until he'd be nothing but a puppet on a string.

As for Rory, Domino believed that you reaped what you sowed, and the human was a sly, greedy, amoral bastard. Domino might be a hedonistic thief and a coward, but after Sean, he'd sworn never to use his ability again, not even to save his pitiful life. He just wanted to be left alone to die in peace.

Ulrike moved to the side of the frame, and Domino understood why the frame hung a few inches off the floor.

Yes, it made it difficult to balance, but it also put their groins at the same level.

The alpha reached out a thick finger and traced the edge of the purple mark on Domino's butt. He gritted his teeth, following a lilting melody in his head.

"Such a shame, without these, you'd be quite attractive. You look like a damn pinto pony," he mused, almost to himself.

Domino gave him the finger with his uninjured hand.

A chuckle rumbled from the alpha's chest. "Your aunt said you were bolshie, but with these" —he pulled the amulet out of his shirt— "there's no need to keep quiet; you can't influence us, and there are no innocent humans around.

Ulrike huffed out a laugh. "Innocent humans, now there's a conflict if ever I heard one. It always surprises me that humans claim that demons are the evil ones when a human will sell you out even faster; and for pocket change too.

"Tunstall will be dealing with that little problem for us right now. He has a real talent for making a body look like an authentic wild animal kill." Ulrike looked from side to side as if checking for spies. "He even takes a few nibbles, just to make it look good, you understand."

Killing innocent humans was an immediate prison sentence for supernaturals if you were caught. Domino's people avoided the issue by the careful selection of victims and body disposal, although Domino hadn't known that, not until after.

FIVE YEARS BEFORE...

This was Domino's time, the only chance he got to experience the life-giving ocean without revolting anyone with his freaky body. The combination of a male body and his huge power marks made most of the sorority avert their eyes and hurry away. The cove was hidden, only accessible by sea and the tunnel at the rear of the underwater sea cave.

After an hour of swimming within the magical barrier created to keep young sirens from straying too far, Domino sat with his back against a boulder at the base of the cliff, playing his tin pipe. He poured his longing for freedom into the music as he'd heard his family do, but unlike them, Domino only ever played alone.

Rhythmic splashing disturbed him, and the pipe left his lips. The lithe figure swimming around the headland, sparked fear, excitement, and overwhelming curiosity. Domino knew he should hide, should flee back to the house and tell someone. Instead, he tucked himself behind the half-submerged boulder to watch.

He'd never seen anyone outside the sorority. His sisters, aunts, cousins, and mother protected him from the other sirens they claimed would kill him if they knew he existed. Domino obeyed, hid, wore female clothing in case of unexpected visitors, answered to female pronouns, and felt grateful to be alive. Respectful behavior was rewarded by being allowed down here on his own, plus having access to his pipe. This was the first time he'd been here alone for a month.

The stranger kept low in the water, scanning the yellow cliffs that backed the small cove. Then they walked out of the sea and Domino's life changed.

Defined abs, muscular chest, not curves, not breasts.

Chin length, curling blond hair glistened with drops of seawater. His skin... it took a few seconds to confirm that the man had no power marks. *Human, he's human.* The sheer life in the young man tightened Domino's abs.

"Hey, kid, don't bother hiding, I've already seen and heard you. You play really well. I bet you're spying on the girls from the school too, right? I hear they all go skinny dipping." A bright smile lit the young man's face together with a conspirator's wink. "Don't worry, I'm not going to say anything. I shouldn't be here either."

Domino dived into the surf, but instead of swimming for the safety of the underwater cave entrance, he hung just under the surface. He watched, lungs screaming, until the tanned vision left.

That night, instead of imagining one of the porn actors he'd seen on Melody's tablet, he dreamed of touching, of being touched, by the hard body of the stranger.

Domino was back on the beach at dawn, pipe in his hand. Sirens didn't become strong enough to influence others until their third or fourth decade, but maybe the young human simply liked his playing.

He'll come back, Domino told himself, he had to come back.

"It's a shame about your pet," Ulrike continued, "but it can't be helped. If he gave you up that easily, he'll blabber to anyone. He's a damn good fuck, but my knot gave him a bit of a surprise. Although knowing him as you do, you know a bit of pain just sends him higher. One session yesterday afternoon and he couldn't stop jabbering about you. I bet he would have come along even without the promise of money."

Perhaps the world would be better off without Rory, perhaps not. Whatever happened to the human, Domino knew the world would be better off without a male siren in it. It was time to get on with making that happen.

Having the more volatile shifter here, the youngest one, would have been better, but maybe he could push Ulrike far enough too.

Heart thumping, Domino tried for a bored expression, circled his good hand, and rolled his eyes. There wasn't a great deal more he could do cuffed naked to a metal frame without using his voice.

Domino's breathing stalled as the shifter's jaw tensed and he crowded forward until his chest pressed against Domino's back. The alpha was several inches taller, out massed him by nearly half again, and could have more than a hundred years of life experience to draw on.

"Think you can fool me, boy? Even though I'm not in fur, you reek of fear." A meaty fist landed in his wet hair and jerked his head back, exposing his throat.

Domino closed his eyes, swallowed. *Do it, you bastard, just do it.*

A nose ran up the soft, exposed flesh of the side of his throat. Heat radiated against Domino's naked skin through the shifter's now damp clothes.

"Fucked a lot of things in my time, but never a siren," the alpha rumbled against Domino's skin, then pinched the flesh over his carotid artery with his teeth. The pain teased rather than threatened.

Despite the humidity, Domino shivered. This would be his future, except the sirens would force unwanted pleasure from him while this shifter merely wanted to get off.

"Still not talking? Well, maybe I can persuade you to beg, although I might have to use a blindfold so I don't see these fuck ugly marks." The shifter paused as if waiting for Domino to speak.

He didn't know what the man expected. Begging not to be hurt, to be released? Bargaining? The only currency Domino possessed was his voice and that wasn't happening, even if it couldn't affect the shifter.

A hand stroked down his back, grabbed, then squeezed his ass hard. "Do you want it, siren, is that why you won't talk? Will you run like your pet if I let you down, or are you going to stick this ass in the air for me?"

Domino held still, relaxed as possible, trying not to give the shifter anything.

"Tough guy, huh? I can appreciate that. I wouldn't give a shit for that human either."

A hand closed around his balls, squeezed. Pain spiked, and Domino let out an involuntary squeak.

"So you can make noises, nice to know. But these are what your aunt is willing to pay a million for; she doesn't give a shit about what you can do with your voice, but I care. I care a great deal. My brothers and I, we're in the bounty business, and it seems to me that you telling someone to stop or give us information is a hell of a lot easier than doing all that running. Less bloody for all concerned too. A few easy marks and we could make that million your family promised without a problem."

Helping these shifters was the second to last thing he'd do, but he needed them to let their guard down. Hopefully, they'd consider him escaping the biggest risk, but without his talon, he'd need something sharp to finish the job unless he could goad one into ending it for him.

Fighting wouldn't get him anywhere apart from hurt,

but he couldn't stomach toadying up like Rory. Besides, it didn't seem to have done the human any good.

Shutting down, not reacting in any way, no matter the provocation, until an opportunity presented itself was the only strategy he had.

Bracing himself not to react, Domino closed his eyes.

"Stick your ass out."

Domino hesitated, mind and belly churning at the thought of being fucked by Ulrike.

"Your choice is obeying, or I'll be pissed when I fuck you. This is going to happen either way. I'm horny, and Tunstall is probably munching on the only other available hole, and not in a fun way." Ulrike's cocky smile made Domino want to kick him in the nuts. Instead, he gave a blank look and turned his head away.

Don't react, whatever he does, don't react. Boring, you're boring.

The imprisoned residents of the tank circled their communal cell, playing their never-ending power games. He wondered how often the staff had to replace fish killed by their fellow prisoners. In the wild, subordinate individuals could move away, find a less desirable territory, here, they'd be harried to death.

A calloused hand palmed his butt cheek, pulled it aside. Domino suppressed a shudder.

"Nervous? You should be. Even bitches have trouble taking me, and they're built for it. If you ask nicely, I'll make it easier; prep you real good."

Domino swallowed, kept his mouth shut.

"Have it your way."

Ulrike prised Domino's cheeks apart, hawked, and spat. Domino couldn't help it, his hole tightened against the invasion.

"You're a shy little thing, aren't you? I like that. Don't worry, we're going to get to know each other real well."

Domino screwed his eyes shut at the sound of a zipper being pulled down, clothing being removed.

Fuck, he's really going to do it. Not even a flicker of desire curled in his belly, unlike the only other time he'd bottomed. Then his lust had been incandescent, lighting up the night like a shooting star.

Heat against his back. A finger testing the way, then a broad, blunt head. *Too big, that's too fucking...* Pain lanced through Domino's hole. Mouth open in a soundless scream, he scrabbled with his toes, trying to lift up away from the tearing pain. Slipping on the wet frame, he lost his toe hold. His entire weight dragged on his wrists and the shaft stabbed in deeper. Ulrike wrapped a heavily muscled arm around Domino's waist holding him up. The alpha's other hand gripped the frame above Domino's head. Shifter behind him, in him, and front welded to the frame, there was nowhere to go, no way to escape.

"I'm going to wreck you, boy." Ulrike's words invaded Domino's ear as his cock violated his body.

Regret filled his soul more than the pain. He should have killed himself as soon as Melody told him his future. Instead, his selfish desires had directed his actions. The story was repeating itself, but this time, Rory was the victim. Domino swore to himself that it wouldn't happen again as Ulrike thrust against him, grunting in pleasure.

But I said that last time too.

CHAPTER SIX

A low growl followed by a human shriek from the rear of the building meant Jude's time was up. Thankful that his feet were already bare, he ripped off his shirt and jeans. Going up against a Karnak as an unarmed man would be even riskier.

His paws hit the ground running, the anticipation of the hunt thrumming through his veins. But was the canine playing with its human prey or hunting for real? The first might mean the Karnak would be more focused on its environment; it would be thinking about herding its prey, making it run, rather than a killing bite.

Following the growls, Jude lifted his muzzle, detecting the slight breeze with his whiskers, then padded around to the downwind side of the building.

Slowing to stalking pace, head still, he placed his paws silently.

"I get it; you're strong, fucking awesome in fact," The human let out a desperate laugh. "I can be useful, believe me."

The human begging for his life gave Jude cover to stalk

around the building's corner, almost on his belly. Every nerve thrumming, every muscle coiled to spring. Quick and deadly, his prey seldom even knew they were being hunted before he was on them, and that went for food as well as bounties. A well-fed house cat might play with its food, Jude never did. Even the most innocuous prey could escape and end up killing you. The only safe prey were dead prey.

Dogs went after their prey full throttle, running them down, exhausting them through blood loss, maybe even hamstringing the poor fuck while the rest of the pack caught up. Sticking together, in and out, nip and harry, never exposing one member to too much individual danger, was their technique. It wouldn't help them against an enemy in the dark who could take them down one by one.

The breeze ruffled his short, dense fur. Jude froze, just in case his scent carried. When the low growling didn't pause, he crept forward again.

The human balanced against a tree in the moonlight, the right leg of his jeans torn and bloodied.

A red-furred dog, bigger than Jude, stood in front of the human hackles raised. Snarling, the dog inched closer, head held low.

"Please, I'll be good. I was good, right? I did everything you asked." Sweat shone on the human's pale face. As the other brothers hadn't been called, this wasn't a drawn-out chase for shits and giggles, but an execution.

No sympathy stirred for the human, and the increased growl volume said the shifter agreed. Rory was a bottom feeder, happy to sell his lover for whatever the Karnaks had offered.

"Ulrike's in charge. He... he'll be–"

If Jude had been wearing skin, not fur, he would have rolled his eyes. The human not only flung his arm out towards the building like an offering to be bitten, but also tried to drive a wedge between pack members. Packs might argue between themselves, but when threatened by an outsider, they closed ranks like nothing else.

A glint of silver around the red neck proved the air elemental's theory; the Karnaks were using some sort of protection talisman. As it hadn't protected Rollin from him, Jude assumed it had a specific function, probably counteracting the siren's abilities. It explained how they'd caught him. Although it didn't explain how Ranulfo had died. The stab wound to his throat had been almost surgical.

Tunstall leaped, grabbed the human's wrist, shaking it for all he was worth. Powerful haunches bunched as he pulled backward. The human didn't even scream as he got dragged to the ground like a ragdoll. The dog released his grip only to lunge for his victim's neck.

Jude jumped, knocking the dog sideways as he fastened his teeth around Tunstall's throat. The mouthful of fur wasn't pleasant, but he held on tight. The dog stumbled, staying on its paws. Jude might have neutralized the dog's main weapon, its teeth, but Tunstall was still dangerous. Fortunately, cats had five natural weapons, not just one.

Falling to his side, Jude brought his back feet up, raking the dog's soft belly, tearing, ripping. Tunstall twisted, but with the weight on his throat, he couldn't get up, and his paws were useless with Jude this close.

Flesh rippled in Jude's mouth as Tunstall shifted. Fists pounded at his flanks, his head; Jude hung on for grim death. Letting go now might well cost him his life. The canine outweighed him, and if Tunstall alerted his brother, not even Jude's claws and teeth would protect him from two dogs. Jude was fast in fur form, but he was built for stealth, ambush, not long-distance speed with fangs snapping at his ass.

The next punch lacked the force of the previous ones, and if Jude had been able to smile, he would have done. Instead, he clamped down ever harder on his victim's throat. Tunstall grabbed for Jude's throat, hoping to strangle his attacker back. The heartbeat against his tongue slowed, the body relaxed. Jude hung on, ten seconds, thirty. The pulse faltered, stopped.

If they'd been alone, he would have kept his position for a minute or more, but more enemies could be lurking in the dark. Still holding Tunstall's limp throat, Jude got his paws back under him, stood up, listening hard.

Wind in the treetops. The whimpers of a badly mauled human. Jude dropped the body. Wide staring eyes. Black holes where his teeth had punctured a pale throat. Blood on his tongue. He licked his lips. It would be so easy to give in, to feed on the hot, fresh meat he'd just killed. He didn't. The supernatural council didn't think highly of carnivorous species feeding on other sentients, although it was fine for many of the demon species. Still, most of them left their prey alive and physically unharmed.

"Please, please don't hurt me." The human's whisper screamed of his weakness, his vulnerability. Feline instincts urged him to take down injured prey.

Jude turned golden eyes on the heavily bleeding man. During the fight, Rory had dragged himself to a tree and now leaned against it as if it could save him. The human didn't have a bounty on him, hadn't faced trial. Killing him could lead to an investigation, but no one said Jude had to save him, even if it were possible.

He cast one last look at Tunstall's body, then turned to the building. Time to finish the job.

CHAPTER SEVEN

Jude shifted so he could open the rear door to the building. Fur might be faster, but having hands gave a lot of advantages in the human world. Unfortunately, his pale skin in human form wasn't one of them. The alpha would spot him in a split second.

Back in his fur, Jude was glad he'd been the odd one out in his family. Melanistic leopard shifters weren't common and often were shunned by their golden brethren. He still had spots as a cat, but they were hard to see unless you were up close. A golden coat might be an advantage in a desert or savanna environment; black was an advantage when dealing with humans. The silver chain around his neck might make him more visible, but he hoped his thick fur disguised it a little.

Moving slowly, and with the strong scents in this place, Ulrike hopefully wouldn't notice him until it was too late. Like his older brother, Ulrike would likely win in a face to face fight, but Jude wouldn't give him that advantage.

Padding down the dark corridor, he sensed the life around him. This area contained four-foot square tanks, with single species exhibits. It reminded him of the supernatural prison but on a smaller scale. Although these inmates hadn't done anything to deserve incarceration.

Soft light came from further down the corridor. The archway into a cavernous space bore a seaweed and fish mural with the legend "Pacific Ocean" at the apex. This was the main attraction, a vast tank you could walk through via a tunnel.

A whimper of pain and a jangle of chain came from an open doorway to his right emblazoned with "Staff Only". Jude froze, exploring with his other senses. Under the strong damp scent, he picked up the musky odor of a canine. He sniffed again, trying to pick up a second scent. As much as he disliked Ulrike, he didn't picture the alpha making those soft suffering whimpers, but was it another unfortunate human or the siren?

"I told you it would hurt. If you ask me to stop, I'll get it to go down sooner rather than later. Or I could expand it. Do you fancy that, boy?"

Jude crept into the room. Light filtered through the water from the other side of the huge aquarium. Ulrike's body obscured most of the smaller one before him, but one of the pale arms visible above the shifter's head bore a purple mark.

"Have you split already? Are you wondering if that's jizz or blood dripping down your leg? Go on, beg me to stop. Just a word, that's all it'll take."

Although the cuffs wrists trembled, one finger rose from a fist, gave a little twist. If Jude had been in human form, he would have laughed out loud at the defiance. His amusement vanished; perhaps the siren wanted to encourage Ulrike. If the siren had masochistic tendencies, the poor bastard didn't have a clue what he'd got himself into.

Curiosity won over the urge for immediate action. The canine shifter wouldn't be going anywhere for at least a few minutes due to his knot. The awkwardness, the danger, of being physically tied to a partner via your cock didn't bear thinking about. Maybe that was one of the reasons canines felt more comfortable living in packs; there was always someone around to protect you. *Well, not this time.* Still, knotting might be better than his own issues. Even incubi looked nervous when he mentioned his fur form.

Belly low to the ground, Jude crept around the outer edge of the maintenance room until he could see the cuffed man's side.

The siren's forehead rested against one arm, curling dark hair obscured his face. The rest of his body almost glowed; it was so pale, but the dark marks swirled across his side almost like those of a clouded leopard. Just like that almost legendary cat, the siren was rare, precious.

Ulrike's arm snaked around the pale body, grabbing at the siren's groin.

"You're not enjoying this at all. Not that it matters, because I fucking love it." The shifter's hand abandoned the siren's junk and moved up to the slender, pale throat.

"Tell me to stop, make a noise. I know you can."

The siren fixed his gaze on the slowly circling shark in the tank. The dim light reflected off a tear trickling down his cheek. Jude could almost hear him thinking, *'Endure, survive. Just a little longer.'*

Jude shifted into his skin form. "Let him go."

Two heads twisted towards him. Anger replaced the initial surprise on the alpha's face. The siren looked... disappointed.

Was I wrong, did he want it? Whatever the siren wanted didn't matter now. Jude had played his card.

"They sent you too?" Ulrike's lip lifted in disgust as he focused on the chain around Jude's neck. "Damn sirens never trust anyone. I told them I wanted an exclusive contract."

Jude shrugged. "Stealth over numbers seems to be a winning combination so far. Although numbers don't matter if you don't stick together."

The alpha stilled, then gave two sharp barks, almost against the siren's ear. The youngster remained frozen as if hoping that not moving would mean he'd be forgotten.

Jude approved the behavior. He didn't know what would happen if Ulrike tried to pull himself free before his knot went down, but it left Jude with a dilemma.

Right now, his prey was pretty much immobilized, an easy kill if he acted quickly. He glanced at the siren. How would he react if Jude killed Ulrike mid tie? He pictured the body falling, maybe remaining attached to his victim.

Fuck. Having that much weight on the knot might cause the kid to prolapse. One thing was certain, Ulrike wouldn't stand there, patiently bleeding out to save the siren injury. Waiting until Ulrike freed himself would mean having to fight the big canine in this enclosed environment. None of those options appealed, but the last could mean game over for Jude, not Ulrike.

"It's just us; your brothers were pretty occupied last time I saw them."

"So, how's business, Moreno? Still rounding up pick-pockets for the council?"

The delaying tactic couldn't have been clearer if Ulrike had said, 'How about we just chat until my pack get here and I'm free so I can chew your throat out?'

Jude circled behind the pair, and Ulrike played right into his hands by twisting to keep him in view. The siren moaned in pain. Ulrike could move his upper body, his feet, but he remained fused to the siren who balanced himself on the frame. The canine had left the frame a few inches from the ground to make it more comfortable to fuck his captive.

"Hey, Moreno, keep where I can see you. We need to discuss where we go from here. You know I've always admired your work."

"Why would I do that when this angle is so much better?"

Ulrike chuckled. "Why, Moreno, I never knew you cared."

"I didn't, not until I saw your brothers playing with that human. He got quite a long way before they caught him. You Karnaks are... interesting."

Giving the alpha the idea that his brothers still lived might give him a little more time. Like any pack animal, Ulrike would prefer to wait for back up before attacking.

The alpha let out a bark of laughter. "Hang on for a few more minutes, kitty, and I'll see what I can arrange. As it happens, I have an unexpected vacancy that might just suit–"

Jude pounced. Claws extended, he buried one fist of talons in Ulrike's throat and swept the other down the canine's belly, but with only one claw extended.

Ulrike let out a gurgling shriek as he collapsed backward, hands going to his throat. Jude swiveled out from behind him as he fell, blood pumping from both his throat and groin, where Jude had severed his cock.

Blood covered the siren's pale backside and thighs, every muscle taut.

"Get it out! Get it the fuck out of me!"

Jude wasn't sure how a siren should sound, but this frantic sharp babble wasn't it.

"Breathe, relax, it should–"

The siren turned his head, dark eyes blazed into Jude's. "Relax? Are you fucking kidding me? There's a severed cock up my ass." Those bright eyes closed, he drew in a shaky breath, then opened them again. "Reach down, grab that thing, and pull it out. Now."

The back of Jude's head buzzed. Without conscious thought, his hand reached out, palmed the tight buttock–

Jude stumbled back, panting and sweating. Even with the charm around his neck, the siren had controlled him for a second.

The pale body turned away, almost convulsing as he vomited to the side, one heave, then another. A bloody mass fell from the siren's ass, joining the small pile of puke on the floor.

From a distance of a few feet, Jude said, "It's gone, and he's dead. So are his brothers. But if you ever, and I mean ever, try to thrall me again, I'll–"

The siren turned to him. "You'll do what, kill me? Be my fucking guest." Reddened lips pressed together, and he hung his head.

"You want to die? Is that why you didn't try to thrall the Karnaks? With the power you have, I'm sure it would've worked on one of them, even with the charms."

The siren didn't reply, but he slumped against the frame. Blood and vomit slicked his legs, and Jude abruptly remembered his age. *Shit.*

"Let's get you free and cleaned up. Do you know where the key to the cuffs is?"

The siren didn't look at him, but as he hadn't collapsed, he remained conscious. *Probably traumatized, and with good reason.*

Jude cast around, spotted a pile of clothes that had to be

Ulrike's. A quick search found the key, a wallet, a phone, and another amulet. *Must be Ranulfo's.*

Even that brief thrall had completely weirded Jude out. Maybe there was something about working in a group after all. He slipped the silver chain over his head, trying not to wince as the second fingerbone touched his naked skin; it hadn't felt this bad in fur form.

The amulet around Ulrike's neck would be covered in blood, just like the one on Tunstall. It would have to be removed so Oroshi could transport the bodies. Given time, he could probably string all four on one chain, although he damn well hoped silver wasn't a requirement. Not being able to use the elemental's transport services would suck, but not as much as being turned into a permanent puppet.

Going over to Ulrike's body, he pulled the chain over the dead man's head. A nearby empty aquarium provided somewhere to wash off the blood. Yes, both he and the siren needed a full body wash, but he wasn't going anywhere near the youngster without all the protection available. He slipped the chain over his head, where it joined the other two. *Just Tunstall's to collect now.*

He eyed the big tank briefly as a possible place to wash, then dismissed it. Water didn't bother him as much as it did some cat shifters, but he had considerable blood on him, and he'd seen more than one shark moving through the gloom.

The cuffs clanging against the frame caused Jude to look over. The siren raised his eyebrows and tugged on the cuffs again.

"Sorry, yeah, I've got the key. Just looking for some way to clean us up. I don't suppose taking a paddle with the sharks would be a good idea."

The siren looked pointedly at the wall in front of him then down at the floor between his feet.

There was a drain in the concrete a few inches in front of the bottom edge of the frame. Jude walked around the frame, skirting the small puddle of vomit, and peered into the gloom. A hose reel hung on the wall. It made sense to have water readily available in an aquatic exhibit.

Jude turned back to the siren and realized he didn't even know his name.

"I'm Jude, Jude Moreno. I'm a leopard shifter, and I'm here to–"

The siren turned away. "Ok, I get that this is amazingly fucked up, but we need to tidy up and be out of here before the human staff turn up." He paused, waiting for an answer, or a glance of acknowledgment. He got neither.

"At least tell me your name."

That made the siren look up. His brows drew together, head tilted.

"You think it's odd I don't know your name? The sirens didn't send me, I–"

The cuffs rattled, and Jude's gaze rose. The siren pointed emphatically at the hose.

Embarrassment welled up. "Right. Sorry. Blood and..." Jude shut up and grabbed the hose. He thought about undoing the cuffs then glanced at the bloody detached lump of flesh still inches from the siren's slender feet. Yeah, seeing that probably wouldn't do the guy's mental health any good.

Jude turned the tap on, tested the gently flowing water with his hand. "Sorry, it's pretty cold."

The siren looked at him, with eyes far older than his age. Jude recognized the expression from looking in the mirror, but not for many years. Hopelessness. The man cuffed to the frame wanted to be clean, but beyond that, he didn't care what happened to him.

Jude sluiced himself off, then wordlessly turned the

spay on the cuffed man. The siren didn't even twitch, just closed his eyes. If he hadn't witnessed his impassioned outburst earlier, Jude would've assumed the siren utterly without feeling.

Moving behind the bloody, battered man, Jude kicked the severed cock towards the body it'd come from and hopefully out of immediate sight. After dealing with the remnants of vomit, Jude played the water up the slim, muscular legs and over the rigid ass. The blood sluiced away as he moved the hose higher. Satisfied that he'd removed all the traces of abuse he could, Jude pointed the hose back at the floor.

Pink lines made their way down the siren's pale inner thighs.

"You're bleeding."

CHAPTER EIGHT

As if I didn't know that.

"Stick your ass out. I'll see how bad it is."

Despite his determination to close himself off, to not feel anything, every muscle tensed at the thought of anything else going near his hole. It was bad enough being on display like this. Either way, Domino couldn't do a damn thing about it.

Jude clearly wanted to gain his confidence, and for a few moments, Domino teetered on the verge of believing him. But the last comment just enforced that he'd merely changed captors, and it sounded as if this one wanted to abuse him just as much as the previous lot.

Jude groaned. "Fuck, that sounded bad. I'm not like them; I just wanted to see if you need medical attention."

So you can get a bonus when you turn in a healthy bounty and get your jollies at the same time? In your dreams, kitty.

Domino hoped he managed to convey all of his thoughts in the single brief look he shot the shifter. He rattled his cuffs, asking the cat to prove what he said with actions.

Body heat against his side, not his back, was the last thing he expected.

"I'll let you go, but only if you promise not to run. In a few minutes, I'll be calling an air elemental to transport–"

Domino thought he'd be ready, that he could face his fate with courage, but the prospect of being face to face with his family in the next few minutes froze his marrow.

Throwing himself backward, he pulled on the cuffs. He couldn't spend his remaining days and years being sneered at, being used by women he disgusted, he couldn't end up as bits of bone–

"Hey, hey, calm down, I'll uncuff you. If you don't want to see an air elemental, you don't have to. Do sirens have something against air elementals in general, or is it just you?"

Body heat against his side, first at his ankles then wide hands reaching up to his own, the flash of a silver key. The last cuff fell open. Domino stumbled sideways, away from his new captor, away from the mutilated body of the last. Every muscle ached, and pain spiked in his hole, his hand.

Jude stood between Domino and the exit, hands spread, naked except for the three amulets around his neck. If he could shift as fast as the Karnaks, Domino wouldn't have a hope of escaping, not in the cat's terrestrial element. Running would only excite a predator who eyed him like a tasty morsel he wanted to chase down.

Domino backed slowly away until his back touched the huge tank. He covered his groin with one hand and the big mark on his upper chest with the other. Tilting his head down, his hair hid a little of his face, but it wasn't enough, not by a long way.

"I really am an idiot." Jude tried a smile. His nose was broad, a little crooked, and a scar cut through his eyebrow.

This man was a fighter, a hunter, and he'd protect his prize for as long as it took to deliver it.

"I forgot non-shifter species aren't comfortable with nudity."

Keeping between Domino and the exit, the shifter moved over to Ulrike's pile of clothes, picked up the plaid overshirt, and held it out. "It's way too big, and I can't do anything about the smell, but you can use it until we get something better?"

Domino didn't move.

Does he think I'm stupid? Then again, if he does, that could work to my advantage. But the elemental's coming. I've got no time to work on him.

The balled-up shirt landed at his feet. He looked up.

Crouched on his haunches, Jude looked just as dangerous as when he'd been upright maybe even more as he could spring from that position.

"Look, I know you're scared, hurt, and you've been through one hell of a crappy experience. But please, believe me, I don't work for the sirens."

But you work for someone. Using his toes, because the only alternative was crouching and with the way his ass felt that was out, Domino grabbed the shirt and transferred it to his uninjured hand.

"You sure you're a siren, not a monkey shifter?"

Domino put the shirt on, waited for the cat's next move. Ulrike's scent surrounded him, and he couldn't help staring at the body. *One moment alive and strong, the next just meat, because of me.*

Jude followed his gaze. "Yeah, I think it's time we got rid of that distraction too. I'll tell the air elemental not to go near you, ok? It won't do anything I tell it not to. It owes me for dealing with the Karnaks; they tortured and killed its kin."

That's why he's here? He's not here for me? Hope swelled in his chest like a wave. *Maybe he's telling the truth. Maybe he does just want to help. But I'm not taking another chance. Time to man up and stop avoiding the end.*

His knowledge of other supernaturals was sketchy, but one thing he did know was that air and water didn't mix. The thought of flying terrified Domino almost as much as fire. An air elemental probably had an even more extreme aversion to water.

Jude closed his eyes and mumbled. It was all the distraction Domino needed. Sprinting to the ladder Tunstall had used, Domino was up it and diving into the tank before Jude finished calling, "Stop!"

The tepid water surrounded and cocooned him. Feeling safe for the first time since spotting Jude at Blaze, Domino swam down to the floor of the tank a few feet from the wall separating the water from the maintenance room.

A painfully thin being with pale blue, almost translucent skin stood next to Jude. Both stared at him.

"So that's a male siren. Bit funny looking." The absurdity of the comment from a being who looked like sticks tied together had Domino giving it the finger.

Jude frowned. "Do you think he heard you, or is he lip reading?"

"Oh, he heard me all right. Things probably sound clearer to him underwater than they do on land." The elemental shuddered. "Ugh, I can't even think about all that water pressing around me. The humidity in here is enough to make me droop on its own. The only thing worse would be being buried alive. Even being indoors makes me twitchy."

"How long can he stay under?"

Blue tinged eyebrows drew together. "And why do you think I'd be an expert on sirens? Air elemental, not water, remember? Let's get this over with so you can chase Tunstall. I always thought he'd be the last." It moved over to Ulrike.

"Ulrike was the last. Tunstall's outside, but you'll have to wait for me. He's wearing one of these." Jude touched the amulets around his neck.

The elemental recoiled with a hiss. "Do you have to do that? That's enough silver to kill me three times over. I can almost feel the burn from here."

Jude glanced over at Domino, then angled his body away from the tank. "Do you think silver is necessary for them to work? When I was only wearing one, he almost thralled me. If I can put them on something else, I–"

"Again, do I look like a witch? I'm an air elemental," it enunciated carefully. "I ride the winds and transport things through the gaps between gases. Try taking them off and see what happens," it said and turned to the body. A choked noise of disgust came from the blue lips. "Ugh, did you have to cut his cock off? I appreciate the suffering, but couldn't you be less... inventive? I've got to touch it now."

Jude snatched up Ulrike's jeans, picked up the severed cock with the inside, and tied the legs loosely around the neck of the body.

"There. Don't be such a baby. It's only meat like the rest of him."

"Your fashion sense is extraordinary, but I think my sibling would approve of your inventiveness. Death by severed cock is a new one. I'll meet you outside, but you'd better get a move on, this place opens in a couple of hours and the staff will be here before that."

Jude nodded towards the tank. "Can he affect you?"

Domino almost laughed as the blue being rolled its eyes, crouched, touched Ulrike's shoulder, and vanished.

Sitting on the sand, life-giving energy seeping into him, Domino felt better by the second, his ass no longer stung and his thumb only throbbed a little. It sucked that he couldn't simply stay here. Having a man swimming about in their exhibit, a man who only breathed every ten to fifteen minutes would cause quite a stir. But spending the rest of his short life as a lab rat didn't appeal any more than being a sperm donor for his fellow sirens.

Most of his kind simply swam into the deep ocean when they felt their time coming. The phrase, "They've taken their last swim," was a gentle way to inform a relative that someone had died. This wasn't the ocean, but it was a damn sight better than an overdose of heroin in a bone-dry desert grave.

A dead body at the bottom of the tank would make far more sense than a live one, and maybe some of the permanent prisoners would enjoy an extra snack. As his body would be taken to a human morgue, it also meant his family wouldn't get it. A win-win situation, except for the death part. He'd already been under long enough for his lungs to ache more than his hand. *Just a little longer.*

Frantic banging forced him to open his eyes. Jude stood against the outside of the tank. Eyes wide and dark, he jerked his thumb toward the surface.

Domino smiled, shook his head, closed his eyes. The banging resumed.

He opened his eyes again, annoyed that his last moments wouldn't be as serene as he'd dreamed.

Jude held the three chains, amulets dangling from them, out to the side. "Your father sent me; he only just found out about you. He's a mage and can extend your life. Use your voice, ask me if it's true, because I damn well don't want to go in with those sharks to pull you out, but I will if I have to."

The thought of the cat trying to catch him in this environment was laughable... unless he waited until Domino passed out. He'd assumed his father was dead, just like every other siren sperm donor. Their biology just didn't allow for a sire to live beyond conception.

It's bullshit, it's got to be. But I'm special, what if my father was too? Hope dangled like the bones of his ancestors from the chains. Domino didn't want to die, he just refused to be a sorority captive and the reason the whole world went to shit. *But if there's a chance...*

Domino mimed throwing overarm.

Jude balled the three chains and tossed them into the tank. Two black tip sharks surged towards the flashing metal as it sank, shimmering, towards the bottom.

Domino launched himself up, snatching the amulets before they were swallowed. One shark swerved away, the other took a punch to the nose before it gave up. His head broke the surface and he drew in a shuddering breath. It felt good, like a new beginning.

Goosebumps covered his skin as he left the warmth, the security, of the water.

Jude held out a hand to help him down the ladder. Domino ignored it.

"Still sulking? We're going to have to get you over that. No one likes a sulker."

The absurdity that he'd care about being liked made Domino shake his head. He'd never met anyone quite like this before. Deadly one second, cracking jokes the next, and all the time as naked as the day he'd been born and completely comfortable with it.

Domino pulled the dripping shirt around himself a little tighter, angling his head so his wet hair covered his face as much as possible.

"This way." Jude padded off into the darkness, muscles moving under his bronze skin. Even if Domino hadn't known he was a cat shifter, he might have guessed from the way he moved —controlled and loose at the same time. The canine shifters had vibrated with tense energy.

The cold breeze chilled his wet skin as Jude opened the door to the outside, but Domino paused at the sight of hazy mountains in the distance. The town where he'd been hiding had been on a flood plain. The only good news was there were no mountains within two hundred miles of where he grew up. It didn't mean that it hadn't been the Karnaks' destination or that they weren't taking him to another sorority.

"Over there." Jude pointed into the trees. "We've got to take off Tunstall's amulet before the elemental can move him."

Enough light filtered through the coniferous trees for Domino to see the blue figure standing next to another naked corpse.

"Go on, add it to your collection." Jude nodded towards the bloody corpse, rubbing at his arms. It appeared the cat shifter preferred a warmer climate.

Domino felt clean, almost pristine from his swim. The thought of getting any more blood on him caused more of a shudder than the frigid temperature.

Who is this man who treated violent death like it happened to him every day?

Maybe it did.

"I haven't got all day," the elemental ground out.

After another glance at where Domino stood, arms wrapped around himself, Jude went over and ripped the chain from the torn throat. "Be a good..." Jude paused, frowned. "What are you anyway, male or female? I can never tell."

"Does it matter?"

Jude shrugged. "Not to me. 'It' just seems a bit rude."

"I'm male, for now. So can I go or do you need a lecture on the reproductive strategy of my species?"

"No, I'm good. But wiping the CCTV would make the Council happy."

The elemental gave an exasperated sigh and nodded. "If that's all?"

Jude smiled. "I think that about covers it."

The elemental stood. "Judah Moreno, you have the thanks of the air elementals. Your fifty journeys start from now." He glanced at Domino. "And passengers count as additional journeys. I'm not running a coach service." The body and the elemental vanished.

"We're going to have to use the van the Karnaks had. There must be some clothes you can use in there. We just have to fetch my pack and we can be off."

Domino couldn't quite believe what he'd seen and heard. These two were treating this as if it were an everyday experience. Maybe nearly dying and murdering people was for them. Domino felt as if he were in a murky pool, trying to make it to clearer water. Nothing made sense.

Jude cocked his head, frowned. "Damn, I thought he'd be gone by now. We can't leave him in case he can still talk when the staff arrive."

Confused, Domino followed Jude through the trees

perhaps thirty steps, then his feet became rooted to the needle-strewn earth.

Whimpering, Rory pulled himself a few inches with one hand, the other wrapped around his middle. Pinkish grey ropes poked between his fingers.

Jude blew out a breath. "Shit. Go wait in the van; it's right outside the front entrance. I'll join you when I've cleaned up this mess. With any luck, the local police will think it was a bear or coyote attack."

Domino grabbed his arm. Rory was an immoral fucker, but killing him in cold blood?

Jude turned dark eyes on him. "He's got a severe gut wound. It'll be infected, even if his bowel isn't perforated, which would be a miracle looking at that wound. Even if he makes it to hospital, he's got a couple of days of slow agony before he dies." Jude looked Domino straight in the eyes. "And yeah, I think he deserves that for what he did to you, but he might also talk about what he saw. We don't need another supernatural scare among humans. Don't worry, the supernatural council will approve this. I work for them occasionally. Their primary aim is to protect our existence."

Jude stepped towards his next victim. "Hey, Rory. Time's up, I'm afraid. I'll be quick, I promise."

Rory let out a visceral gasp of fear and frantically clawed at the ground, kicking with the one leg that still worked as he tried to move faster.

"Please, I won't say anything, I won't–"

It was so damn tempting to let Jude take the responsibility, but Rory was terrified. As much as Domino thought the human was a waste of space, if Domino hadn't met him, Rory would still be hustling in Blaze, cheerfully sucking cock in dark corners.

He caught Jude's arm. The cat shifter raised an

eyebrow.

Before he changed his mind, Domino thrust the amulets at Jude's chest. Using his ability to ease Rory's passing was one thing, hurting anyone else wouldn't happen.

"You want me to put these on?"

Domino gave a long-suffering blink and nodded. *Why do people always think I'm stupid because I don't talk?*

Jude took the chains, but Domino didn't wait to see if he put them on. Stepping in front of the shifter, he approached the man flopping on the ground like a landed fish. Rory's body was almost more familiar to him than his own. He'd enjoyed looking at Rory, especially when he writhed underneath him. Domino never looked at himself, except when fully dressed, and then only to check all the marks were hidden.

"Hey, Rory," he said and sat in the dirt next to him. And fuck did his voice sound odd after all this time.

"D...Dom?"

"Yeah. Wanna hear a song?"

Rory's eyes widened. "They said you c... could control people with your voice."

Pressing his lips together, Domino nodded. "I can stop it hurting while we wait for the ambulance. You just have to relax and let it work."

"You'd do that for me, after I..."

"Sold me out?" Domino managed a weak smile. "Yeah, but I get to boast about dumping your ass when we get back to Blaze, so it's all good."

"Wha–" Rory coughed; his tense body screamed of the pain it caused.

Domino started singing, low and soft, pushing his need for Rory to relax, to sink into himself, to give up into every note.

CHAPTER NINE

Jude expected a remarkable, commanding voice, but the soft honeyed tone wrapped around him like a familiar blanket. What he didn't expect was Meatloaf's 'Two Out Of Three Ain't Bad'. But only after a few words, tension leached out of the human. He leaned into the siren, a slight smile on his lips.

Remembering that Rory had called the siren "Dom" broke him out of his momentary stupor. He hadn't got any alpha vibes from the man, if anything, he seemed to be on the other end of the spectrum.

As the pair didn't seem to be going anywhere soon, and knowing he'd easily get caught up in the music, Jude retrieved his pack and jacket from the tree. The physical activity helped him focus, but the silky voice followed him, drifting through the dawn light and over the swelling bird song.

Apart from the nap in the car, he'd been awake for over forty-eight hours. When his bare feet touched the ground again, the deep bed of pine needles called like an expensive memory foam bed.

A gust of wind reminded him how much he hated the cold, and it was even worse without his fur. Blinking hard, Jude jogged over to the blue van to get his clothes. The driver's door hung open, ready for the last driver who would never return.

Jude shrugged back into his shirt and jeans that he'd left near the rear wheel but decided against putting on his socks and boots. As always, after he'd spent time in his fur, clothes, especially footwear, felt alien and constraining.

His new charge didn't know where to put his hands to hide his nudity, and Jude's single change of clothing wouldn't fit the siren, but too big was better than none. If Rollin had brought clothes, they might fit. The other three Karnaks had been larger than Jude. At least the driver's door being open for the last few hours had aired the vehicle.

In the back, he found a cylindrical plastic tank taking up much of the space behind the driver's seat. Set on brackets two inches above the floor, it had a tap in the center. Four packs were thrown on top of each other against it. Like him, it looked like the Karnaks traveled light.

A canvas chest further down the vehicle drew his attention. The clothing inside had been disturbed, searched. It varied from ultra-plain to vibrant, but all the shirts were long-sleeved and high necked. The various masks and balaclavas couldn't belong to anyone else but the siren. This must be his vehicle. A sleeping bag and a pillow were tucked next to the chest. No wonder no one had been able to track him down; he'd been living in a van.

Jude looked a little closer at the cylindrical water tank. Something poked out from underneath it. It could have been a piece of stray clothing, but the creases in the Siren's clothes pointed to someone who looked after his possessions, rather than throwing them around.

Jude went down on his belly, reached under, and pulled the muddy brown, surprisingly soft roll of cloth out. Unfolding it, he found a full syringe and a tin whistle.

The siren's two most precious possessions. For most people, the functional, inexpensive instrument would be a simple way to make music, entertain, and while away time. For a siren, it could be a weapon. He put the pipe back and transferred the syringe to his pack. It could be medicine the siren needed, but with the single dose and the suicide attempt in the tank, Jude would be stupid to take a chance on it being lethal. He transferred it to his own pack for safety, intending to get rid of it if it proved to be a "get out of life quick" plan.

After checking the shifters packs for anything useful, and being revolted at their level of hygiene, he dumped them out onto the parking lot. The humans would enjoy puzzling through them as they investigated Rory's death, at least Jude hoped he'd passed by now. If he hadn't, he'd probably have to do it and that might upset his twitchy charge.

The siren's voice still drifted through the oddly still air; Jude paused, listening for signs of wildlife. No birdsong at all.

Were they simply listening to the siren too, or had his voice affected everything without an amulet that could hear him?

A mauled body, bloodstains, and mysterious packs with no owners were a puzzle, but when combined with dead wildlife it could cause international interest.

"Shit." Walking over, he picked up the small brown feathered body he'd spotted. Birds always felt so much lighter than they looked. Its throat fluttered.

Asleep. Fuck, is that all he's trying to do to the human? Laying the bird down, he carried on.

As soon as he caught sight of the pair propped up against a tree, he knew the man in the siren's arms wasn't sleeping. There was a certain "nothingness" about a corpse, a lack of muscle tone that didn't happen when sleeping or unconscious.

The siren's eyes were closed as he sang, "There ain't no way I'm ever gonna love you." A single tear tracking down his face spoke of sadness, regret, not overwhelming heartbreak.

"He's gone," Jude said gently.

The song stopped between one word and the next. Seconds ticked by. Jude itched to check his phone for the time when the siren wordlessly eased out from underneath the body. He didn't spare Rory a glance but walked past Jude, head down, hair obscuring his features, shoulders hunched, hugging himself.

Jude turned and followed him. Strength, natural elegance, even in such a dark place. *I want to see him smile.*

Jude called out, "This trip is going to be a barrel of laughs if you're going to give me the silent treatment the whole way."

The siren's shoulders straightened. He held up a single finger, giving it the deliberate twist Jude had seen earlier.

Jude chuckled. Not a smile, but he'd take it, for now. Today just kept getting better and better. Five bounties gained, four paid out, and one to deliver, and that one wasn't exactly hard on the eyes.

Ulrike's damp shirt clung to the siren's sleek, muscled torso and ended halfway to his knees. Another one of those intriguing purple marks painted the rear of one impossibly pale thigh. Jude remembered how it curled around his butt. Ulrike had called the marks ugly, the siren's body language agreed. Jude wanted to map them, with his tongue. The fantasy pulled up short. This was a bounty, a dangerous, distressed one, not a hook-up.

"Jump in the back and get changed; I'll drive." His silent companion hadn't asked for the amulets back, and Jude wasn't stupid enough to offer. He wouldn't be handing them over even if the siren asked. He'd been lucky so far, but if his bounty switched out of this passivity, he wanted some protection.

The side door slid shut. Jude glanced behind to check the siren was inside and then turned his attention to the road. They had a long way to go.

Ten minutes later, a jean-clad, black hoodie-wearing long, lean form climbed, make that flowed, into the passenger seat. All Jude could see of him were the ends of his fingers and slim, pale, naked feet.

Is he playing me? Going barefoot was a shifter habit, and to Jude, it was sexier than being naked. It teased, promised, like lace underwear. Whatever the case, he wouldn't fall for it.

Many of his quarries were plain evil, deluded, or merely stupid. Finding out their stories passed the time if an air elemental pick-up wasn't immediate, or if it wasn't a council job. Sometimes, bounties thought his friendly, bantering manner meant he'd cut them some slack, maybe he'd even let them go. It never did.

There was enough hate in the world, and Jude saved his for those who mattered. He calmly hunted down the bounties on his list and disposed of them according to council regulations. Dead bounties were safer and keeping immortals in prison had to be expensive. Even the coffers of the supernatural council weren't limitless, and Jude wanted his share. But first, he had to get this bounty banked. He estimated it'd take four, maybe five days to deliver this one, and the more rapport he built up the lower the chances of trouble. Besides, he still wanted to see a smile or any reaction apart from silent depression, and the landscape around here sucked.

"So, Rory called you his Dom? I must admit, I'm not getting any dom vibes from you."

The siren disappeared over the back of the seat again.

"I was only asking; no need to get pissed."

Traffic built up as they neared the nearest town to the aquatic center. It was small, only ten thousand residents, but it'd have somewhere to eat. Jude's belly grumbled at the thought. He almost regretted not snacking on the thralled bird.

The siren slid back into the seat.

"Over your sulk? Good. Even I find it difficult to hold a one-sided conversation, although I am the most interesting guy I know."

The siren tapped an ivory domino on the dash. Jude glanced over before concentrating back on the road. "Can't do much with only one. What is it? A souvenir? Come on, you've got to give me more than that, I suck at charades."

A sign with "May's Diner" appeared as if Jude's belly had conjured it.

He pulled up outside the establishment identical to hundreds of others he'd been in over the years. Booths near the large windows and stools at the counter. This one boasted a garish orange and blue theme.

"I'm not sure how sirens work, but do you need to eat? Not that it matters because I could eat a horse."

The domino tapped on the dash then the siren pointed at his own chest.

The end hitting the dash had six spots. "Your name's

six? Bit odd, but I've heard worse; you could have been lumped with Flipper or something."

Jude tried to keep a straight face as the siren, as Domino, leaned his head back as if looking to the heavens for help.

"So, food? Not sure if they have seaweed here." Jude opened his door and looked down. "Shit, forgot my boots; they're in the back. Grab them for me? You'd better put yours on too. Humans tend to notice if you're not wearing shoes when it's below freezing."

Domino gave him a long-suffering look and climbed effortlessly over the seats. That prolonged immersion certainly seemed to have done him good, but Jude still wanted to check his charge's injuries, particularly his hand.

Domino found the boots, proffered them with his uninjured hand then frowned as he glanced between Jude and the back of his seat.

"Yeah, I could've got them myself." Jude grinned. "I just wanted to watch you climb over again. You're so... bendy." Domino's expression blanked, and Jude hastily added, "And I have never, ever, slept with a bounty or with anyone who didn't want me." He held up two fingers. "The first because it's too damn complicated, and the second because can you think of anyone who wouldn't want this?" He waved a hand at himself.

Domino stared at him through his hair like a shaggy dog.

"Huh, tough audience. Stick something on your feet, and I'll try to wheedle information out of you over a fish burger or whatever you salty types eat. Me, I'm having the biggest rare steak they have."

Domino looked a little green as he shook his head and waved Jude away.

"No appetite? Look, I get it. It was pretty horrible back

there, but you have to eat, right? Even if you don't, I do, and leaving you out here on your own isn't going to happen. You did just try to drown yourself, and Daddy won't pay for a DOA."

Domino's mouth opened, and then his jaw clenched shut. The urge to speak, to communicate, rolled off him in waves, but he still didn't make a sound.

Jude lifted the four chains around his neck and shook them. "You can talk. You can't affect me, remember?"

Domino jabbed a finger at a couple walking into the diner, then at the windows where patrons were visible.

"Yeah, you might affect them, but what are you going to do, make them all want the same breakfast as you? Cause an unprecedented run on filet o' fish?"

Domino's eyes narrowed. He tapped his chest and pointed to the floor.

"Pout as much as you like but you're not staying in here. I've seen the sort of trouble you can get into when you're on your own."

Domino stared out of the window, the very picture of teenage stubbornness.

"You're right, I don't understand what it's like to be you, but I want to."

Domino raised his uninjured hand and rubbed his thumb against the two first fingers.

Jude got out, walked around, and opened Domino's door. "Yeah, I do this for money, but that's not all. Your father, Orcus, is a pretty powerful mage, and he thinks he can help you."

Domino grabbed his own nuts, shook them a little.

Jude chuckled. "Well, if it proves to be balls, you can say 'I told you so' and I'll admit I was wrong, which doesn't happen much. The only choice you get right now is coming in with me, or I park at the back of the lot, tie you up, and gag you while I get food to go."

Domino got out, skulked into the diner, and slid into the first empty booth. Hunching down, he pulled his hood forward, obscuring his face further.

Jude could've kicked himself. Domino's reluctance wasn't due to worrying about affecting the other patrons. This was about his birthmarks.

Domino scooted in even further as Jude slid in next to him, shielding him from anyone walking past. This early, the chances of anyone sitting opposite them were low.

Domino held his hand out palm up and tapped on it. When Jude didn't immediately reach for his phone, he pointed at Jude's pocket.

"If you want in my jeans, I'm sure we can sort something out later." To his disappointment, Domino didn't continue the banter, he just slumped down a little more.

"What can I get you, folks?" The brightly smiling girl stood poised with her pad and pencil. Jude hadn't even picked up the menu yet.

"You got any steak?"

"Sure thing. We've got some nice rump in."

"Sounds good. I like it big and rare."

"And on the side?" Servers always pushed the sides, but anything apart from pure meat could upset his belly. Not fun on a road trip.

"Just the steak, please."

"Ookay." She made a note on her pad. "And for you, sugar?"

Keeping his head down, Domino pointed at the pad with his good hand. The other remained under the table.

"Sorry, honey, I don't understand. Do you want something not on the menu?"

Jude knew what Domino wanted, but curiosity about how he'd obtain the means to write without asking made him hold his tongue.

Domino mimed writing on the table.

"Ooh, you want to color, sweetie? You wait right here, and I'll get you some crayons. We have a children's menu too; I'm sure they'll be something on there you'll like." With another saccharine smile, she hurried away.

Domino's jaw clenched, and Jude bit his lip to keep the laughter inside. A sharp elbow in his ribs proved the straw that broke the camel's back.

He let out a bark of laughter. Rubbing away the pain in his side, he said, "Mind the ribs, I bruise easy. It's not my fault she thinks you've got learning difficulties. Just tell the lady what you want."

CHAPTER TEN

This captor didn't give Domino choices any more than the last ones. Although instead of assaulting him, this cat got his jollies by embarrassing his prisoner in public. It didn't matter, Domino was twisting a mental knife in his own guts anyway. He'd broken his vow, had used his voice, and he didn't know what he had left now that he'd lost even that tiny shred of integrity.

Murderer, coward, thief, betrayer, and now vow breaker. He wondered what else would be added to the list before he managed to die and that might be a lot harder than he'd planned with Jude around.

The woman came back with a pack of crayons and a sheet of paper with an outline of cartoon characters surrounding the diner logo. She proffered a menu plastered in the same idiotic characters. He shook his head.

"Ok, sweetie, let me know if you want anything," she said and left them to it.

Domino turned the paper over, chose a blue crayon, and started to write.

"You really like coloring, huh?" Jude said, twisting the knife further.

My father's dead.

Jude looked everywhere but at what Domino had written. Probably checking for other hunters coming to steal his prize as he'd stolen from the Karnaks. Or maybe he was just being a dick. Domino tapped the table, causing Jude to glance down.

"And how do you know that? Sirens don't exactly have a good track record with their baby daddies. I bet he high-tailed it out of there as soon as he did the deed."

Domino turned his attention back to the window. There was no point in trying to explain something so complicated with a fucking crayon to a guy who gave zero shits about anything apart from his bank balance.

He hadn't found his phone or his damn thumb in the van. The entire top joint had been removed. The area was red, raw, and tender, but it'd healed over thanks to the healing seawater.

Which I never should have left. I'm such a fucking coward.

Right now, it could've all been over. No more stares, no more anxiety or pain. No more cocky, fucking irritating cat shifter brightening up the world one quip at a time.

Jude's meal arrived. The juicy lump of meat nearly overflowed the plate. The cat shifter tucked in with relish. A few minutes ago, Jude's meal had been raw meat, like Rory and the Karnak brothers.

Jude groaned in delight at the first mouthful. "So damn good, you sure you don't want some?"

Domino's belly knotted. It could have been hunger or revulsion making it squirm, but whatever it was, he wanted out of here.

"Suit yourself." Jude put another huge bite into his mouth. Domino wouldn't have been surprised if the shifter picked the meat up in his hands and just gnawed on it.

Eating would only prolong things. Right now, his captor didn't know he needed to eat. Domino didn't require monstrous amounts of food like Jude was devouring with obscene relish, but he did need some for body maintenance. Seawater provided energy but the water in the tank would be stale by now, depleted and useless. Starvation wouldn't be an easy way to go, but with Jude watching him like a hawk, it might be his only option.

He eyed the serrated knife in Jude's hand, picturing stabbing it into his own throat or belly. His stomach heaved, remembering the sight and stink of Rory's guts.

"Sorry if this is bothering you, but we really can't risk not being together, and I have to eat. I've got a very fast metabolism, comes with being a cat shifter. We need meat regularly."

Thank you for sharing that piece of fascinating trivia. Mental and physical exhaustion dragged at Domino until he wondered if he'd actually dissolve into the seat. *Should've stayed in the damn tank.* Resting his head on the window, he closed his eyes and listened to the humans chatting around him. Sleep called, but he couldn't, not here. One word, one shout because of a bad dream, and everyone within earshot could die.

He'd never slept beside any of his hook-ups, never slept in the same room, let alone the same bed as anyone, even as a child. He usually left his partner sleeping soundly and returned to his van. He'd drive to a different isolated location every night, so he wouldn't affect anyone if he called out. Staying awake until he found a non-verbal way to communicate with Jude depressed him further.

The shifter only seemed to have two modes, bloody, callous murder or irreverent banter. *It must be nice not to care, not to worry.* It was why he'd spent so much time at Blaze, but even there, he could never fully forget.

"Can I get you boys, anything else?" Domino sank down a little further at the woman's voice. Her curiosity, her pity, pecked at him, wanting to know his dirty secrets.

"I could do with a takeout box. Any kind of meat, doesn't matter what, if you've got anything ready?"

"Just meat, no bread or salad?"

"Yep, I'm an all protein kind of guy."

The server tutted. "Those faddy diets won't do you any good in the long run."

Jude spread his hands. "Do I look like I'm suffering?"

She gave him a long slow appraisal, then leaned forward, exposing her cleavage. "No, you certainly don't. I've got a break in a little while if you–"

Jude gave her a grin that would melt the underwear of anyone remotely interested in cock and slung his arm around Domino's shoulders. Every muscle tensed, but Domino managed to stay still. "Sorry, but I don't play on your team."

Her eyes went wide as she glanced between them. "But he's..." she paused, wrinkling her nose.

"Sexy when he's playing at being a kid? Yeah, I know. Daddies and littles, right? Got to love the kink."

What the living fuck?

Jude gave him a grin. "Aw, don't get all salty on me, my little guppy, not unless you want a spanking?"

Domino could do sweet fuck all apart from sit there and take it. If he reacted, Jude would humiliate him even more.

The server hurried off, her face red.

"Time to go," Jude announced. "Looks like I'm not getting my takeout." He dropped a few bills on the table and slid out of his seat. "Well, come on, before the good old boys decide they need to hurry us along. Of course, you could tell them to sit down."

Domino looked in the direction Jude nodded. The waitress stood next to a table of four men, arms clasped to her chest as if she'd suffered a horrible shock, chattering and nodding in their direction.

Despite the banter, Jude drove off as soon as the doors had shut on the van and his gaze flicked to the side mirrors for several miles.

Domino stared out the window at the wintery, bleak landscape. So damn static. The sea never stopped moving, always alive, never dormant like this. He imagined sitting on his rock in the cove, watching the waves, playing his pipe before his life had gone to shit before the human called Sean.

Jude pulled off to the side of the road. They'd come down from the low hills and were making their way along a seemingly endless straight road through snow-dusted sandy scrubland. Dry, dead, cold. It looked exactly how Domino felt, except this land waited for spring to live again.

"Right, in the back."

Domino tensed. *Not again, I can't do that again.*

"Let's get this clear." Jude held up a finger. "I am not going to molest you. I don't get my jollies that way. I've stopped so we can sleep, nothing more. I'm knackered, so are you. I don't know about sirens, but healing from injuries tires me out. As your thumb looks pretty damn good and sitting doesn't bother you, you've done a lot of healing too. You can tell me why they took the top joint of your thumb when we wake up. Oh, and you'll be cuffed." Jude gave the cocky smile again. "I can't have my paycheck wandering off, can I?"

Domino merely stared back. Jude's grin faltered. "I can't work out if you've got a damn good poker face or if you really don't give a shit, but I'm looking forward to finding out. Do you need to piss before we bed down?" He paused. "Do sirens even piss? If you don't eat or drink, I guess–"

Domino climbed over into the back, pulled out the sleeping bag, and climbed in.

"Not going to share? Bit mean. It's going to get damn cold in here."

Domino circled his hand, then touched his chest.

"All this is yours?"

After jabbing a finger at Jude, he gave him the bird then jerked his thumb at the outside of the van.

"And if I don't like it, I can fuck off?" Jude pouted. "You're quite the charmer. It's a good job I've got fantastic self-esteem, or I might start thinking you don't like me very much."

Domino couldn't help huffing in amusement. He wobbled his hand from side to side.

Jude grinned and bent to his pack, pulled out a pair of metal handcuffs. "I prefer leather myself, but you couldn't believe the number of prisoners who gnaw through them. It was costing me a fortune."

Domino's ass clenched, stung.

The van moved a little as Jude crouched down. "It's either this, or I get in the bag with you. I'll shift first if that makes you more comfortable." He paused, eyebrows lifted. "I'll even purr if it helps you relax."

He'll have to be naked to shift, what if he shifts back once I'm asleep? But I really don't want those cuffs on, and the chances of getting away from him when–

"You know what always relaxes me? Reading." Jude reached over and pulled a black tablet eReader with a stylized red cat on the cover out of his pack. "Along with the cuffs and a change of clothes, this is essential luggage. Bit like your flute. I'm just happy I don't have to lug a barrel of seawater around with me."

Someone else touching his pipe was almost as bad as being raped. He felt violated, fouled, and a dunk in seawater wouldn't help. Stretching out, he grabbed the cloth, almost ripping it open to check his pipe had survived. It looked... ok. Reaching out a finger, he hovered it over the shiny chrome. He hadn't touched it since he'd left home since he'd used it to... He also couldn't bring himself to leave it behind. His heartbeat lowered, then bubbled back up as he realized the shifter had witnessed his panic. Wrapping the pipe back up quickly, as if being exposed would damage it, or make the memories flood out, he held it to his chest.

"I didn't touch it; I just made sure it wasn't a weapon, which thinking about it, it might be. But I guess as you won't use your voice, you won't use that either. Oh, and I got rid of the syringe, heroin, right?"

In his panic about the pipe, he'd completely forgotten about the heroin.

To Domino's surprise, Jude didn't ask him to explain or belittle him again. The shifter simply stretched out on the floor beside him, opened the cover of the tablet, and started scrolling.

It looked like Jude really did want to spend a few hours

here. He reached for the simple cloth gag he'd fashioned from a bandana. It wouldn't stop him making noises, but it'd stop him forming words. If he had a nightmare, someone who heard him might become distressed, but they wouldn't be forced to do something against their will.

Jude didn't look away from the device as Domino settled back down. "So, what do you like reading? Thrillers? Peril on the high seas? Romance? Poetry? Well, it doesn't really matter because I'm in the middle of *The Martian*, so you'll have to put up with it." He cleared his throat and started reading. "Log entry Sol 39."

Jude's voice might as well have been magical as Domino found himself hanging on every word of the story. A man alone, fighting for survival. Domino would've swapped places with him without hesitation.

On the few occasions when Melody loaned him her phone, Domino hadn't wasted time with reading. He'd either researched the human world, how to drive, how they interacted for when he left home, or he watched gay porn.

An occasional passing vehicle made the van rock a little. Domino pictured how the van looked from the outside, abandoned, dead, serene in the empty land. Over Jude's low voice, he pictured dark rolling waves, the sight, sound, and scent of the ocean, and drifted.

CHAPTER ELEVEN

FIVE YEARS BEFORE...

Sean licked his lips. They weren't puffy or pouty like those of Domino's kin, they were strong, masculine, like the rest of him. Domino couldn't stop imagining kissing them, seeing them wrapped around his cock.

This was the third time they'd met, the second time they'd spoken. This morning, just after dawn, Sean swam around the headland of their rocky island home. Domino nearly expired from excitement where he hid behind his boulder. Domino had prepared himself to talk to him, to be appealing. His belly fluttered with nerves. He'd never seen a human before Sean, let alone spoken to one.

"Hey, I see you back there. Come on out," the bronzed godlike human called.

Taking a deep breath, Domino stood up from where he crouched behind a boulder. Sean blinked.

"Erm, hi. I'm Sean. I was just..."

"Trying to steal a look at the school?" Domino blurted

one of the lines he'd memorized. It'd sounded cooler in his head.

The way Sean blushed was adorable. "Yeah, I guess. Do you live there?"

"My family run it. How about you?"

Sean seemed content to talk about himself, which was a hell of a lot easier than if he'd wanted to know about Domino. He'd prepared something about being a handyman for the school, but the story had holes an oil tanker could sail through. The truth was, Domino didn't do anything, wasn't allowed to do anything even remotely dangerous. Sean was studying coastal landforms for his final year geology project at Edinburgh University. He was from Ohio and doing a year abroad. Domino simply sat, listened, and watched Sean's hair change to the color of ripe wheat as it dried.

All the bronzed young man asked about, in his wonderful soft rolling accent was the "school" on the cliffs above. The island was almost a dozen miles out from the mainland, and they used high fences and magical charms to keep unwanted visitors from the small hamlet away. Domino desperately wanted to find out about Sean's life, about how humanity worked from a real human rather than a phone screen. Unfortunately, his only source of information had a one-track mind.

"So, you're the only guy amongst all those girls? I bet you get a lot of action, even with–." Again, Sean's eyes strayed to the power marks on Domino's face, his exposed torso, and thigh. It was as if the human couldn't see past them, any more than Domino's kin could see past his gender.

Sean blushed. "Sorry, that was rude. I've just never seen

port-wine stains as extensive as yours before. Have you tried laser treatment? I've heard it can be really effective."

Port-wine stains? Did humans having their own term for power marks mean they knew about sirens, or did humans have a similar thing? Domino filed the term away for later thought.

"I do ok. Not a lot of choice for them." Domino lifted his chin towards the top of the cliff.

"Would you..." Sean took a breath. "Would you introduce me to some of them? On the quiet? All those girls stuck here with only one guy for company?" He wiggled his eyebrows up and down.

Telling him the "girls" were hundreds of years old and literally fucked men like him to death didn't seem a good way to prolong their interaction.

Domino found himself agreeing to Sean's proposal and arranging to meet that evening, although he had no intention of taking him up through the caverns. Sean wouldn't survive meeting any of Domino's kin.

If Domino got caught sneaking out, he'd be grounded for months, but he wanted to spend as much time as possible with Sean. He watched until Sean was out of sight before diving back under the surface to the entrance of the cave.

Domino spent the day holed up in his attic room, but this time he was thankful he wasn't allowed to go to lessons like his sisters and cousins. Even practicing his pipe held no interest. Instead, he imagined Sean spread out on his bed, naked, with his cock bobbing against his belly and leaking for him.

A knock sounded on his door. "You ok, freak? You didn't come down for dinner, or lunch for that matter. Your mother sent me up." Despite the insult, Melody didn't sound pissed about being ordered to check on him.

"Not a freak," he called out for the umpteenth time.

The door swung open to reveal his brunette, blue-eyed cousin.

Her eyes dragged over him. Domino reached for his shirt, pulled it on.

"Would you stop looking at me like that? I'm a guy, not a freak. There are plenty of us in the world."

"Not like you. And I have to say, I think I hit the jackpot being your cousin."

Out of all his kin, Melody was the best. Yes, she ignored him in public, but at least she didn't treat him as if he was stupid because he had balls. Plus, she "forgot" her phone sometimes. This was new though, she'd never mentioned how she felt about being related to him before.

After a pause that made his skin prickle as she watched him, he asked, "Care to enlighten me?"

"After you've eaten. Come on, up and at 'em."

"Not hungry. I went down to the cove this morning. My ban for cutting this," he ruffled his curling dark hair that again neared his chin, "finished."

"I meant proper food. Youngsters need it, you know that."

His belly silently rumbled, but he wouldn't tell her the reason why he hadn't fetched food from the kitchen. He'd never live it down if he popped an erection in public as he'd done randomly ever since he'd first seen Sean. The mention of food made him squirm as he imagined Sean licking his fingers after popping something tasty into his mouth. Nope, staying up here until tonight was one hundred percent the best call.

"Maybe I'm just growing out of needing three meals a day."

"Don't start playing grown up yet, short stuff," she joked, but her amusement didn't reach her eyes.

"I'm eighteen, Mel, not a kid anymore."

She came over, sat on the bed, and to his shock, ruffled his hair. "I know, but think about pretending for a bit longer, ok?"

Now that confused him. "I thought me being old enough to get out of all your hair is what everyone is waiting for."

With a sigh, she flopped back on the bed. "You think the restrictions you've got now are tough? You just wait until they find out your balls are working."

Unease fluttered in his belly. "What do you mean?"

She propped herself up on her elbows. "You're hot property, kid. Why do you think we've been increasing security around this place? We've never had electric fences, constant patrols, and magic protections before. I watched a crusty old human spell the cove and the grounds when you were five. You wandered out of the gate one day and Tethys had a fit."

His breath caught for a moment. "Me?"

She chuckled and ruffled his hair again. "Yeah, you. There's a prophecy that says a siren born from two siren parents will rule the world with just a word. And every, and I mean every single siren who knows about you and isn't a close relative will want to jump your bone. Being the mother of the ruler of the world? Big," she held her hands apart, "huge, ambition."

He blinked at her. "You're kidding, right?"

"'fraid not, kid. Your future is a bedroom in a sea cave with hot and cold running booty, morning, noon, and night.

And don't worry about quickening the pregnancies, that's only necessary with humans, or that's what they're saying." Her tone said she didn't believe it.

Conjuring up a line of eager, curvy sirens all grabbing for him did a great job of deflating his half-hard cock. He'd never considered that a siren pregnancy only implanted when the sire died might apply to him too. The thought of being with a woman left him feeling a little nauseous so had assumed it wasn't something he'd ever have to worry about.

Suitable human males were encouraged, magically, to mate with as many women as possible over a two- or three-day period, and then they vanished. Domino got locked in his room on the two occasions a human had been captured. He'd listened to the laughter, the mating party, then their screams. There was one huge flaw in the plan Melody proposed.

"But... I don't like girls. I'd never be able to–" The words fell out of his mouth before he could stop them.

She patted his leg. "I thought as much. Phones have search history. Not a lot you can do about being gay or what's going to happen though. You're stuck with both." She rolled her eyes. "Siring the ruler of the world is your destiny; the reason you exist. Which is a load of crap as far as I'm concerned, but the rest of them believe it. You, freak, are the most important thing that's happened to this sorority, our species, in centuries.

"The protections are as much about keeping you in as they are about keeping other sirens out. Our mothers are planning world domination as we speak. Seems I get to be your primary keeper, seeing as I'm the last on the list for baby duty."

Domino swallowed. "Last?"

"Yeah. They have a schedule set up and everything."

Melody stopped talking, but Domino didn't notice as he tried to get his head around what she'd said. He came up with the only plausible explanation.

"Great joke, Mel, you really had me going there."

Her lips pressed together, and his heart fell. "I'm not kidding. So you'd better get your ass down to the cove and play with your pretty human boy before they notice. It wouldn't go well for either of you if they find out. I'll cover for you."

A smile lit her features as she reached out a finger and shut his gaping mouth. "Did you really think you were alone down there earlier? Sweetie, you're watched everywhere except when you're up here."

With a full moon rising, Domino sneaked out his bedroom window.

"By Poseidon's balls, Cowrie, what makes you think you get to go before me? We're both his cousins." Melody's voice rose from the main living area. He certainly owed her for this, and his mind played over what she'd said.

A prophecy. About me. It shouldn't make sense, but the more he thought about it, the more it did. He'd thought they made him hide because they were worried about having a "freak" in the family, but Melody's story held a ring of truth.

As the argument continued, he sprinted across the wide lawn that looked like no man's land rather than a manicured garden feature. Being locked up here for his entire life, being forced too... he shuddered. The humans had drugs for such things. He doubted Aunt Tethys would balk at using them, or any other means, to get him to perform.

He'd thought his life sucked so far, but he'd always assumed he'd leave the sorority at some point and make a life for himself among the humans.

It would be a little more difficult now, but it didn't mean it'd be impossible. *Sean, I can get Sean to help.*

As usual, Domino left his thigh-length tunic, he refused to call it a dress, just inside the entrance to the tunnel. Luminescent lichen on the walls lit his way.

He didn't even give his customary shudder of revulsion as he passed the eyelets embedded in the floor where the tunnel widened into a cave. It'd never been discussed with him, but he was sure this was where the quickening ceremonies took place. He didn't want to think about how many beautiful human men like Sean had their lives cut short here. But this human was for him, and Sean would leave safely at the end of this night.

In his excitement, Domino hardly felt the chill of the water as he swam through the underwater cave entrance in his trunks.

Even though night had fallen, and the chill air stimulated his skin, the water was the same warm temperature it'd been during the day. Swimming at night always gave him the thrill of the forbidden, and tonight... Tonight was the biggest risk, the biggest thrill of his life. Domino's entire body tingled with life as he pulled himself through the dark, energy-giving water.

Domino surfaced with barely a ripple, keeping close to the cliff to not draw attention. The cave entrance was always submerged, but at the current low tide, about thirty feet of rocks were exposed at the back of the small cove.

In the moonlight, he could see a shadowed figure at the base of the cliff, looking up. Jealousy twisted. Sean wasn't here for him. All he wanted was pussy. Domino still didn't think twice about walking out of the water.

"Hi." He kept his voice low, but Sean still jumped like a

scalded cat. Palm on his chest, the human spun to face Domino who still stood up to his thighs in the gentle surf.

"Jesus Christ, you nearly gave me a heart attack. Do you always creep about like that?"

Domino waded out of the water, gaze mapping the way the moonlight highlighted the planes of Sean's body, his shoulder, his hip. Domino halted when the water came halfway up his calves. Somehow, being even partially immersed swelled his confidence.

"Voices are powerful." Why he'd recited the warning his cousins were constantly being taught, he didn't know. Maybe he wanted to prove to this human, this lesser being, that despite his utter lack of experience he was more than Sean assumed. That he was worthy of Sean's attention.

"Uh-huh, the girls like being chatted up? Got it." Sean grinned, almost vibrating with excitement. "Are any of them waiting? I thought you might bring them with you. I've been looking, but I can't figure out how to get up the cliff." Sean indicated the rock with a wave, but his eyes focused on Domino's chest.

Yes, he thinks I'm hot too. The adrenaline shot of excitement flatlined as Sean's upper lip lifted.

"Would you stop worrying about the birthmarks?"

Sean's tanned face lost the slight disgust. *I did that with only a word.* Domino rolled the thought around for size. Maybe Melody had been right, he was more than a freak of nature. His kin had to sing, usually in groups, to influence humans. But he didn't want to think about anything but the man in front of him right now, especially if this was his only chance to be with a guy.

The reason why his kin enticed human males shone from Sean like the midday sun. Strong and beautiful,

Domino wanted to lick him all over; wanted to have him in his body like his kin would.

Sean only got the same gleam in his eyes when he spoke about the "girls". The girls who would use, then kill him. His kin were group predators, pure and simple. Domino had always felt more comfortable being alone. He hoped his magic would work the same way. Young female sirens came into their abilities gradually, usually starting at puberty. Even without the outward sign of body hair humans boasted, Domino's reaction to Sean proved he'd passed into the life stage when the magic of most sirens developed. Domino wasn't most sirens though.

The girls attended daily vocal lessons, honing their harmonies. Domino had never been encouraged to sing. Mother said his voice grated, but it appeared he didn't need harmonies to affect a human.

"Do you think they'll like me?"

Domino's gaze strayed down Sean's tight abs and his lightly haired thighs.

"They'll love you," he said, carving his heart out with every word.

"So, which one are you going to introduce me to? You'll tell her it's a one-time thing though, right? I'm heading out for a tour of Europe tomorrow."

Sean was almost rubbing his hands together in anticipation. Choking jealousy surged. Overlooked, ignored, and dismissed as a person, even by a human.

Looking into Sean's green eyes, he took a chance. Either this would work, or Sean would leave in disgust. "You want me more than you've ever wanted anyone."

Sean's eyes lost their focus, staring blankly. Domino shut up, horror rising as the seconds ticked by. Only the sound of the waves disturbed the frozen moment.

Oh fuck, I broke him. Mother always tells the girls not to go too far, not to–

Sean stepped forward into the water, stroked a palm down Domino's shoulder. Leaning in, Sean brushed their lips together, and all thoughts of morality evaporated. The heat of Sean's skin soaked into him. Imagining that heat inside his body nearly had Domino pushing the human down to the rock. But if this was how Sean wanted it, he'd cope, maybe. Fingers traced Domino's back and sides making him shiver. Reaching up, he put his arms around Sean's neck, wanting to press himself against all that wonderful warm skin.

"No, stay still."

Domino obeyed willingly, probably for the first time in his life. Sean rewarded him by turning his attention to Domino's neck. With lips, teeth, and tongue, Sean teased, worshipped. He moved down, outlining the power mark on Domino's chest, the mark that had revolted him a few minutes before.

Domino tried to pull away, not wanting to experience that disgust again, but Sean held on firmly, kissed him a little more before letting go. Domino looked at the purple patch on his arm, guilt rising. Sean didn't want him; this was siren magic, nothing more. He still couldn't bring himself to stop it. *Just a few more minutes.*

Using his fingertips, Sean tilted Domino's chin up until he looked into serious green eyes.

"You're stunning, and I knew from the start about your birthmarks. They make you even more interesting, not forgetting your wonderful tight muscles and great ass."

Domino's heart pounded, and Sean must be able to feel it. His fingers were on his wrist, reading his pulse as if it were Braille.

"Do you want me to kiss you again?"

Domino let his gaze slide over Sean's tanned chest, his sculpted arms and shoulders. Sean's baggy swimming trunks hung low on his hips, revealing a line of pale sandy hair running from his navel downwards before it disappeared into the waistband. The overt sign of masculinity stole his breath. Sirens didn't develop body hair at puberty, and he couldn't wait to explore what else made a human male different from every other person he'd ever met.

"Fuck, yes, and don't hold back. I want it all."

Sean claimed his lips, forcing his mouth open. Domino melted against him, happy to go along for the ride. It lasted for only a few moments before Sean broke away leaving Domino breathless and ready to beg for more. His body buzzed, his cock so hard it ached.

Domino couldn't believe this was happening. The attic boy was getting kissed stupid by a guy hotter than any of the porn stars he'd seen, and he vowed to enjoy it as much as he could, while he could.

Domino wanted to drop to his knees to see, taste, what those shorts contained, but issuing any more instructions risked breaking the thrall. Only the most powerful sirens could force compliance with speech; most had to sing in groups to impose even a general emotion on others, and they needed constant practice to get the harmonies right.

He pictured himself lying naked over the rock, his pale skin against Sean's darker form as the human pumped into his ass, arms bulging with effort.

When he'd first met Sean, he'd wanted to be acknowledged, a little consideration, an attachment, no matter how fleeting. Not anymore. Breathless, Domino glanced over to where anyone coming out of the cave would surface, hyperaware of the heat and size of the man next to him.

Sean would be leaving tomorrow. Domino had maybe an hour before Melody or, god forbid, someone else came looking. If they caught Sean... Even the human being here now was dangerous, but Domino wanted... by Poseidon's balls he wanted so much more than kissing.

"Fuck me."

Sean tensed. Domino swallowed down his fear that his magic wasn't strong enough to overcome Sean's preferences. If he'd failed, Sean would leave, with or without a parting punch. Domino would cope with the rejection, just like all the others he'd suffered. What he wouldn't risk was wondering, "What if?" for the rest of his life.

Reaching out, Domino traced the golden line of hairs disappearing into the swim shorts. Sean's breath quickened, but he didn't move away, didn't say no.

"Sit down."

Sean moved to Domino's favorite rock, the one with a flattened top near the cliff wall and sat. Domino kneeled between Sean's knees and put his hand on a hairy thigh. Moving it up, he slipped it under the leg of Sean's shorts.

A large hand landed on top of his. "I'm not–"

Domino put every ounce of emotion into his next words. "I'm everything you've ever wanted." As he spoke, he pulled his hand away and went for the waistband of Sean's shorts.

The bigger man grabbed his wrists, squeezed, but Domino wasn't giving up that easily. Sean hadn't hit him, hadn't told him to stop or tried to escape. *He must want this; he just doesn't want to admit it.*

Sean groaned, but stayed still, almost as if his body refused to obey him. "You need to stop. This isn't right."

"You want it, I know you do."

Sean's Adam's apple bobbed as he swallowed. "Domino,

I… I'm not going to take advantage of you; you're just a kid. You haven't even got any body hair."

That's the problem? Domino could certainly do something about that.

"I'm plenty old enough. I just wax because I'm a competitive swimmer. I told you that, remember?" He hadn't said anything of the sort, but Sean nodded anyway. The thrill of being powerful for once dragged Domino's desire even higher. This human was his, not theirs.

Despite the humidity, Domino shivered as he teetered between the promise of mind-blowing pleasure, of forcing this man to do something he didn't want to or releasing him.

I should let him go. I should be better than–

Sean reached out, dragged a thumb down Domino's smooth cheek. "Tell me what you want."

Every shred of morality vanished at the soft question as if Sean were the siren, not Domino.

"I don't want to think; I just want you to fuck me so hard I'll feel it for days, remember it for a lifetime."

"Shall I tell you what I want?" In the moonlight, Sean's eyes were black.

"Don't care," Domino blurted, "as long as it involves my ass and your cock."

Sean gripped the back of Domino's head, slammed his mouth against his, invading, punishing with his tongue. The ache in Domino's cock flared as Sean moved his lips to his throat, then bit down hard enough to make Domino hiss.

"Like that, just like that."

"Shut up, I don't give a shit what you want," Sean growled, sending Domino even higher. "What I want is my dick in your ass and your cum in my hand," Sean murmured as he pulled Domino's trunks down, and let his cock spring free.

The world spun as Sean lifted him with hands under his armpits and turned, forcing Domino to lay back on the flat rock, not that he resisted.

"I can't believe I've never done this." Sean stopped talking as his mouth enveloped Domino's aching shaft.

With a groan at the wet heat surrounding him, Domino arched up, forcing himself deeper. Sean pulled off. Domino mourned the lack of heat, although the slight breeze on his now wet cock felt good.

"Want to fuck my mouth?" Sean wiggled his eyebrows, and Domino nearly lost it. This was all his wet dreams come true.

"Hell, yeah."

Sean closed his lips around him again. Domino thrust up, and Sean gagged and pulled off. "Ugh, guess I need a little more practice."

"Don't you like it?"

Sean froze, his eyes going wide.

With fear spiking that he'd broken the thrall, Domino blurted, "You like it, love it. The only thing you'd rather do is fuck me."

Domino found himself on his hands and knees before he registered that he was moving.

His trunks were yanked off his legs then his thighs were prised apart. Spit hitting his hole was the last thing he expected. It was so damn dirty. Domino moaned, "Fuck, that's hot; do it again."

Sean hawked and spat again, then buried his face in his crack. The rough treatment and abrasive stubble against his tender skin felt fantastic. The next second, Sean's fingers pressed against his puckered hole. Blowing out a breath, he tried to relax. Two seconds, five. No movement, no words.

"You ok?" Domino asked.

"I've never done this to a guy before. I don't–"

This can't stop now, not when I'm so damn close.

"You've always wanted to. You think about it all the time, you–"

A thick finger pressed into him, quickly followed by a second. There was no teasing, no tender care. It was animalistic, dirty, and raw. Domino's leaking dick tapped against his belly; his balls threatened to explode before Sean's cock had even entered him.

Don't come, don't come.

The third finger made Domino hiss through his teeth; the pain helped rein in his spiraling orgasm.

"Ah, shut up; you know you want it," Sean growled, fucking him with his fingers.

Domino did, more than anything. And to show it, he pillowed his forehead on his elbows, widening his stance. He didn't dare speak in case he said something that stopped this.

The three fingers pulled out after only a few thrusts. With his dick hard as a rock and his balls aching, Domino looked over his shoulder. Sean concentrated on his own cock, spreading spit on it in preparation for fucking the living daylights out of him.

For the first time, Domino wondered if he could do this, that cock looked damn big. Sean didn't give him time to think as he pressed against Domino's hole, forcing himself inside.

Domino gasped, squirmed at the pain, but Sean's hard grip on his hips didn't let him move an inch. The pain focused all his senses down to that small area of his body, an area that didn't seem so small right now. He bit his lip so he didn't voice anything that might break the thrall.

One slow withdrawal, one considered push in. *I can do*

this. But that was all the kindness Sean gave. He pumped, hard and fast, not showing an ounce of mercy. Having his fantasy fulfilled turned Domino on more than ever. He wanted it to last, needed it to be over before someone came looking for him.

Domino's hand dropped to his own dick. It wasn't easy keeping his balance using only one hand as Sean fucked him like a steam train, but he managed it. Sean's heavy balls hit his with each sharp thrust. Domino tensed, feeling his balls draw up, knowing he was about to tip over the edge.

Sean pulled out and flipped Domino over so fast he thought his back would bruise when it hit the rock. His hand got slapped away from his dick. A hot mouth closed over the tip while Sean used just his finger and thumb to jerk him.

The orgasm wrenched from him. Crying out, Domino grabbed Sean's head, forcing him to take more as he shot into his mouth. Gasping like a landed fish Domino let go and watched Sean rear above him.

Between one heartbeat and the next, seeing Sean come was the purpose of Domino's existence.

The human held his gaze in the bright moonlight, mouth open, lips wet with Domino's climax, every muscle tense as he worked his own shaft. With the nearly full moon behind him, he looked like a Norse God.

"You want it?" His impending climax added rawness to Sean's voice.

"Go on, do it; shoot all over me. I wanna rub it in."

Sean's body tensed, twitched. A hot pulse hit Domino's chest, then another, and another. When it was over, Sean leaned his head back, looking up to the top of the cliff.

Where my kin are, where he'd rather be.

"Did you enjoy any of that?" Domino asked.

Sean's eyes widened. He bent over, retching as if trying to throw up his entire stomach.

A trembling finger pointed, Sean's face twisted in horror, disgust. He didn't look beautiful anymore.

"What, what the fuck did you do to me?"

Anger, shame, and guilt swirled, combined.

"I gave you a good time." Domino wiped his fingers in the cum on his chest and held it up. "See?"

Sean retched again; the sound cut through the peaceful night. "You're sick" he gasped, stumbling back, wiping at his mouth with the back of his forearm. "All you faggots are sick. The world would be a better place if you all fucking died."

This was meant to have been his time, maybe his only time, to be appreciated, admired. Years of being dismissed, being told to go back upstairs, to cover up, coalesced, took root, then exploded.

"News, you just fucked me, so if you hate faggots so much, how about starting by killing yourself?"

Domino expected Sean to storm off towards the sea, then he could drag his sorry ass back to his lonely bedroom and work out how he felt about this.

Sean turned towards the cliff face and smashed his head against it. A sickening dull crunch echoed through Domino's soul and the body collapsed.

CHAPTER TWELVE

Domino couldn't move, he just watched, willing Sean to make a noise, to stir. So damn quiet. The waves kept lapping the shore as if nothing had happened.

Slow clapping came from behind. He spun. Aunt Tethys and mother were walking out of the water. Both women looked to be in their late twenties, early thirties. They were ripe, with gentle curves, flaring hips and trim waists. Both had long hair, his mother was dark, Aunt Tethys blonde.

Both wore satisfied smiles.

"Well done, Domino. Sister, I told you your boy was more than he appeared."

Domino swallowed, tried to cover himself. "I...he..."

"Shh, son. Don't talk. You need to be careful about that now." Mother walked towards him, hands out to the side as if he were a rabbit about to bolt.

"You are clearly powerful, but in males, that power has a price, a big one. All siren power is linked to life energy. Female power is gentle, and we sustain each other, absorbing it from each other. But you..." She gave a little hiccup of distress, her lips pressed together and her eyes shone in the moonlight.

Aunt Tethys wrapped an arm around his mother's shoulders. "Shh, Aria, you knew this was coming. We prepared; we can do this."

"I didn't mean to; he–"

"I mean it, don't talk," Aunt Tethys snapped. "Every utterance where you use magic takes a little of your life force. And unlike females, male sirens can't recharge. Now you've released your power, every time you speak brings your death closer. You are so important to us, to our entire race. You have no idea how–"

He zoned them out. Neither woman had even glanced at the man he'd just killed. All that beautiful life, that energy and future, gone, just gone. *It's my fault. If I hadn't been so damn selfish, he still would be alive.*

His aunt stood beside him. Stroked his hair. His mother cupped his face.

"Domino, can you hear me? It's me, your mother. None of us meant for this to–" He tried to focus on her and failed. Nothing mattered.

"He's in shock, sister, but the amulet will cloud his mind. All this news, it was bound to affect him. We always suspected males were delicate, but this... this was more than even I expected. Melody has a lot to answer for. Let's get him home."

"How are we going to get him home, he can't swim like this."

"Pop back up and bring the skiff around, I'll stay with him. While you're up there, send someone down to deal with the body. Although if he stays like this, it might make things easier. Accepting his future, even though we tried to shelter him from things he could never have, would have been difficult."

Domino could hear them, but their words didn't make sense. All he could see was the horror on Sean's face, the contrast between his full of life body a few minutes ago and the stillness now.

Multiple voices urging him to move, a rocking boat. His bed. More soothing harmonious voices.

Time passed, or it might have done. Domino floated, eating, drinking, sleeping as instructed by the harmonizing voices. Always three, sometimes more.

"Is he done yet? This has got to be the most boring duty ever, and it's going to be even worse if we keep him down here permanently."

That's Lark. His half-sister sounded pissed off. Domino had no idea why, and he didn't much care. The lower half of his body sat in seawater, and it was dim, damp. Light filtered in via the water. *I'm in the sea cave.* Memories drifted in and out. He'd been here like this before, a few times. He sat still, not having any urge to move. The energy seeping into his skin tingled, like tiny fish nibbling at his skin.

"Oh, shut up. You two are always going to have a privileged position. Us cousins will have to take our chances with the rest of the sorority," Cowrie said.

"And you think not getting the chance to be the mother of the siren Queen is worth being a permanent babysitter?" Domino's other half-sister, Sonata, grumbled.

"Or King, it could be a king," Lark added.

Cowrie laughed. "You really think a male can lead us to rule over the world? Don't be ridiculous."

"I heard Mother talking to Tethys. She said he

controlled that human with spoken words, not even a hint of a song."

Silence reigned for a few seconds before Sonata spoke. "Well if he did, it cracked his mind."

"By Poseidon's balls, haven't you wondered why he's gained a necklace? It's a thought clouding amulet made from his sire's bone. All the time he's wearing that, he's a zombie. It's the only way to control him. Tethys thinks he could even thrall one of us if he really tried."

Lark snorted. "Sirens can't thrall each other."

"Sirens can't thrall humans on their own either."

"It was a young, weak male; we don't even know if he did thrall him. He could've..."

The arguing continued, Domino ignored them, enjoying the energy flowing into him from the living water. He imagined swimming, being surrounded by comforting pressure, by life, but for some reason, he stayed still.

A dark head broke the surface as if the water had given birth, but her chin remained submerged. Melody put her finger to her lips and beckoned. *How long had it been since I've seen her? Why is her blonde hair brown?*

Melody frowned, her head disappeared, but he could see her swimming nearer under the water. The water was deep here, especially at high tide like now.

Rising up with a splash, she grabbed his arm, pulling him into the water, and yanking at his neck. The water felt lighter, clearer than thin air. Melody wore dark, skin-tight clothes, it looked so odd when all he'd seen before was flesh.

She tugged him toward the light and he quickly got the idea. This was a kidnap or a rescue; it didn't matter which, it only mattered that he was getting out of here. He broke the surface to see a small motorboat bobbing a few feet away. The sun was low in the sky. A siren with dark hair sat in the boat wearing the same black form-fitting leggings and a matching long-sleeved shirt as Mel. At least, he assumed she was a siren, without her skin on show he couldn't see any power marks.

"Here, come here," the older one called out, beckoned frantically.

He glanced out to sea, getting in the boat would separate him from the lifegiving water, and he didn't know or trust this strange siren.

"Ugh," the siren growled. "You can't swim across the barrier; you've got to go over it." She leaned over holding out her hand.

"Melody, what about Melody?"

"Forget her; she knew this was a one-way mission. Come on, let's go."

"Not without Mel." Feeling more focused than he had since the night Sean died, he ducked back under.

Cowrie lay still, halfway out of the water. Lark stood over Melody, a knife in her hand. Sonata was nowhere to be seen.

"Think you could just sneak back in here and steal him for those cheating bitches? There's nothing lower than a traitor."

Melody swallowed, struggling to breathe. Her hand pressed against her abdomen. "He's not a thing, to... be traded. He–"

"Won't get far. As for you–" Lark raised the knife. Melody gasped, shrank back.

"Stop!" Domino called out. Lark froze. He waited, but Lark didn't move a muscle. It was eerie, like she'd been turned to stone.

He threw himself out of the water, dread making him stumble. Instinct made him reach out a hand to stop himself from faceplanting on the unforgiving cave floor. His shoulder hit Lark, knocking her to the ground.

Heart in his mouth, he rolled Lark's limp body over.

Don't be dead, fuck, don't be dead. Her eyes stared, fixed. Blank. Lifeless.

"Domino, you–" Melody coughed, blood trickled from the side of her mouth. She tried again. "You've got to get out of here. Sonata went for help." She winced, swallowed.

Stepping over Lark's body, he touched Melody's bruised face. One hand clutched her belly, the other twisted at an unnatural angle. "No, I'm not going anywhere without you. Your friend's waiting in the boat, we'll get you to a doctor, get you–"

"See, see that loose rock over there, a foot to the right of the tree-shaped lichen?"

He glanced over. "Yeah, but we–"

"Move it. There's a box inside."

Maybe it's a healing amulet or potion. He scuttled over. The ancient wooden box, the size of two clenched fists, had the sorority rune, a trident bisecting an infinity symbol, burned into the lid. A silver knife with a mother-of-pearl handle and the rune carved into the blade lay next to the box. Wincing, he pushed the revolting object aside: It had to be the weapon used to sacrifice men in the quickening ceremonies.

He drew the box out and opened it. Even in the diffuse light from the water, the gemstones glittered. They didn't look like healing amulets to him, but then again, he'd never seen an amulet.

"Which one?" he asked, hurrying over.

Melody coughed, gasped. She blew out a tight breath then spoke. "Not amulets, just gems. Take them, get away, start," she swallowed, "a new life. I lied before when I said they wouldn't kill you. They wouldn't take the chance of the pregnancies not implanting. They'll use that knife on you just like they do on all the men. She coughed, winced. "Don't trust Kelpea."

"No, no, I'm not leaving you. I–"

A shaky smile curved her pale lips. "Don't worry, freak, we'll be in Poseidon's kingdom together soon enough, even if they don't catch you and carve out your heart. No male siren has ever made twenty-five," she coughed again. "Ugh, now fuck off and live a little."

Footsteps pounding down the tunnel.

"Go, you idiot; if you get caught I did this for nothing."

He leaned down, pecked her on the cheek. "I'll raise hell, don't you worry. Gonna miss you, Mel, and... thanks."

Eyes prickling, he dived back into the water, one hand clutching the box to his chest.

He surfaced next to the boat. Something stung his cheek.

"Idiot! You nearly hit him," Aunt Tethys' voice came from the cliffs above. Ducking back down, he swam under the boat coming up on the far side.

Kelpea poked her head above the side of the boat. "What are you playing at? Get the fuck in!"

He pulled himself up on the side and the siren reached down, grabbed his trunks, and hauled him in. "Keep your goddamned head down," she snarled and crawled towards the bow.

Another bullet pinged against the hull next to where the siren crouched, one hand on the small wheel. She pushed the throttle forward. The boat vibrated, lifting up at the bow as it shot forward. Domino was sure the siren couldn't see where they were headed, but as long as it was out to sea, he guessed it didn't matter. The breeze raised bumps on his skin, and he risked a glance over the side of the boat. They were passing out of the cove. Freedom, or at least it would be until Kelpea got to her destination. Then it'd start all over again, but this time, without Melody.

A minute later, Kelpea glanced back at him. "Come over here. They could still shoot, but they won't risk hitting the golden goose."

Domino preferred "freak," at least the way Mel said it anyway. They would have found her by now, and if she wasn't already dead, she soon would be, but not before they made her talk.

"Where are we going?"

"Don't worry, it's not where Melody thought, it's a lot nearer. My sisters have a larger boat out to sea; we're taking you south, you'll be safe with us. Better weather too. Our sorority might not be as big or as rich as yours, but we're fighters."

"Where did Melody think you were going?" He put all the need, the desperation to be free into his words.

Kelpea froze, let out a squeak.

"Tell me now," he pressed.

"Bridgeport, on the mainland. We have a car there. We were going to an airstrip." Kelpea gasped as if in pain. Bridgeport was due west, the nearest town to the island.

"And your ship?"

"Four miles out, due south," she gritted out.

"Turn off the tracker." He didn't know that the speedboat had one, but her hand reaching for a button on the dash confirmed it.

He had money, transportation... now he just needed clothes and this siren gone.

"Strip."

Movements stiff, she pulled off the black pants and shirt.

"We'll find you," she said as she stood there in just bikini bottoms. "There's no point in–"

"Over the side." She hesitated. He hadn't put as much need into that instruction. Stranding her a half a mile from shore meant she could still be at risk from his kin, but he didn't care. She hadn't cared about Melody and she wanted to use him just as much as his kin did.

"NOW," he growled. She almost slipped in her haste to throw herself into the gentle swell.

Not looking back, he pushed the throttle to max and headed up the coast. As soon as he thought he was out of sight, he turned the boat due west. When the engine ran out of petrol, he'd use the oars tucked under the seats. The New World had far fewer sirens, and no one would expect him to try to cross the Atlantic on his own.

All he had to do was keep quiet to prolong his life as much as possible, and stay one step ahead of the sirens until he joined Mel in Poseidon's kingdom, hopefully never having sired a child who could subjugate the world.

CHAPTER THIRTEEN

Sleeping beside bounties could be uncomfortable. Some tried talking him out of turning them in; others tried escaping when they thought he was asleep. Occasionally one would attempt to seduce him. Jude didn't mind that so much, not if they were cute guys anyway. Their reaction if they didn't know about cat shifter anatomy always gave him a smile.

Like many people in this stressful situation, Domino twitched, moaned, and frowned his way through his dreams. The siren's subconscious didn't look pleasant. *Is he reliving his time with the Karnaks, the human's death, or something else?*

After an hour, Domino settled into a more peaceful sleep. Jude stripped, shivered, and shifted. Fur was always warmer. He let himself drift, dreaming of a warmer climate. When on a case, he got by with napping, but between cases, he loved to soak up sunshine while catching up on proper sleep.

Coffee wasn't a usual part of Jude's sunbathing sessions. He sniffed. Definitely coffee, although it smelled like instant rather than anything fancy. Opening his eyes, the first thing he registered was being alone in the back of the van and a breeze from the front of the vehicle. Either he'd slept unusually deeply, or the siren moved damn quietly. No one had snuck out on him in years. He cursed himself for not using the cuffs as he'd intended, but he hadn't wanted to distress his innocent bounty more than necessary. Domino wasn't a criminal, just a confused, frightened, and maybe dying kid.

He poked his head over the seat, without bothering to shift. If Domino had done a runner, chasing him down in fur would be a hell of a lot easier. The chains around his neck swung, rubbed against each other, reminding him how dangerous his charge could be despite his demeanor. People who thought they had nothing to live for were some of the most dangerous.

A few feet in front of the vehicle, Domino crouched next to a fire, poking it with a stick. A grey metal pot sat in the embers. At least Jude assumed it was Domino; he couldn't see any skin except for fingers because of the all-black outfit of pulled up hoodie and jeans.

Jude's breath formed clouds even inside the van. Staying in fur would be so much warmer, but it sucked for conversation. After shifting, stiff with cold, Jude pulled on his jeans, shirt, and jacket, then reluctantly added socks and boots.

Shivering, huffing, he got out via the side door and stomped over to the fire.

"Couldn't you have picked somewhere a little warmer to hide? One day, one of my bounties will decide to hide in a luxury tropical resort. It might take me a week to make sure they're the right person."

"Sorry, you'll have to have it black."

Jude only realized he hadn't replied when Domino's back stiffened, but damn, silent all day yesterday and now he wants to talk about coffee? However, spooking Domino back into silence was the last thing he wanted. There were things about this case that didn't quite add up.

"Black's fine. Not all kitties like saucers of milk."

Crouching down, careful not to let his ass touch the freezing ground, he accepted a steaming mug, took a sip. Domino laid the kettle aside.

"So, talking now?"

Domino's shoulders stiffened, then shrugged. A pause. A swallow.

"Yeah. Someone needs to know. Before, well, you know."

"Your father says he can do something about that. It's one of the reasons I'm here."

"Whoever sent you isn't my father. Siren pregnancies only implant after the death of the sire. If I'm alive, my father's dead."

Domino poked the fire, didn't look at his companion. Every fiber screamed defeat. "That's what'll happen to me if the sirens get me. I'll be made to service as many of them as possible until I die. If I reach the end of the queue, they'll kill me. I've seen the knife, heard it happen to others."

"I won't let that happen." The words were out of Jude's mouth before he thought about them.

Domino's huffed breath mingled with the smoke spiraling up into the clear pale sky.

"Whatcha goin' to do, kill me first? I hope you're better

at it than I am. Although, thinking about it, I have my moments."

The self-pity might be justified, but it pissed Jude off. You couldn't change the past, but you could make sure the same shit didn't happen to other people. Justice took action, not passivity.

"You've got nothing to beat yourself up about over Rory. That was his choice, his greed. He deserved what he got."

Domino sank a little lower. "No, no, he didn't. Neither did Ranulfo, the first human I killed, or my sister, although there's a possible argument about my sister." He threw his half-drunk coffee over the fire and stood up. "Shall we get going?"

Jude remained hunkered down. From this angle, he could see Domino's face. Resignation, depression. Soft full lips, a straight, sharp nose, high cheekbones, black eyes, the large dark purple patch on the right side of his face. The siren turned away, hiding his features.

"The marks don't bother me any more than tattoos would."

Domino held out his hand for Jude's now empty mug. "Tattoos are a choice; they're wanted and considered. These are a curse."

Jude watched him walk back to the van, rinse the cups with water from a ten-gallon bottle, and climb into the passenger seat.

Jude stood, circled his shoulders against the residual stiffness that sleeping on a hard surface caused. His belly rumbled, reminding him of something else that didn't seem to bother the siren.

After checking the fire was out, he went over to the van and opened the passenger door where Domino sat.

"How often do you need to recharge with seawater?"

"I'm fine; I don't-"

"If I think you're lying, I'll contact the siren representative on the council. She might get suspicious or could pass on my question to the wrong people. Is it worth it?"

Domino let out a long breath, leaned his head back on the headrest, exposing his throat. Fisting his hands stopped Jude reaching for the pale column. *Does he know that's damn erotic? Is he playing me?* Whatever the case, it'd been a damn long time since anyone had successfully played Jude, and he wasn't stopping that winning streak now.

"Well?"

"At least once a day. Other sirens can last longer, but I'm... not usual."

Jude took a step back, waving a hand to indicate Domino should get out. "Have at it. I deliver healthy bounties."

"Apart from the dead ones." If Domino meant to shock or make Jude uncomfortable, it didn't work. Jude knew what and who he was, an asshole who did a necessary job, one he happened to enjoy most of the time.

"True. But I wanted those ones dead. You, I want breathing. Now move."

Without another word, Domino slithered over the back of the seat. The movement might have exposed a little skin in a different climate, and Jude found himself cursing the weather yet again. He wouldn't do anything about this niggling attraction, but enjoying the view was allowed.

Water splashed into a bucket, the scent of the sea rose, then the side door opened.

Jude turned, leaning his back up against the van. Domino hesitated, holding the black bucket of water, but he didn't look at Jude. Maybe it was a case of, "If I can't see you, you can't see me."

"You don't have to watch," Domino ground out.

The embarrassment was cute. "You watched me eat yesterday."

"You didn't give me a choice."

Jude grinned. "True. And I'm not giving you one now. Go ahead, strip, or whatever you got to do."

"Fucking perv. Any skin contact works, and even if I don't feel the cold like you, it's not exactly tropical sunshine out here."

"But all-over feels better, right? You were positively glowing in the aquarium."

Domino hesitated, pulled up his sleeve, and turned his back.

"Ah, ah, I need to see. You've got a major case of death wish and–"

Domino turned back around. If looks could kill, Jude would be frying. "You get nothing for a corpse. So sorry for wanting to put a dent in your retirement fund." With one swift movement, he poured the water over his forearm in a rush.

Jude cocked his head. "I like fast food as much as the next guy, but that's ridiculous."

Domino rolled his eyes and seemed to have forgotten his embarrassment about his birthmarks. "And you're an authority on sirens now? It works, that's all you need to know. I thought we were in a hurry? Don't you want to feed that bottomless pit of a stomach?"

"No, yes, and yes. But you're driving. I've got some research to do."

Domino put the bucket back in the van but didn't bother wiping off his arm. "Happy to, although I don't have a license. Kinda tricky what with this face and the staying off the grid thing. And where are we going?"

"That way," Jude pointed along the road, "to see your daddy." At Domino's glare, he added, "to the guy who claims to be your father and who says he can save your life, which, personally, I think is a good idea even if you don't."

Without a word, Domino got into the driving seat and started the engine. Jude hastily climbed in. Being left on the side of the road would be damn embarrassing.

"Don't worry; I'm not going to do anything drastic. If I had the balls to kill myself, I would've done it while you were snoring." Domino checked the mirror then pulled out.

"I don't snore. That was unconscious purring."

Domino snorted a laugh. "Riiight. And I'm the fucking little mermaid."

"I'm glad you're not. Driving with a tail would be damn difficult, and a seashell bra must be fucking uncomfortable." He paused, then asked, "Do you miss it? The ocean?"

Domino's lips pressed together, and he nodded.

Way to go on busting the mood, Moreno.

"You seem pretty good at driving for someone who hasn't got a license."

"YouTube is a wonderful thing. I also know how to castrate domestic animals, including cats, and wallpaper a room."

"And I do not want to know why you looked up those things." Leaning forward, Jude turned on the radio. It was set to a popular music channel, and a ballad poured out.

Jude set himself up with his phone and tablet. The tablet wasn't ideal, but it was small enough to be portable and had a better screen than his phone.

He'd already told Orcus that he'd located the target, but not about catching him. Given what Domino said, he wasn't about to hand over an innocent to a man he knew little about. And then there was the issue of the human killing

Domino mentioned. Had the victim been one of the few humans supernaturals were allowed to cull to survive?

There were a few species, blood demons, reapers, and now it seemed sirens, that needed, or thought they needed, death to survive.

Usually, such beings had arrangements with human authorities. People with life-limiting conditions could sign up for a huge payout for their loved ones, or criminals sentenced to death got a choice. He guessed many siren fathers were criminals looking for a little paradise before they passed. Had the person Domino killed been one of these? Or was there something more sinister going on? Technically, Jude wasn't a law enforcement officer, but if he let a human murderer go free, he might not find many more Council contracts coming his way.

If they find out.

Contrary to what Domino assumed, his pay didn't go into a retirement account. All his cash went into a reward fund for information on the Scibetta rat pack who had killed his family. The nightmares no longer bothered him, but it had taken years before they faded.

"Penny for your thoughts?" Domino asked.

That was another thing he wanted to find out. Watching carefully, he asked, "Why have you gotten so chatty? You knew I had the amulets yesterday, but you weren't talking."

Domino didn't even hesitate as he shot back, "What can I say, your conversation is so scintillating. I couldn't help myself."

Jude let out a belly laugh. "Oh, you have got some sass, boy. I like you." His own words shut him up as the truth rang like a bell.

"Not enough not to turn me over, though, right?"

"Enough to make sure he is who he says he is and can help you before I do."

Domino's head whipped sideways. Their eyes met, and an unspoken question buzzed between them. *Can I trust you?*

He raised his eyebrows. "Looking at the road when driving is usually a good idea."

Domino turned his gaze forward again, his hands flexing on the wheel. If he'd been screaming his discomfort, it couldn't have been clearer.

A few minutes later, Domino pulled into a rest stop. "I'll gas it up; you get some takeout."

"Yes, sir. What did your last slave die from?"

"My voice."

Jude was left gaping as the van door shut behind the siren.

CHAPTER FOURTEEN

All the information says a siren pregnancy only quickens with the death of the sire.

Do you have him?

Jude didn't pause before answering the mage's text question. Domino had carried on driving while Jude ate his takeout breakfast of sausages and researched his employer.

You looked very alive the last time we spoke. I don't work for liars.

He'll die unless you get him here.

How about I just take him to the council and let them sort this out?

I don't pay for non-delivery.

The implied insult that he was only in this for the

money didn't sting as much as it had when Domino said it. Jude waited, knowing he held all the cards. The landscape they passed through had turned a little greener as their altitude came down. Jude hadn't given Domino any more details about their destination other than which way to go when they came to an intersection.

He's my grandson.

A plausible answer, but it threw up even more questions.

I've looked you up. You have over a dozen children and countless grandchildren, most of whom you've never met. Why this one?

So many questions about someone you don't have yet.
You wouldn't be lying to me, would you, Mr. Moreno?
I can find you with very little trouble.
Remember the tracking mark?

Jude's gaze flicked to the back of his hand. His skin looked unblemished, but that didn't mean there wasn't a residual effect. Domino looked relaxed, serene, as he drove towards another possible shitstorm, one Jude had created.

I want to help him, not hurt him; you have my word.
Bring him as soon as you can; his time is limited.
I can send a plane or a helicopter to you.
Even an elemental if it's an emergency.
Is it?

Jude looked at the less than reassuring words. "Hurting"

could take many forms, and not everyone's definition would be the same. If Orcus told the truth about being able to track him, Domino could be in danger just by being near him. But if he left him alone... There would be others like the Karnaks, like himself, out there, and all they'd see was the price on that curly, snarky head. At least with Jude around, he'd have someone in his corner.

Moreno?

He hesitated over the device for a few more seconds.

We're crossing into Maine. Should be with you in three days.

He pressed send then regretted it. He'd never been this indecisive about a bounty before. It bugged him.

"My turn to drive," he announced. At least if he were driving, he wouldn't be trying to catch a glimpse of Domino's face every few seconds or admiring the way his jeans hugged his thighs.

If I ever get a place of my own, I'd build a tank for him to swim in so that I could watch him all the time.

And where the fuck did that thought come from?

The rest of the day went pretty much as the day before, except Jude didn't get any more than a general conversation out of Domino. That night, the siren crawled into his sleeping bag again without offering to share. Jude's disappointment annoyed him.

Domino hesitated instead of resting his head on the pillow. "Are you going to read again?"

Jude's jaw creaked as he yawned. It always felt so much better in his fur form. "Want me to read aloud again? I thought you'd be sick of the sound of my voice by now." Silence stretched. Jude thought Domino might have dropped off to sleep.

"I kinda like it."

"Did anyone read you bedtime stories as a kid? My mom read to me and my sister; it's one of my most precious memories."

"I used to listen to the singing downstairs in the evening. Unless it was freezing, I used to leave my bedroom window open so I could hear better."

"Sounds nice. So they sang every evening?"

"Yeah. All sororities do it; it's a bonding thing."

"But you weren't allowed to join in?"

Domino didn't answer, just snuggled down. Jude got his tablet out.

Domino spent the day either dozing or filing his nails, particularly the one on his right thumb. Either that file was dull, or siren's nails were a hell of a lot harder than Jude's. Maybe that's why the Karnaks had clipped the top joint of Domino's thumb, to remove a weapon.

When the sun sat on the horizon the day after, Jude pulled over. Domino had been drooping for the last hour; he probably needed a recharge. Yes, they could have stopped at the motel in the last town but being around people made the siren twitchy. Knowing they'd be camping again; Jude had bought some supplies at their last stop.

Sirens might not need to eat, but a flame-seared steak sounded perfect.

Domino's hunched form didn't stir as he leaned on the window, curled up on the seat like a kitten. Even asleep, he'd made sure his hood covered his face like a security blanket. He looked so damn peaceful, so young and vulnerable. If Jude had been in fur, the urge to go over, hold him down, and groom him would've been hard to resist. Then again, being licked by a giant cat you'd seen kill probably wasn't the most relaxing way to be woken up.

Instead, Jude nudged Domino's shoulder. "Come on, kid, time to eat and catch some proper z's."

Domino jerked, sat up, head whipping around.

"S'okay, just me. We're miles from anywhere, no other people around."

Domino deflated, screwed up his eyes, and then opened them wide. Despite the cute facial exercises, he didn't look awake. In fact, he looked damn tired. There were circles under his eyes.

How much sleep is he getting?

Domino had fallen asleep before Jude the last two nights, but he'd been up first.

If sleep was the issue, they could do something about that, but if his poor condition was more about his impending death, they'd have to cut this road trip short and take faster transport.

"I'll start the fire; you go do your bucket thing. There's a stand of trees you can use for privacy over there, but unless you want to be knocked down by a two hundred pound pissed off leopard, don't run off.

The siren's eyes narrowed, but he didn't speak.

"Just you and me here, Salty. There's no need for the silent treatment."

"You really think I couldn't affect you if I tried? I almost got you at the sea life place."

A slow smile spread across Jude's face. Domino wasn't threatening him, rather, he sounded resigned to hurting everyone around him.

"You're welcome to try, but you might break that pretty voice of yours. Bigger and uglier people than you have tried to hurt me without success."

Domino got out and filled his bucket from the back. He took two steps before halting. "You don't want to watch?"

"Do I need to?"

"Guess not." Domino turned towards the small stand of broadleaved trees at the edge of the road. Jude heard the cry for attention loud and clear.

"I've changed my mind. Take your top off; I'll do the pouring this time."

For a second, Jude thought he'd have a fight on his hands as Domino tensed. Then he put the bucket down, pulled off his hoodie along with his shirt, and bent over, hands on his knees. The marks contrasted against the rest of his skin even more than they had at the aquarium. *Is he getting paler or are the marks getting darker?*

Domino's choice of a sideways position lacked potential, but having him half-naked and willingly bent over still had desire curling in his belly. Pushing things was probably a bad idea, but Jude couldn't help it. "Your jeans are going to get wet."

Domino gave him the bird.

Jude chuckled, picked up the bucket, and stepped around so Domino's head was only about six inches from his groin. The siren started to straighten.

Jude put his hand on the back of Domino's neck, holding him down. "Don't get your shorts in a knot; I'm just trying not to get your jeans wet. Besides, didn't your mother teach you that making rude gestures isn't the way to make friends?"

Before Domino could reply, Jude tipped the bucket, pouring the water over his head, neck, and shoulders in a steady flow. When he finished, Domino stood up and shook like a dog. His long hair flung water all over Jude.

Holding up his hands to prevent the splatter proved pretty useless. "Hey, watch out, cats don't like water." He sniffed. "Especially smelly water. That stinks."

Domino grabbed the bucket and returned it to the van, but this time he grabbed a towel and rubbed it over his head.

The styling lasted about a minute before the towel joined the bucket. Domino reached for his shirt and hoodie.

Banter had gotten a positive reaction before, and Jude hated to change a winning formula.

"That's it? Didn't your mother teach you about styling?"

Domino looked him straight in the eyes, and for a second, nerves bubbled.

"My mother taught me to hide and to look like a girl in case an unexpected visitor caught sight of me. She tried to convince me that being locked in an attic and ignored meant she cared. Now if you'll excuse me, I'm-"

"Going to sit with me while I build a fire and cook my dinner. You might have fed; I haven't. Come on, let's go get some firewood."

Domino looked like tramping around in the cold was the last thing he wanted to do, but if he refused, Jude's assessment that the siren was barely staying on his feet would be proven.

The water in the van wasn't having the same effect as that in the aquarium, and yet, the siren was still going through the motions.

Jude bet that even if he took the top off the tank somehow and lay Domino full-length in the water, it wouldn't provide any energy. It appeared seawater lost whatever nutrients it provided over time, just like mundane food.

Domino trailed him into the copse of trees, picking up the occasional twig or fallen branch as Jude bent to the task with enthusiasm. When he had his arms full, he glanced over at Domino's pitiful bundle.

"Is that it? Seriously, if I hadn't seen you in that club and the aquarium, I'd assume you're a sloth shifter."

Domino simply turned and began plodding back towards the van. Orcus had more energy than his grandson right now. If this was going to stay a live delivery, Jude needed more information.

After beating Domino back, he dumped his pile of firewood and then went to find his phone. The siren simply added his small bundle to the collection and squatted down as if moving any further would be too much effort. He also had his arms wrapped around himself, the first indication that Domino even felt the low temperature.

Who to call only took a few minutes thought. Anyone on the Supernatural Council was out. If anyone caught a sniff that he'd found a male of the species, the siren delegate might find out. From what Domino said, that wouldn't be a good idea. Milo was too damn nosy; he'd want to know all the ins and outs of what was happening.

A smile tickled Jude's lips. Ezra Erotes. The youngest incubus and all-around shady character. Ezra wasn't exactly the most upstanding citizen. He bent the rules but had yet to be caught breaking them, even though the head of the Supernatural Council had taken him under his wing.

A year and a half ago, Ezra had been up on charges of

human abuse and unwilling addiction, but he'd been cleared during an epic trial. If the governor of the Supernatural prison hadn't been sent to bring in the incubus, Jude would've taken the case. A rogue incubus could be as much fun as he sounded.

They hadn't met in the flesh until Jude spent a memorable vacation on an island in the Mediterranean last summer. Sex, sunshine, and relaxation without worrying about when and where he could shift. The place was a haven for all species of supernaturals and knowledgeable humans. Milo was damn lucky to have hooked up with Ezra permanently. He dialed.

"This is damn early for a booty call." Jude grinned at the gravelly voice.

"It's never too early or too late for you, Erotes." Rustling of sheets and a few disgruntled male voices pointed to the fact that Ezra wasn't alone, not that Jude expected him to be. Sex demons with a harem seldom slept alone.

Jude heard a door click before the demon spoke again.

"Moreno? That you?"

"It warms my heart that you remember my name."

"I remember your cock, that's not something anyone forgets easily. Are you coming for a visit?" The hope in the demon's voice made Jude smile.

"Not for a while, I'm afraid. Did you get that problem with Finn sorted out?

"Oh yeah, with bells on. What's up?"

"I'm after some information."

A heartfelt groan came down the line. "If it's information you want, talk to Pixie. You remember the pink-haired, acid-tongued fae, right? Information is her bag, not mine."

"This has got to be between you and me."

"Do tell." Ezra sounded like a little boy being told a

naughty secret. Although the demon was decades older than Jude, in terms of lifespan, he was a teenager for his kind. Demons could live for a thousand years or more, not the three hundred or so for shifters.

"Ever had a siren?"

"Four, in one go, but only once. Why, have you picked some up? You'll need a damn iron lung to satisfy them, and they like to ride, but I'm not sure they'll enjoy what you're packing."

"You did, quite a lot if I remember."

"You were certainly memorable, I'll give you that. But in case you hadn't noticed, sex is kinda my thing."

Jude moved to keep an eye on Domino as he stood on the other side of the van. The siren had managed to light the fire and was poking at it with little enthusiasm. He needed to get on with this.

"Do they eat?"

"Sucking your cock would be a challenge for–"

"No, I mean food, proper food." He paused; sex was food for Ezra. "Mundane food."

The incubus chuckled. "Well, I wasn't taking them out to dinner first. Although I bumped into them in the resort restaurant; they were eyeing up Finn as if he was dessert. And no, I didn't let them near him; he is still human."

"So they ate mundane food?" Jude pressed. He could almost see Ezra rolling his eyes.

"Yes, they ate, and we fucked. They were here for three days, and when they weren't eating or swimming, we fucked, forwards, backwards, upside–"

"They swam a lot?"

"Ugh, what's this about, Jude? I haven't had my morning glory yet." Keeping a hungry incubus away from his breakfast when he had a bed full of willing feeders wouldn't gain him any points.

"I've got a bounty, a siren, who claims their species doesn't eat and can survive by pouring a bucket of at least five-day-old seawater over themselves twice a day."

"Then I suggest your bounty doesn't want to live long enough to be turned in."

It was about what Jude figured. Either through depression or via a considered plan, Domino was slowly killing himself.

"Thanks for the info, I'll try and get back to–"

"Is she singing or playing an instrument?"

Jude bit his tongue before he corrected Ezra about Domino's gender. Of course, the incubus had assumed the siren they were talking about was female.

"No. Does it matter?"

"Every siren I've met hums, sings, plays an instrument, talks, or their mouth is occupied some other way, eating, underwater, or they're asleep. I've never met a more oral species. Although I've found a few ways to shut them up, usually involving my cock and their–"

Jude interrupted Ezra; hearing yet more sexual exploits wouldn't solve his problem.

"Thanks for the info, I'll be sure to book up a vacation soon." He broke the connection. Time to call for a delivery.

CHAPTER FIFTEEN

It took far longer than Domino expected for Jude to return. He didn't look happy. The shifter held a bag of groceries and the sleeping bag. Keeping quiet seemed like a good idea, not that he felt very chatty.

The sleeping bag landed on his head. "Wrap that around you; it's not a request."

Domino complied. It did feel good. In fact, just keeling over on his side sounded like a fantastic idea. Sitting down, Jude took four sticks from the pile and set about sharpening the ends with a half-shifted hand.

His talons reminded Domino of his lost thumb. Maybe if he'd been able to retract his talon, he might not have lost it for killing Ranulfo. Then again, as the bone was missing, he guessed they'd had another motive for taking the joint. The bone amulets were hidden under Jude's ancient black leather jacket, but Domino knew they were there. Bits of sirens. His relatives. If he'd had anything in his belly, he probably would have lost it.

When he finished sharpening the sticks, Jude pulled a

large, wax paper wrapped slab of beef from the bag. That last truck stop must have had a much more extensive inventory than it appeared from the outside.

Jude sliced through the meat as if it was butter, stuck chunks on the sticks, and dug them into the ground so they hung into the flames. Then he pulled a bottle out of the bag along with Domino's two mugs. After pouring, Jude proffered one to Domino. He didn't take it.

"It's just an energy drink." When Domino still didn't reach for it, he waved it up and down. "If I was going to hurt you, I wouldn't bother drugging you first. I'm bigger, stronger, and faster. I'd just tie you up. Drink it."

Domino took the mug and eyed the orange liquid with suspicion. "What's in it?"

"Electrolytes, glucose, all good stuff." To prove his point, he took a swig himself. "Mmm, yum."

Domino took a sip. "It's very salty."

"That's the electrolytes. Drink up."

With Jude watching him, he drank the rest. He felt foggy as if he'd drunk alcohol. Anxiety melted away to be replaced by sleepy relaxation. "Would you mind if I went to bed now?"

"Yes. I like company while I eat." He poured more of the orange stuff into Domino's mug.

"I thought cats were solitary, apart from lions," Domino said and looked Jude over. "You don't look like a lion to me."

Jude's brows drew together. "I bloody well hope not. Lions are grade-A assholes. Always in groups, chucking their weight around. King of the beasts, my ass."

Domino lowered his head to hide his smile.

"And what are you grinning about?"

"You. At the center of a lion gangbang."

"And how the hell is that funny?"

Domino laughed. The lion thing wasn't funny but turning the tables on the confident shifter tickled him. He shook his head and took another few swallows of the energy drink. It was certainly living up to its name; energy seemed to be diffusing into his body with every mouthful.

"Laugh it up, Salty. Here, chew on this and shut the fuck up." Jude thrust a stick with a lump of seared meat on it at him.

Still chuckling, Domino took a bite and groaned in pleasure as hot meat juices exploded in his mouth.

"Good?"

"Fuck, yeah," he said around the mouthful and grabbed the mug from Jude who had just filled it up again.

They ate in companionable silence for a while, before Jude got up and walked back to the van. Domino laid back on the ground, listening to the silence and looking up at the now visible stars. Full, sated, and content. He didn't know how Jude had done it, but gratitude swelled, bursting from him in clouds like his breath in the cold.

"Hey, Salty, over here."

With a sigh, Domino rolled to his feet. Jude had opened the side door of the van. The water bucket sat on the ground in front of it.

"Sit." Jude pointed to the floor of the van.

"I've already–"

"Doused yourself with stale water? Yeah, I saw and smelled it. Sit. Down."

Domino sat.

"The diner had a fish tank. I thought you could do with a fresh meal. You have to ask if you need something." As he spoke, Jude squatted, lifted Domino's foot, and took off his shoe and sock.

No one had ever done anything like this for him. Yes, his family had ensured he got what he needed, but that was all. Even with Melody, he hadn't been certain her help had been more than trying to ingratiate herself with the golden goose. Yes, she died during the rescue attempt, but he'd always wondered what she would have done with him if she'd survived. This, and the reading the two previous nights, was so much more than ensuring Jude got his paycheck.

Jude tugged on Domino's other foot, and he realized the shifter wanted to remove his shoe and sock.

"Sorry," he mumbled and lifted his leg. Once both his feet were bare, Jude rolled up his jeans and guided both feet into the water. The rush of energy pulled a groan from him. It felt like a pure shot of alcohol, short, sharp, and it warmed his body.

"Good?"

Jude's comment pulled Domino's eyes open again. He nodded, not trusting his voice, not wanting to hurt or influence Jude. The shifter was doing this because he wanted to, not out of any obligation or magical influence. Domino didn't understand, but he wanted to.

Jude stood up and perched beside him in the van doorway. "I'll accept a tune or a song as a thank you."

Domino swallowed; his throat suddenly dry. Bowing his head, his thoughts raced. He couldn't influence Jude, not much anyway. Singing for Rory had been... wonderful. He'd felt the magic rise, warm his chest, before it heated the air around him. He'd enjoyed it so much that he'd continued even after Rory passed. If Jude hadn't come back, he might have sung for hours.

The wrapped cloth containing his pipe appeared in his lap. "Why did you pick that Meatloaf song for Rory?"

The question tugged a smile from Domino's lips. "It was his breakup song. When he got fed up with a guy, he used to get up on the stage and dedicate it to the poor bastard. I heard it every night for ten days when I first went to Blaze; then he picked me."

"And that's all I want to know about you and that nasty little human. What I want to know now is what you're going to play, or sing, for me?"

The cloth begged him to open it. There was no one around apart from Jude, and if he didn't pick the wrong song, he could play again. It might be the last time.

With a flick of his wrist, he opened the cloth. The chrome pipe glinted in the moonlight. He picked it up, caressed the holes. Over the last five years, sometimes he got it out, held it, fingering the notes he remembered, without playing them. It was never enough.

Raising the pipe to his lips, he began the opening to 'Hey Jude'. He could almost see the magic rolling off himself like smoke. A smile tickled the shifter's lips, his expression interested, not blank.

Fuck, those amulets really work. I can do this. One last time. Anticipation, excitement curled. He couldn't swim out into the deep ocean but playing one last time would be nearly as good.

He only intended to play the pipe, but after he'd run through the melody once, he couldn't resist singing. Although he changed the female lyrics to masculine.

The power rose, expanded, and he gave himself over to it. When 'Hey Jude' finished, he went straight into 'Don't Stop Me Now' by Queen, followed by another rock ballad, and then another. Old and new, fast and slow, the songs didn't matter, only the singing counted. The moon was high in the sky by the time dizziness set in. He stopped, and fatigue hit him, but he foggily tried to think of something else to sing, anything at all to keep the magic flowing like charged nectar in his veins.

"You could make a fortune with that voice. I could feel the emotion in every song." Jude's low tone held admiration, even devotion. Domino's good mood evaporated. *Sex and songs, that's all anyone is interested in.*

With stiff movements, like he'd done a hundred times, he re-wrapped the pipe, wondering if Jude would bury him with it or if it'd end up abandoned, unloved, and unappreciated.

"It wouldn't be a long career, even if everyone who heard me had one of those amulets."

"Why?"

Domino hesitated. *Does it matter now?* The fresh seawater had perked him up, both in the bucket and probably in the drink Jude gave him. Underneath the energy and the euphoria singing produced, bone-deep exhaustion pressed in on him.

The sand timer of his life was running out and he didn't want Jude to blame himself, not even a little bit. The last few days had been the most peaceful and relaxed Domino could remember. He owed Jude the truth.

"Because using my voice or playing drains my life force. Every word and note takes minutes and hours from me. Female sirens can recharge themselves. Males have a finite pot; when it's gone..." He made starbursts with his hands and a crashing noise.

Jude closed his eyes, heaved a sigh. "And I just let you sing for two fucking hours."

"I wanted to. It felt good. Thanks for the–" He stopped as Jude put his finger on his lips.

"How long?" Jude asked, then groaned. "Don't answer that. From now on, you go back to signing and writing."

"No point. I'd rather–"

Jude slapped a hand over his mouth, staring into his eyes. "I will gag you if I have to; just shut up and let me think."

Jude got out his phone, started scrolling.

It hadn't felt cold at all when he'd been singing, but the water in the bucket was only cold fluid now; it held no energy. Taking his feet out of the water, he dried them on a towel then climbed inside the sleeping bag, hoping the world would just piss off and leave him alone to die in peace.

Domino drifted, not listening to Jude's quick words. With the amulets around the shifter's neck, he doubted he could stop him doing anything. He couldn't outrun him, and the van keys were in Jude's pocket.

"Domino?" His shoulder was shaken. He gave Jude the bird without opening his eyes.

"Hilarious. Orcus is sending a plane to an airfield an hour from here in the morning. We'll be with him by lunchtime, and he can work whatever magic he intends to use to save you."

Domino sat up. Stress showed in Jude's tense shoulders.

"This Orcus guy isn't my–"

"For fuck's sake, stop talking, and Orcus said he's your grandfather, not your father, although why he lied, I'm not entirely sure."

"Father's closer. I suppose he–"

"Ah," Jude's sharp utterance had Domino rolling his eyes. Jude paused, lips pursed. "Actually, hang on."

Stepping over Domino's legs, he opened the lid of the chest where Domino kept his clothes. A quick rummage produced what Domino feared. The cloth gag he used to prevent affecting any passing humans while he slept.

"You're going to condemn me to that on possibly my last–"

Flat on his back with a snarling man on top of him had Domino's adrenaline spiking, it felt too much like being back with the Karnaks, but Jude didn't have to know that.

"You will stay quiet or I'll–"

Domino grinned and waggled his eyebrows.

Jude opened his mouth, then shut it, chuckled, and got off him. "You're dreadful, and not getting around me with promises of sex. I'm not an incubus."

Domino tapped his wrist where a watch would have sat if he'd had one and gave his best puppy dog eyes. Flirting without words was a hell of a lot easier than doing it verbally after all this time.

"A last request because your time's running out?"

Domino nodded at Jude's correct interpretation. The shifter cocked his head, sniffed.

"Don't try to bullshit a bullshitter." Jude paused, swallowed, then carried on. "You might have a magic voice, but I've got a magic nose. You're not turned on, and you shouldn't be. Canine shifters aren't the only ones with different cocks."

Domino's gaze dropped to Jude's jeans. Even in the gloom, he could see a sizable bulge.

What the fuck did he mean by different? Bigger? Wider? Ulrike had torn him, and repeating that experience wasn't on his to-do list. But Jude wasn't the only one in the van with a cock. That hairy, controlled, muscled body at his command would be quite an experience.

The cat shifter sniffed again, and his face creased into a wicked grin. "I'd love to know what you're thinking, but I'll do a deal with you. One week from now, after you've seen your grandfather, I'll fuck your brains out. Deal?"

Domino gave a slow smirk, decision made. He indicated himself with his thumb, stuck his middle finger up, then pointed at Jude.

"You think you're going to top me? I'll tell you what, let's get you to Orcus and next week first, ok?"

Domino flopped down onto his back.

"Yeah, I know it sucks, and not in a good way. But seriously, you must say if you're feeling unwell. I can get the air elemental to transport us, but these–" he patted his chest over the amulets, "would have to stay behind."

Domino's expression must have given him away. "Yeah, I'm not exactly keen on the idea either, but if it's a choice between that and you pushing up daisies, I'll cope. I can always post them on. Now, let's get some sleep."

To Domino's disappointment, instead of getting out his tablet, Jude turned his back, made a pillow out of his arm, and went to sleep. Two days of being read to in his life, and he missed it so fucking much. It probably would have been better if he'd never experienced it. Domino forced the thought out of his mind. No, he couldn't regret that happening.

Although Domino's limbs felt heavy, the high of singing for the first time in years made sleep impossible. His thoughts kept turning again and again to the man sleeping next to him.

Maybe he should have been thinking about his grandfather, about the promise of life. Would Jude simply leave after he'd made the delivery? Domino knew nothing about his supposed grandfather, and no relative, except Mel, had ever wanted to help rather than use him, and he wasn't entirely sure about her either.

For the first time, he considered being alive this time next year. What would such a life be like? Would he still be hunted by the sororities? He guessed so. You didn't give up hope of being the most powerful race on the planet easily. He still wouldn't be able to go out, have a job, or socialize when and where he wanted. Even if the sirens stopped hunting him, his power would always attract people who wanted to use him.

The best he could hope for was an isolated home by the sea. He drifted, imagining a guard on the gate, passing out the amulets to visitors. No more than four people at a time. Count them in, count them out.

For an introvert, it'd be heaven on a plate. For him, it'd be an upmarket prison until the day he died, but it had to be better than the alternative. Would Jude be one of the visitors?

No, that's so damn stupid. Why the hell would a free spirit like Jude ever let himself get saddled with me? Maybe if this imaginary place is a tropical island, he might visit. He likes the sun, the heat. Maybe if it was a small island, the other residents might even get used to me. Yes, I'd have to keep quiet, but...

He flipped again between hiding, possibly living longer, and packing in as much as he could, while he could. It'd been the story of the last five years.

Dancing on a beach with Jude, barbeques, swimming together, maybe even learning to surf. It was a damn good fantasy.

Jude twitched in his sleep, once, and then again. A gasp of fear passed his lips. Whatever haunted the leopard shifter's dreams, it wasn't pleasant. Given their conversation right before he went to sleep, Domino imagined Jude fighting phantom attackers, trying to keep him safe. The urge to give something back bubbled up.

Keeping his voice low, barely audible, he started Bob Marley's 'Three Little Birds'. 'Every little thing's gonna be alright' might not be true in real life, but hopefully, it could be in Jude's dreamworld.

CHAPTER SIXTEEN

"JuDAH. I said, pass me the juice."

"DeliLAH, I said, this is mine, you drank yours," Jude growled back. The twins knew using the other's full name pissed them off, and it didn't help that Del was in the middle of her adolescent growth spurt. Right now, she was two inches taller than him, and when she wasn't using his full name, she called him "Titch".

"And I need more; don't forget I shifted again this morning."

Jude pressed his lips together and handed over the bottle of juice. He had no comeback against that argument. He'd been horribly jealous when Del managed to shift for the first time a month ago. The ability to shift came with sexual maturity and girls got there before boys. The compensation that he'd be bigger and stronger than her as an adult didn't help now.

This car journey was the living end. Every year, their mom made the eight-hour journey to visit her mother and dragged them along, but this time the move would be permanent. Mom was pregnant again, this time with triplets. She said she couldn't cope with five kids on her own; he agreed but didn't like it.

Shifters lived a long time; she could have waited until her current kids were grown before having more. That's how all his aunts arranged their families.

He and Delilah were thirteen and quite capable of looking after themselves and helping out. He'd argued passionately against the need to move. As always, his male opinion didn't carry much weight when it came to wider family matters.

The thought of living with Grandma, three aunts, and a whole bunch of young cousins made him shiver. Most cat shifter families were matrilineal. Males came and went, but the female relationships stayed fierce and strong. They expected him to leave, and maybe not ever return, sometime in the next decade. Males traveled and had little responsibility as far as the women were concerned.

For all he knew, he and his twin could have different fathers. It didn't matter. Their mother probably knew the names of the male or males she'd mated with although she'd never said. She'd let them know for genetic purposes when they were old enough. Their father might contribute to their family income, or he might not even know he had offspring.

Males of his kind were either loners or formed tight bonds with one or two other males. They didn't get involved in rearing cubs, or rather the females closed ranks when one was expecting.

If one of these "brotherhoods" came across a fertile receptive female, they would likely all mate her. Fun and then walk away with none of the wranglings. It sounded damn good.

Jude gazed out of the window as the damp, barely visible fields and trees passed by, wondering what it'd be like to be part of a brotherhood and away from all these females. His eldest male cousins vacated Grandma's house when it'd been decided they were moving in. Spending more time with the three older boys had been the only good thing about this, but the trio moved out together last week.

His aunts and Grandma were so damn obsessed with details. What the hell did it matter if his shirt matched his shoes or not? He sighed, imagining endless discussions about interior decoration and food preparation. It was bad enough with just Del and Mom. If the meat was no longer moving and had been near some sort of high heat recently, Jude was good to go.

In their small city apartment, he'd shared a room with his twin. Yes, they argued, but they understood each other, could almost tell what the other was thinking. Mom might think they were bickering, but they were just checking in, making sure the other was ok.

In Grandma's sprawling old house, he'd have his own room as the only remaining boy. Del would bunk in with two of their cousins. She'd get closer to them, further from him. It was the way of their kind, but he wasn't ready to move on, not yet. This first step towards adulthood had been forced upon him, and he didn't want it.

Why can't I remain a kid forever?

Jude checked his watch, another hour to go. They'd get to Grandma's around eight pm, just in time to eat supper and go to bed. All their possessions were following on behind by truck but wouldn't arrive until tomorrow.

The car braked, throwing Jude against his seatbelt and cutting Del off mid-sentence.

Jude swallowed. Looking at his twin, he could see her wide eyes in the thin, early summer evening light.

"Mom? What's–"

Their mother twisted in her seat, shoving her phone towards Jude. Her teeth were elongated, showing white in the gloom. "Del, shift and run. Jude, find a tree, climb as high as you can, and call Grandma. Got it?"

She waited for Jude to nod, then his beautiful mother undid her seatbelt, and ripped open her dress. She opened the door, but a golden spotted cat exited the car, not a blonde woman.

A shiver went up Jude's spine as his mother growled. He'd never heard her make a noise like that; she sounded magnificent. Nothing could stand against her, against them.

Before he could say anything, Del was out of her seatbelt, stripping off her clothes like mom, her face set with determination. She looked so much like mom, fierce and strong. No wonder the men of their kind backed off when a female was in protective mode; he wouldn't want to tangle with either his mother or sister.

Delilah shifted, pawed at the door. He guessed it took a while to get used to what you could and couldn't do in fur. Jude threw himself sideways to open it. Del slipped out sleek and beautiful, although she wasn't as muscled as Mom. He felt defenseless, angry that he couldn't join them. The tingling Del had talked about before she shifted had yet to happen to him.

"You just have to really, really want it," she'd explained. Well, he damn well wanted it now, and it still wasn't happening.

Looking out the windshield, Mom stood, crouched and ready to attack six wiry male figures. Jude swallowed. *Mom's tough, but six?*

"Looks like we get three for the price of one." Higher pitched than most males, this guy's voice scratched at Jude's ears. "And just in time, by the look of it. A few more weeks, and there'd be even more damn cats."

"Aren't you going to shift too, little tomcat?" another said. "Abner should never have messed with the Scibetta pack. Our rug display will be the talk of the rat world. Father, mother, and two little stools to warm our butts."

Mom's growl rose to a screech. Muscles bunched, she flung herself forward.

All the men shouted, grabbed for their pockets. Jude snarled, imagining her claws, her teeth, tearing their throats out. He wanted to join in, to rend the man who wanted to skin them, might have already killed his father. At least that's who he assumed they'd meant by the name Abner.

A bang split the evening air. Heart exploding in his chest, Jude stared as his mother took the man to the ground.

Another man pointed at Mom; a second bang rang out. His beautiful, vibrant mother lay still. Hope pinged through him as she moved, but it was only the man underneath her pushing her body away.

"Get the fucking kits," he growled, wiping at a bloody gash on his face.

Jude stood there for a second, trying to process, then turned and ran blindly, jumping over a wooden fence at the side of the road. A dog barked frantically in the distance.

He found himself in a field, the ground uneven with cow dung. The animals themselves huddled at the far side, under some trees. He knew he needed to call for help, needed the might of his extended family, but curses and shouts came from behind him. Two, maybe three, of the men were chasing him. He couldn't see or hear Del, hopefully, she'd gotten away and gone for help.

The running footsteps were getting closer; these rat

shifters were small but fast. His breath rasped in his throat. They'd catch him, skin him, like–

His foot caught. He went down on his belly, hand hitting something that squished, stank. Scrabbling to his feet, he ran again, but their footsteps, their panting breaths, came from right behind him. His back itched, imagining a touch, a bullet.

Outnumbered by faster opponents, waiting for the sound of a gun, tearing pain, he flung himself toward instinctive safety, the small copse of mature trees where the black and white dairy cattle sheltered.

"For fuck's sake, just shoot him!"

"Not until he shifts–"

A scream came from behind him. Spinning, he saw a spotted cat on the back of one of the three men; the others were both aiming guns at Del.

"Shift, Del, shift!" he shouted. Golden spotted fur turned into pale naked skin, but his sister still spat and clawed.

One man pulled back, his hand clutching his face that bore three claw marks. "My fucking eye!" He brought his gun up again.

The man next to him knocked his hand down while the third man tried to contain Del. Jude ran toward them.

"Help, get help!" Del screamed.

While she stayed in skin form, Jude hoped she'd be safe, but she was right, they needed help.

"Ah fuck, she bit me. She's a damn hell cat just like her fucking mother."

With Del keeping the men occupied, Jude ran for the trees again. Even though the rats were small for adults, Jude was still smaller, and tree climbing was a cat ability.

As he neared them, the cows ran, tails held high,

bawling in panic. The barking dog sounded closer, but not close enough. Besides, a dog might attack him as easily as the rats. Using the wooden fence, Jude vaulted up into the branches, climbing twenty feet before looking down.

Del still struggled between two of the men. One held her from behind, her hands pinned behind her back.

"Get your fucking hands off me!" *She's angry, not afraid; my Delilah wouldn't be scared.* The lie didn't help.

Pulling Mom's phone out of his pocket, he hit the name at the top of the contacts list. Three rings felt like a lifetime.

"Late again, Bella? I swear if you–"

"M...Mom's dead. They've got D...Del–" He swallowed, trying to control himself; he'd stuttered, he never stuttered.

"Judah, listen to me, we can't help unless you tell us where you are." His grandmother's to-the-point voice calmed him a little, but mom had sounded like that too. And now, now she was–.

"Judah Moreno, talk to me right now. Where are you?"

"I don't know; we're about an hour from you, it's a–"

Del screamed; Jude nearly dropped the phone.

"Judah, are you safe? Can they get to you?"

"I'm in a tree, but Deli... Gran, they're t...touching her. I need to go down; I can't–"

"Judah, stay right where you are. You can't help Delilah right now. We're on our way. Stay put, do you hear me?" Gran sounded frantic. "Tell me everything you can about who attacked you."

"There's six of them, all small guys. They stopped the car, mom... They s...said they were going to use her as a ru..." He swallowed, unable to complete the word. "I... I told Del to shift back, but now they're..."

With a final shriek, Del shifted again. The man holding

her lost his grip, and she ran for Jude's tree, body flexing, pure poetry in motion.

A shot rang out. Del somersaulted, lay still.

A scream tore from Jude's throat, his chest constricted. Not seeing anything else but the men approaching his sister, he slid, almost fell down the tree.

How he got to her side first, he didn't know. What he did know was that they wouldn't take her, not his Del.

Thumping to the grass on his knees, he pulled Del onto his lap, snarling at the three approaching figures. He didn't want to think about what the others were doing to Mom.

"Ready to shift yet?" one asked.

Jude stared at all three, committing their sharp features to memory. "I'm gonna find you and kill you."

The men laughed, chatted to each other as they got closer, guns covering him.

"So brave for one so short."

"Do you think he can even shift yet?"

"Might have to hold him for a few years until he's big enough to make a proper feature."

"Did I hear a call for justifiable revenge?"

How the man in the red shirt and black suit managed to appear in the field, Jude didn't know.

"We're handling it ourselves, demon, so fuck off."

The clean-shaven man frowned. "Dear dear, such unfortunate language, but I wasn't talking to you. Judah, is it? Would you like me to take care of these pesky rats for you?"

Delilah groaned, and hope bloomed. "It's ok, Gran's coming. Just hang on Deli, you're going to be fine." The larger world faded as he concentrated on willing Del to be ok.

One second he was cradling an adolescent leopard, the next, he held his sister's naked body.

"Oh fuck, that hurts," she gasped.

"Do I get an answer?" The suited man sounded bored. "I do have other mayhem to cause."

Jude ignored the man, the demon, whatever he was.

Jude stroked Del's face, wiping away a trickle of blood from her nose. "Don't talk; I've got you. You're going to be–"

"Don't... Don't bullshit a bullshitter, Titch, make 'em suffer, you hear me?"

"Well, if you don't need my services, I'll be going, but just to make it more interesting, you should know there are multiple, rather angry leopard shifters on their way by air elemental. Oh, and the farmer is about twenty seconds away with his dogs and a shotgun. Have a wonderful evening."

When Jude glanced up, the suited man had vanished, and a pair of black dogs were running, barking, at the rapidly retreating attackers.

Glancing back down at Deli, he found she was dressed and gently smiling. The field had transformed into a beach with golden sand. A song, a gentle happy song with a Caribbean twang, drifted around them. He recognized the spot as the island where he'd vacationed with Ezra.

"It didn't happen like this," Jude said, his body and voice that of an adult again.

"No, it didn't," Del replied, looked around. "This is nice, though."

"Yeah." Jude considered all the things he'd wanted to say to Delilah but had never had the chance. "I'm sorry for not saving you."

She turned the blue eyes that he remembered going

blank on him. "I've got no regrets. I saved you. You've grown into a good man, Titch; I'm proud of you."

"This is him doing this, isn't it?"

"Sort of. He didn't want you to suffer anymore. Give up this revenge thing, Judah; it's eating up your life."

He shook his head. "I can't. You did nothing wrong and they killed you because Mom slept with a man one time. They still have their pelts somewhere. I won't rest until they are properly laid to rest."

She pressed her lips together and nodded looking out at the ocean. She looked so innocent, so full of potential, so young.

"Just promise you'll remember to live for yourself sometimes? That's all that me, Mom, and Dad want. You'rc all that's left of us; don't throw it away."

"Dad's dead too?" No bodies had ever been found, but Abner Cullen and his brother Bernard disappeared a week before the attack.

"Both of them. Turns out we were probably only half-siblings."

"Are, Del, are. You're still my sister."

"No, I'm not. I'm a figment of your imagination. Everything I'm saying is coming out of your titchy little head." He smiled at the old insult.

"Not so titchy anymore."

She looked him over. "No, you're not. Your body has moved on; maybe it's time that head of yours does too."

The bright sunshine felt obscene. Delilah's remains were buried at Gran's house. He hated to think where his Mom and the father and uncle he'd never met were. He didn't even know if his father was Abner or Bernard.

"No. Not until it's done, until they rest in peace."

They listened to the never-ending surf, and nerve by

nerve, Jude relaxed. This really was paradise. If Heaven existed, it had to be something like this.

"Have you ever thought about what you'll do when you've finally finished off the Scibettas? Are you going to go after their kids like they did? Dad did them wrong after all."

"I'm not after revenge; I'm after justice. I make a difference, Del. I stop bad people; I prevent what happened to you happening to others. I'm happy."

Her eyes twinkled as she looked at him. "Now, now Titch, how many times do I have to tell you not to bullshit a bullshitter? You're lonely and you know it."

"Is that you talking or him?"

"Domino?"

He nodded.

"Everything is one hundred percent you; this is your head after all. You like him, he likes you, and you could make a real difference in his life; what he has left of it anyway. You could do a good thing here, and you know it wouldn't be long term." She patted his leg. "Think about it." Pushing to her feet, she yelled, "Last one in the sea is a dirty dog," and took off down the beach, blonde ponytail flying in the breeze.

Grinning like an idiot, Jude took off after her. This was his dream, and he intended to enjoy it.

CHAPTER SEVENTEEN

Jude's easy smile as he wandered over to where Domino brewed coffee eased the bubbling anxiety. The shifter appeared unaware of his interference last night.

"Morning. Did you sleep ok?" Jude asked.

Domino shrugged, nodded, and handed him a mug of coffee.

Jude took a sip, glanced around at the chilly damp field. A single car approached and carried on without stopping. It was the first vehicle to pass in over half an hour, and it broke the spell that they were alone.

Even though they'd only known each other for a matter of days, Domino felt that Jude knew and understood him better than anyone had in a long time. *Because we talked, a boon I no longer possess*. He found himself wondering if his mysterious mage grandfather could do something about that too.

Jude hunkered down, easy and relaxed. "I slept better than I have in a long time, after having a very vivid nightmare which turned into..." A smile curved his lips. "Something pretty damn wonderful. You wouldn't have had anything to do with that, would you?"

Domino smiled, shook his head.

"Liar."

Domino mimed texting. Jude handed over his phone without a word. For now, they could talk using text, but it would be impossible on the road.

What was the dream about?

Jude took another mouthful of coffee. "Have you had your morning feed?"

Domino nodded. He'd found the half-full plastic barrel at the back of the van. There wasn't any point in calling bullshit on Jude's claim that he'd picked up the water at the last diner. The spindly elemental must be stronger than it looked to have transported all that seawater.

He could feel Jude assessing him, so he sat up a little straighter. The shifter threw the remains of his coffee into the fire, making it hiss.

"Let's go get some proper breakfast."

Domino could tell an "It's none of your business" when he heard one. It seemed Jude wasn't as into being friendly as he'd thought.

"Hey, Salty. I'll tell you, it's not a secret, but I'd rather do it when you can't interrupt. It kinda has to come out in one go."

I can't exactly interrupt you with your fucking talking ban. Domino just nodded, the unspoken words smashing against each other in his head as usual.

"You ok with driving?"

Another nod. *I'm going to turn into a fucking nodding dog at this rate.*

They cleared the campsite and got in the van. Domino drove for two minutes before Jude spoke.

"I was thirteen, scrawny, irritating, and pissed off at the world. I didn't appreciate what I had."

Jude told the tale of his childhood. He couldn't help grinning as the shifter related his love-hate relationship with his twin. The envy died as he explained how she'd died. Losing Mel had been bad enough, but the other half of your soul? Domino couldn't imagine that.

"So that's why I do this. I'm biding my time, honing my skills while I wait for the next lead on the remaining two."

How could you ever smile after that? Yes, he'd been treated as a thing, a steppingstone to a possible future, but to have known such love and have it ripped from you? *How the fuck is he so cheerful?*

Eyes watering, Domino pulled off the highway on the edge of a town, turned the engine off, undid his seatbelt, and simply climbed into Jude's lap.

Strong arms went around him, rubbed his back. There were no words. Even if he could talk, he didn't know what to say. He just wanted to change the past, but if that hadn't happened, Jude wouldn't be with him now.

Does that make me grateful that his family were murdered?

The tap on the window sounded like a gunshot. Domino shot upright from where he'd had his face buried in Jude's neck, taking in the comforting scent of the scratchy skin.

A beefy guy wearing a thick navy-blue sweater stood almost against the window, face twisted in disgust. He looked in his forties, rough, a working man.

Domino tried to get off Jude's lap, but the shifter held him in place by his hips. Domino pulled his hood up, bowed his head, skin itching with the unwanted attention of a stranger.

Jude wound down the window. "Can we help you?"

"What do you think you're doing in my town?"

Jude gave him a sunny smile. "This is a hug. It's what people tend to do to express sympathy, joy, or affection."

The man's lip lifted in a sneer. "Do you want a beating, faggot?"

Domino could solve this problem with one sentence. *These are not the gays you are looking for*. A squeeze on his wrist told Jude's opinion of him getting involved, but the shifter rolled his hips, just a little. It wasn't enough to alert the asshole who had snuck up on them, so it must be meant to tell Domino something.

He dismissed the hot but dangerous idea that Jude wanted to keep flirting. It clicked. *He wants to be able to shift easily.*

"We're not doing anything wrong. We're both fully clothed, just having a break from driving. Would you like to see my license, officer? I'm particularly proud of the photo. I think it really captures my essence."

Domino had to give Jude points for offering his own license, even though Domino had been driving. His lack of any identification documents could be a problem.

The man's lip lifted. "I'm not a cop. I get sent to deal with problems my brother-in-law can't sort legally. We don't like your kind in our town. I'm giving you one chance to keep on driving."

Keeping his movements as small as possible, Domino inched his hands to the button on Jude's jeans, slipped it through the hole.

"Fucking queer, trying to feel him up while I'm fucking talking to you? I ought to put a bullet in both of you, but I guess I'll just settle for beating the crap out of you. Less paperwork for Tommy that way."

The smile dropped off Jude's face, and his grip on Domino vanished. Domino climbed off Jude's lap, giving him room to move if needed.

The bigot's hand went to his gun. "Hands where I can see them, both of you."

Domino raised his hands, keeping his head down. Jude slowly followed. "This is totally unnecessary. We were just–"

"Performing acts of public indecency on the highway, as Tommy would say. Hey you, let me see your face." Domino didn't so much as twitch, hoping the human would somehow forget about him.

"I'm going to get my wallet out of my pocket and show you my license and ID. I'm a licensed private investigator, and my office know where I–"

"So you're an asshole in more ways than one? This just gets better. Got any concealed weapons?"

The man clearly wasn't going to give them a break. He needed to do something; Jude might be quick, but this asshole could pull that trigger any second.

"Look, we–"

Jude's head shot around to face him. "I told you to be quiet." The shifter's fierce expression had Domino sinking back in his seat. The hood shifted; he pulled it down to shield his face even more.

"Hey, don't talk to him like that. Actually, how old are you, kid? Damn fucking paedos."

Domino glanced at Jude, kept his mouth shut.

"Don't look at him; look at me. Out of the van." He twitched his gun at Jude. "You first, smartass. Stay there, kid."

Jude got out, keeping his movements slow and deliberate.

"Hands on the hood, you filthy fucking pervert. Innocent, my ass, your pants are undone. Were you going to make that poor kid blow you or sit on you? I'm calling Tommy."

Jude complied, pleading with his eyes for Domino to behave.

The man lowered his gun, pointing at the back of Jude's knee.

Jude tore out of his grasp, whipped around. The man stumbled back, bringing up his weapon.

"*STOP.*"

Both men froze. Domino got out of the van. The man's face was blank, but Jude's eyes darted around. *Panic or anger?* It didn't matter which. Domino had used his power on him against his wishes, despite the talismans.

He hadn't expected to affect Jude as well, but the evidence stood twitching right in front of him. The thrall could last minutes, even hours and days, on the human, but it probably wouldn't hold the shifter for long.

I could just take off.

The chances that their relationship would continue in the same way after this was zero to nothing. Jude had seen him as a victim, someone to protect. With one word, he'd moved into a "threat" category.

Jude dumping him on the side of the road with the bounty still on his head wouldn't happen, but the shifter might treat him as a prisoner now, like the Karnaks had. And he certainly wouldn't stick around once he'd been paid. This was a betrayal of the worst kind; Jude valued his freedom above virtually everything.

And what about the human? The man was a piece of shit, a violent homophobe.

Turning him loose to do something like this to other

unsuspecting travelers left a bitter taste in his mouth. He dreaded to think what happened to the gay residents of this town.

Domino froze as a growl came from behind him. Back prickling, expecting to be grabbed or knocked over with every passing second, he turned to look.

Jude's butt rested against the front of the van; his arms were folded, jaw tense. *Not a happy kitty.* But he wasn't issuing orders or getting physical, yet. He'd managed to move a little, but some of the thrall must still be in place. For all the faith the Karnak's had put in the amulets, it appeared they were pretty damn useless.

If they were going to have any sort of relationship after Orcus worked his magic, if it worked, they had to have something in common. Justice, punishing evil people, was Jude's reason for existing.

Domino could change the way this human thought, behaved, for a while anyway. Any thrall would eventually fade, but the damage would be done. What did they say about walking a mile in someone's shoes to truly understand them?

He walked up until he almost touched the man's chest with his own and started whispering.

"You've watched the other guys in the locker room at college. All those slick, hard bodies turned you on. You remember hiding your boner, feeling guilty, jerking off to thoughts of them."

The man wetted his lips, Domino felt just a little dirty, but it was exciting too. To make the thrall work, Domino needed to believe in what he said. Two big hairy guys, wrestling, going at it, yeah, he'd want to watch that.

"You've seen Tommy's cock; it scares you a little because you can't help thinking about that thick meat.

You've seen him watching you too, it's time to let him know the truth, that you want him as much as he wants you."

Another growl came from behind him. He looked down, the man's cock strained against his jeans, a wet spot showed against the material. The urge to push this, to get this bigot to molest his equally homophobic brother-in-law rose, but that could end in another death. A beating, having him feel like he made others feel was his aim, not a lynching.

Another car passed on the other side of the road. The driver stared at him.

Domino pulled his hood down, and murmured, "Forget you saw us. Go see your brother-in-law. Watch his cock, his ass. They fascinate you. You want to know what they taste like."

The man turned and walked back to his car without looking at either of them.

Domino turned back to Jude. The shifter's stance hadn't changed, neither had the glare. It was so quiet that Domino could hear birdsong.

"Sorry?"

Jude didn't move or reply. Dread curled in Domino's belly; the thrall was still in place.

His words tumbled over themselves trying to get out of his mouth. "You can move, talk, do anything you like."

"Oh, I know that. The thrall lasted until you started talking to that asshole. I was just deciding what to do about your little stunt."

"I was only trying–"

The way Jude's brows drew together had Domino buttoning his lips. A fizz of anticipation buzzed through his groin. *Is he into physical punishments? Being tied up would freak me out, but a little spanking...* He pictured himself bare assed over Jude's lap. In his imagination, Jude traced the power marks, admired them, then gave his butt a sharp slap.

Domino examined the top of his sneakers. They really were getting threadbare.

"Look at me."

His gaze shot up to Jude's.

"I know you were only trying to help, but I would have handled it. You endangered yourself for no reason, but it was damn creative, I've got to give you that."

"But he–"

Jude strode forward and a finger landed on Domino's lips.

Domino lost the fight against the bubbling arousal, opened his mouth, took Jude's finger in, sucked a little.

Jude didn't pull away. "I told you, we wait until after we get to your grandfather."

That seemed so far away. He was here, Jude was here. Who knew what could change after they met his grandfather? Why waste this chance?

I could make him. An image of Sean's broken body morphing into Jude's slammed into his mind. *I controlled him, even with the amulets.*

He staggered back, Jude grabbing for his arms. Flailing, he tried to avoid the touch, and fell, his butt hitting the loose gravel at the side of the road. Jude bent towards him. Domino scooted back, heart pounding. Physical touch seemed as bad as touching Jude with sound. *Poison, I'm fucking poison!*

Jude stood, hands spread wide. "I'm not quite sure what's going on, but I'm not going to hurt you. Let's just get in the van, go to the–"

Domino shook his head frantically. He'd had it right

before he'd met Jude, he should die, as quickly as possible. The first person he'd spoken to, other than Jude... he could have ruined his life, cost him his life. He didn't even know if the guy had ever done anything like this before. He could have been coerced into it. Domino had assumed, acted.

His brother-in-law could throw him out of town; he might even be married, have kids. Fuck, the cop could even shoot him.

"Salty, you're hyperventilating, you need to slow down your breathing or you're going to pass out. In-" Jude demonstrated a long, slow inhale, "And out."

Pain spiked in his chest. *This isn't a panic attack, it's a heart attack. Finally, it's happening, but fuck, why does it have to hurt so much?*

In the moment, Domino didn't want to die, didn't want to end up as a charm around some fucker's neck.

"Don't... Don't let them have me." He swallowed as if it would help pull in more oxygen. "Don't let them cut me up to make..." Throat closing, he waved a hand at Jude's chest.

"You're going to be fine. It's just a panic attack, just a–"

Roaring, like that of an angry ocean, sounded in his head as the edges of his vision darkened. Jude was coming towards him, mouth still moving, but Domino couldn't hear him. Darkness rolled over him, claimed him.

CHAPTER EIGHTEEN

Pressing the pads of his fingers to Domino's neck, Jude felt the flutter of the siren's pulse. Relief flooded him at the correct diagnosis of a panic attack rather than a heart attack. The next time, they might not be so lucky. It'd take another thirty minutes to get to the airfield, twenty or thirty to get airborne, four hours to the nearest airstrip to Orcus' home on the coast of the Salish sea... Too long.

Leaving Domino where he lay, Jude ran back to the van, grabbed his pack, a change of clothes for Domino, a gag, and his pipe. His hand hesitated on the amulets, but he didn't have a choice. Besides, they didn't provide full protection anyway. Taking them off, he shoved them under the water tank where Domino had hidden his pipe. After locking the van, he headed back to the still unconscious siren.

Kneeling, he checked Domino's pulse again and tied the gag gently around the siren's head. He didn't think the siren would knowingly hurt anyone, but by accident? It was better to be safe than sorry.

"Oroshi, you're awesome."

He counted to ten. When nothing happened, he decided he'd have to go with the original mundane transport option. Relief flooded at the familiar pop behind him.

"Sorry, I'm late. I was having a wonderful chat with a selkie about architecture." Oroshi looked around. "Much nicer than here. The Mediterranean is lovely this time of year." For the first time, the air elemental looked down at Domino.

"The water didn't help then?"

"It did, for a while. Orcus' mansion, please."

"Go here, go there. No one's got time to talk anymore." The elemental's pale blue eyebrows drew together. "Where are those evil silver chains?"

"In the van; you're safe. Now can we get on with it? His grandfather said he could help him."

"Who's that?"

Jude sighed. "Orcus, you know the guy I want you to take us too?"

The elemental snorted. "No way is Orcus his grandfather. Orcus is barely older than the siren."

Jude snorted. "He's over a hundred if he's a day."

Oroshi frowned. "The young guy digging the garden?"

"That was Horace, his nephew."

"Nu-uh. That was Orcus. My kind have a thing about names. I think of a name, and the image of its owner appears in my head. John Smith gives me a damn headache."

"Maybe it's a family name?" Jude offered, fed up with the pointless argument. Whatever his name, the old mage claimed to be able to save Domino, and time was limited.

Oroshi looked skeptical.

"Put us inside, please."

"No can do, he's got wards up, a shit ton of them. I can feel them whenever I think about the place. That's why I dumped you outside last time."

"Just take us, will you?"

"Gonna pick him up? It's snowing at your destination."

Even though it made sense, Jude scowled and bent to pick Domino up; the pack already provided a weight on his back.

Domino groaned as Jude lifted him to his shoulder, and he prayed the siren would stay at least dazed for a little longer. Travel by air elemental took a little getting used to and he didn't want puke down his back.

"Passengers count as a trip. With the water run, which counts as two, there and back, this'll take you down to forty-six."

"Understoo–"

Before Jude finished, his belly lurched, and he found himself standing on the gravel drive outside Orcus' imposing residence. Snow drifted down. It wasn't cold enough to settle, but the freezing slush seemed intent on making its way down his collar.

The door flung open to reveal Ace wearing jeans and a black turtleneck sweater.

"Good to see you, Ace," Jude called.

"Horace, please. Bring him in; time is of the essence."

Jude walked up the stairs, knees protesting at the extra weight.

"Where's your uncle?"

Horace stepped aside to let him pass. "Down in the workroom, getting things ready, but we didn't think you'd be this quick."

As soon as Jude stepped inside, the musty mothball smell he remembered hit, perhaps a little stronger than before. He wondered how Horace and the servants stood it. The place smelled as old as Orcus looked.

"Travel by air elemental? Does bounty hunting pay significantly more than I imagined?"

Shit. He'd officially finished his job by delivering a live bounty. Normally, he'd simply collect his money and move on.

"I've got an arrangement with one. I'd like to stay; see him afterward."

Horace's eyebrows rose. "I'm not running a hotel, but I suppose you staying the night with him wouldn't hurt. The procedure can't happen in the next twenty-four hours anyway."

The easy, flirting banter had vanished from their previous meetings, but circumstances had changed, so Jude let it go. It didn't matter anyway; he wasn't interested in a hook up with Ace anymore. The man he held had become everything to him.

A door slammed further into the building. "Don't mind that; Uncle's got a couple of clients here. They like their privacy. Please don't abuse my hospitality by bugging them. Bring him this way; you can use the same room as before. I'll have food brought up."

Horace unlocked the door to the room that had been Jude's base just a few days before. It didn't look as though the bedding had been changed. It still looked a hell of a lot better than the cold floor of a van on the side of a road.

He laid Domino carefully on the bed, and the man immediately turned on his side, rubbed his head on the pillow, hugged it to him, then relaxed again.

Jude's chest tightened, and he fought the urge to grin like a madman. *He can smell me.*

"Don't... do anything to him. No touching. It could be too stressful. You haven't... already have you?"

"That's a bit of a personal question, don't you think?"

Horace straightened up to his full height, which happened to be several inches shorter than Jude. "I'm his doctor."

"You're his doctor's nephew, the gardener, the last time we met. Lose the attitude, Hor."

Horace bristled. "What did you call me?"

"Hor. Which was what you suggested I call you when we met. Or don't you remember trying to get into my pants?"

Horace paled, turned, and hurried from the room. The lock clicked behind him. "Simply a precaution for the comfort of the other guests," he called out. Footsteps hurried away.

Checking that Domino still slept soundly, Jude couldn't strip fast enough as the shower gave its siren call.

The bottle of shower gel he'd left here was still in place on the shelf at the end of the bath. He climbed in, turned the taps on, and pulled the lever to detour the water to the showerhead hanging over the bath. It wasn't hotel standard facilities, but he'd take it, boy, would he take it. He stepped under the water even before it'd warmed up.

The pipes banged, and the water turned from freezing to almost uncomfortably hot. Jude groaned, lowered his head as the heat seeped into his shoulders. *I'm choosing my next job by climate, not cash.*

The thought brought the realization of the impending end of this job. Or was it? Even when Orcus managed to extend Domino's life, the sirens would still want their errant son back. Could Orcus protect Domino here? Would this musty old mansion become just another prison for the vibrant youngster? A jail with the now creepy Horace as the only company his age?

I could keep him safe, and he'd be one hell of an asset on jobs. He paused, examining his motivation. *Am I just trying to use him like everyone else?*

The bath creaked and his eyes shot open. Domino stood at the other end of the bath, naked as the day he'd been born.

"We can't," Jude blurted even as his eyes roamed the tight, sinuous body. *Fuck, he looks as good as a damn incubus.*

Domino tilted his head, mimed washing his pits, the picture of innocence. It might have worked if his cock wasn't standing away from his body, almost waving for attention.

Gaze on a cock that had an intriguing purple mark snaking around one side, one he wanted to investigate with his tongue, Jude said, "There's not enough room for both of us under here."

Domino lifted both hands, index fingers pointing up, then painfully slowly brought them nearer each other. Jude watched, mesmerized. When the digits were a half-inch apart, and Jude was almost drooling, Domino snapped them together and rubbed.

Jude jumped a little, laughed, wrapped a hand around the back of Domino's neck, and drew him in. When they were nose to nose, he asked, "Do you even know where we are?"

Domino's answer was to nibble at his lips and press his hard cock against Jude's groin. Their height difference meant the tip of his cock reached halfway up Jude's, or it would do if he'd been fully erect. What Domino was doing couldn't be described as thrusting, rather he rolled his hips in a constant motion, never stopping, never jerking.

The thought of that underneath him, squirming and gasping, maybe having to hold him still as he– Jude blew out a breath, trying to stop all his brains descending to his cock as it hardened. He didn't want Domino to find out like this, didn't want–

The siren stopped moving, looked up at him, then a slim hand closed around his now hard cock.

Jude groaned at the delicious pressure, hoping it would last, knowing it wouldn't.

"Bit different, huh?"

At least Domino hadn't jumped away swearing like he'd been bitten. Some guys did. He knew what Domino could feel. When he got really hard, like every other cat on the planet, small, downward-facing spines lifted away from his cock. It was a reaction he couldn't help, like hairs lifting away from skin when you shivered in human form.

Masturbating was fine, once he or whoever was stroking him got the "touch on the way down and release" technique, but fucking hurt his partner. Fine for masochists and incubi, for others, not so much. He had no desire to hurt Domino.

"You wouldn't happen to be a masochist, would you?" he murmured.

Domino's plump lips that Jude couldn't help imagining around his shaft pressed together. Keeping his gaze locked with Jude's, his head shook, then it lowered and he dropped his hand.

Having Domino walk away now, when this could be his last chance, had Jude's hand tightening on the siren's shoulder. Words were unnecessary as Jude lowered himself to his knees.

"I've been wanting to do this since I first saw this," Jude murmured and gave in to the impulse to trace the mark on Domino's lower belly with his tongue.

His skin tasted salty, not from sweat, but clean like the sea. Jude intended to tease, to hold Domino on the edge until sexy noises ripped from his throat, but after one taste, he couldn't hold back. Jude engulfed the cock in his mouth, taking as much inside as he could, gagged, and did it again. Domino tasted like life. More than his own pleasure, Jude wanted to experience the siren's.

He clutched Domino's rounded ass cheek with one hand, wishing he could lick the mark on it, know it as well as the back of his hand. The other hand went to his own cock. Twist on the upstroke, release, repeat.

Domino whined, pushed his hips forward, widened his stance, begging for a different sort of touch. It would be so damn easy to stand up, turn the siren around, and push into the hot, tight heat. He was stronger than Domino, could hold him down and take what he craved, but the siren could stop him with just a word. Jude's cock twitched in his hand. Playing with fire was apparently a turn on.

He offered his fingers to Domino. The siren took them into his mouth, tongue swirling, sucking like Jude imagined him doing to his cock.

Before he entirely lost himself to the fantasy, Jude withdrew his fingers and pushed them between Domino's cheeks. He didn't have to ask if Domino was alright with being penetrated because the moment he tapped on the siren's pucker with a finger, Domino pressed back onto it.

A hand around his wrist prevented him from searching for Domino's prostate. Domino held Jude's head still with a fist in his hair. The siren twisted and trembled, using Jude to find his pleasure. Tiny strangled noises came from above Jude, and he worked his own cock faster.

The water going suddenly cold must have provided the final stimulus as Domino gasped, stiffened, and came down Jude's throat.

A second later, Domino's butt hit the bath. Cold water poured down on Jude; his own erection still begged for attention, but he couldn't help grinning at Domino's punch-drunk smile.

"That good, huh?"

Domino held out his hand, wobbled it from side to side.

"Why you–" Jude lunged for him. Domino scrambled out of the bath, with a tiny squeak of delight.

He didn't doubt that Domino wanted to express himself with sound, would have been restraining himself during the blow job. It wasn't fair. None of this was fair.

Getting up, his mood and boner deflated, Jude turned off the taps. He found Domino wrapped in a bathrobe, looking at the food-laden table set near the window. The cook must have remembered Jude's eating habits as most of the dishes held steaming plain steaks and pieces of chicken, although there was also half a lobster and some boiled carrots and peas.

Whoever had set it, must have heard the action in the bathroom.

He clapped a hand on Domino's shoulder. "Yep, we're busted. I bet Dawkins got a thrill, though."

Domino tilted his head, mouthed, *Dawkins?*

"Your grandfather's butler. That's where we are, his home in Washington state. I got the air elemental to transport us after you fainted, so no amulets."

Domino's shoulders hunched, and he rubbed his brow.

"Yeah, I know, I kinda got used to them too, but let's eat. I seem to have developed a massive appetite. No idea why."

Instead of sitting down, Domino walked over to the window. Jude pulled his clothes on, then walked over. He knew what the siren could see, having spent several weeks in this room.

The light snowfall obscured the scene, but he still had a good view of the rocky shoreline several hundred yards away.

"You want to go paddle?"

Not taking his eyes off the scene, Domino nodded slowly. It wasn't the enthusiasm Jude expected. Although Domino couldn't answer even if Jude asked what was bothering him.

"We can go after we've eaten. Don't worry; I won't let anyone hurt you."

Domino moved over to the table, sat down. Jude joined him, mouth watering. He'd put two steaks and half a chicken on his plate before he noticed Domino wasn't filling his own plate.

Although the hot meat called to him, Jude put down his knife and fork.

"We're not going back to the 'Oh I don't need to eat I'm a siren shit' are we, because I've already busted that myth, my friend."

He knew he'd said the wrong thing as Domino sat back, hugged himself.

You don't hand friends over to strangers for cash. He blew out a breath.

"Look, I'll hang around until after you've had whatever treatment your grandfather has planned for you, ok? Then you can have a proper think about what you want to do next. I don't exactly have a stable existence, and until I catch those last two rats and find my family's remains, that's the way it's got to be. I could come visit though."

Why he tacked on the last sentence, he didn't know, but it earned him a glare.

"Whoa, Salty, crash and burn for the cat." He grinned and bit into the chunk of meat on his fork.

CHAPTER NINETEEN

Why the fuck did I think a little fumble in a shower would change anything?

I should be lucky he thinks of me as a friend, although it's probably a line to keep me quiet while he waits for his money.

The view out the window seemed so familiar except for the details. A cold windswept rock coast, just like home, except he was apparently on the other side of the planet. At this distance, he wouldn't be able to see anyone in the water, but it didn't mean they weren't there. Every siren on the planet would be looking for him.

Is this my life again? Living in confinement with a view of the sea I can occasionally visit with supervision if I'm good?

Jude's smile, his banter, didn't help. However long Jude stayed, he wouldn't be here forever. The man was right; Domino couldn't follow him around, messing up his hunting.

He picked at the excellent lobster, more to prevent

another one-sided argument than any wish to eat, while he watched Jude devour the equivalent of half a sheep.

The loss of the amulets hurt more than he'd thought. It'd taken such a short time to forget the habit of silence. He'd spent so long shut up in himself, all his thoughts and emotions contained, it felt like a prison door had clanged shut again.

Domino moved back to the window. Sirens might be able to affect people, but the wild, living water called to him just as strongly. He needed to surround himself in the energy, needed to swim under the surface.

"Come on, let's go." Jude went to the door. "Dawkins, oh Dawkins," he called.

Shuffling footsteps neared the door and a key turned in the lock.

We were locked in?

The door opened. "Yes, sir?"

The man's face looked as though it needed a damn good iron, make that an iron and at least an inch of wrinkled skin removed.

"Are Orcus' shy guests hiding away, because Domino needs to go paddle in the sea. In case you didn't know, his kind need skin contact with fresh seawa–"

"I'll have buckets brought to fill the bath sir, that is if you no longer require it for.... Recreation?"

Domino cringed but Jude's grin got wider. "Oh, I think we're good for now, but it's a no to the buckets. Domino and I are going down to the beach, unless we're prisoners here?" The cat shifter's light tone hadn't changed, nor had his stance, but Domino felt the threat all the same.

Dawkins lowered his head. "I was merely hoping to save you a cold and unpleasant journey, sir."

"And who was going to get these buckets of seawater,

you, Dawkins? I don't think so. Domino and I are hardy souls; we'll be back before you know it."

"The path down to the beach is unlit, sir. It would be dangerous to traverse when it gets dark in around half an hour. If sir could wait until–"

"I'm a cat, Dawkins. I see better in low light conditions. Now, are you going to stand aside, or do I move you?"

Dawkins moved. "As you wish, sir."

"Excellent choice. Stick some clothes on Salty; we're going paddling."

As Domino pulled clothes on, Jude took his shirt off and reached for the button on his jeans. Domino raised his eyebrows.

"I'm warmer in fur, and I can definitely see better. Can you take the bathrobe though, just in case I have to shift back? The temperature out there will have my bare balls trying to climb back inside."

Minutes later, Domino followed the huge black cat down stairs he didn't remember climbing. He wore the bathrobe over his clothes so his hands remained free in case he slipped. He might be a siren, but wet rocks were slippery whatever you were.

Jude led him to a huge front door, then looked over his shoulder. Domino stepped forward to open it; he hadn't considered the handicaps a fur form might have, apart from communication difficulties.

The snow had stopped falling by the time they stepped outside, but it was still damp and cold. The cat looked pointedly at the warmly lit doorway they were leaving, but Domino shut it with a firm clang. The cat sighed, hung its head a little, then padded off to the right. Domino grinned. It seemed Jude was quite capable of commenting without speaking too.

The path down to the shore wasn't particularly steep, but it would be daunting to an elderly man like Dawkins. The thought of the butler trying to carry a single bucket of seawater up this path made Domino shiver, let alone enough to fill a bath.

Jude led him to a flat, wet rock with a small moat of seawater around it left by the retreating tide. The cat jumped up, fastidiously avoiding getting his paws wet. His outline blurred and a naked Jude sat there.

"Give me the damn robe; it's freezing."

Domino handed it over with a smile. He found it funny that a man who killed without turning a hair trembled when the temperature dropped.

Jude covered up, sat down, and patted the rock between his legs. "Sit here. You can stick your feet in the water while I use you as a hot water bottle."

As soon as Domino sat down, Jude wrapped his arms around him, rested his chin on his shoulder.

The waves breaking on the rocks around a dozen feet away were gentle compared to what the sea could throw at this shore. Even though this was a different body of water, it felt like home. Maybe it was the similar location, the northern, west coast of a landmass.

Jude's arms tightened around him. "Don't wiggle." Domino tapped his chest then pointed out into the bay.

"Not a good idea," Jude murmured. "You're weak, and I don't fancy having to go in that to rescue you. My swimming and boating experience is confined to warm, clear Mediterranean water a hundred yards from beautiful sandy beaches."

The reminder of his last boating experience had Domino tensing. The little boat he'd stolen hadn't been designed for transatlantic voyages. It'd overturned in a storm. He'd ended up swimming for three days, the box of gems stuffed under the tight black shirt he'd stolen from Kelpea.

The reason why he'd made that near-fatal journey still existed. Although there were far more sirens in the old world than the new. The sun was setting, it was damn cold, and he hadn't seen a sign of anyone swimming in the twenty or so minutes they'd been here.

Without words, all he could do was give puppy-dog eyes and mouth "please".

"It's making you nuts, not being able to swim, isn't it?"

Domino tapped Jude's chest, indicated the sea with his thumb, then mimed doing the doggy paddle.

Domino's mouth twitched, and Jude rolled his eyes. "Yeah, I can't swim as good as you, but I can do more than the doggy paddle. Although, looking at all that black water is giving me the shivers."

Domino sighed, let his shoulders sag in defeat, then stood up and indicated the path back up, that was now barely visible. Jude started to pull the bathrobe off, Domino turned, ran across the rocks and did a shallow dive into the water, with Jude's shout of "Hey" ringing in his ears.

As expected, the water was warmer than sitting on the rock, and his clothes provided another level of protection. Even if it'd been ten degrees colder, and he'd been butt naked, this would still have been bliss. Pure, unadulterated bliss. His senses worked differently; sound was both muted and sharper. The surf whooshed around him.

The rocky bottom teemed with plants and animals, but he could only see perhaps six feet with all the plankton and particulates.

The world above felt so far away, both in time and distance, even though he was barely twenty feet from shore.

He pulled harder, loving the way his body slipped through the water, was one with it, as its energy surrounded him.

His lungs ached. It was time to surface if he didn't want to put extra pressure on his failing system, but he didn't want to lose the serenity here under the water. Somehow, he knew this was his last time, and he wanted to make the most of it. He closed his eyes, floated, at one with the sea.

A hand grabbed his collar, pulled him towards the surface. His head broke into the air.

"Shore. Now," Jude growled. "And if you try to get away again, delicate or not, I will beat your ass, black and fucking blue. I hate the fucking cold."

The rest of the short swim back was silent, but as soon as they were out of the water, the orders started again.

"Strip."

Domino glared at the shifter, but Jude's hard look told him voicing a protest would just piss the cat off more. He obeyed the order. Jude picked the bathrobe off the rock and thrust it at Domino.

"Put that on, go back up to the house. And so help me, if you try to run I will thoroughly enjoy chasing you down and taking a bite out of your ass."

As soon as Domino had the robe around him and his shoes on, Jude shifted. When Domino didn't immediately head for the path, he let out a low growl.

"I wasn't in any–" The growl got louder, it rumbled through Domino, almost vibrating his bones.

Domino turned, and holding his bundle of soaking clothes, he headed for the house, the cat padding behind him.

CHAPTER TWENTY

Of all the irresponsible, idiotic stunts... At least Jude hoped that was what Domino had been doing, rather than making another concerted effort to end his life. He'd been so damn lucky to find him in the dark murky water. The adrenaline thrill of spotting him, and then the extra kick when he realized the siren was hanging motionless, the swell moving him like flotsam, still buzzed through his body.

The fear had nothing to do with losing a bounty. Jude knew he shouldn't have given in to Domino in the shower. They couldn't have a future together, even if Orcus managed to save him. How could he keep the impulsive, wild siren safe from his family while he worked?

Milo doesn't hunt physically anymore. The thought of giving up the hunt for the Scibetta didn't produce the visceral self-hatred it usually did. The last two involved, Morris and Eugene, could be dead already. Had his dream of Del been his subconscious telling him to give up the fruitless hunt, to live a little while he could? The idea of living for the living, a future with the man whose cute, tight movements were even now making Jude smile, curled in his belly.

The door opened as they neared the house, a pool of golden light in the growing darkness.

Domino stomped through and headed straight for the stairs.

"The master requests both your presence in the drawing-room when you are ready."

Jude blinked at the human in reply, a little surprised by the man's lack of reaction at seeing a seven-foot-long, two-hundred-pound black cat in the entrance hall. As he padded up the stairs, he concluded that maybe he shouldn't have been surprised. Orcus probably provided spells to all sorts of people.

In this form, the house smelled even worse, but there were a few other scent hints that he hadn't picked up in his human form. Disinfectant. He sniffed again, growled. *Damn place has a rodent problem too.*

The shower was running when Jude entered the bedroom. He shifted and reached for his clothes. Repeating the shower incident wouldn't help matters. Domino had seemed more than happy earlier, then he'd looked out of the window, and things went pear-shaped.

Seeing the sea. That's what set him off. The ocean was clearly something Domino craved and had been living without for several years. He probably hadn't expected to see it again. Yeah, that'd probably turn anyone's mind temporarily.

But even if whatever Orcus intended to do to extend Domino's life worked, the female sirens wouldn't stop trying to get their hands on him. The safest place for Domino was as far from his kind's natural habitat as possible. No wonder he'd felt compelled to experience as much of it as possible, while he could. *And I threatened to beat him for it.* Jude groaned at his idiocy.

Domino came out of the bathroom fully dressed, his hair roughly dried with a towel.

"Look, I'm sorry about what I said; I wouldn't–" Jude was left looking at an open door as Domino marched out of the room without giving him so much as a glance.

Jude blew out a breath. "Salty, you sure are living up to your name."

He found Horace and Domino sitting in two burgundy leather winged armchairs that bracketed a roaring fire. There wasn't a third chair. Jude wondered if they expected him to shift and curl up on the rug like a giant house cat. In other circumstances, he would have done and hoped to get a little petting from Domino.

Both men held a crystal glass of deep amber spirit.

"Do help yourself," Horace said, then took a sip and hummed in appreciation. "Fifty-year-old single malt from near Domino's home; it's excellent."

"Thanks, but no thanks. Should he be drinking in his condition, and where's Orcus? Dawkins said we were meeting him."

Horace took another sip, licked his lips. *Creepy.* Jude wondered what he'd ever seen in the guy.

"One small drink is not going to affect him one way or another, but a swim in almost freezing conditions couldn't have done either of you much good. Domino is positively exhausted."

Domino's glass banged down on an antique side table. He blinked at the fire, head resting against one of the wings of the chair. The blink turned into two, then Domino's eyes didn't open again.

"This will have to wait until the morning," Jude said. "He can't keep his eyes open."

Jude leaned down, put his hand on Domino's shoulder. When he didn't rouse, he shook him harder, fear coiling in his gut.

"Domino, Salty? Wake up." Getting no response, he put two fingers against Domino's neck, under the point of his jaw.

He looked up, Horace still held his glass of whiskey, one leg draped over the other, a picture of relaxation.

"Pulse is sluggish."

Horace sighed, unwrapped his legs, stood up. "I was hoping to have a few more days, but needs must I suppose. Bring him." Without looking at either of them, Horace strode out of the room.

Jude hauled Domino's dead weight up to his shoulder and followed the man who had developed more airs and graces in a few days than he thought possible. Yes, Horace's behavior probably pleased his uncle, but he didn't need to put it on with him.

Jude found him in the corridor, where he waved a hand towards the open door of his uncle's study.

Jude carried his burden into the room, expecting to see Orcus behind the desk. No Orcus.

Horace walked straight past the desk to the door on the far side and opened it, revealing a stone staircase heading down. The scent of disinfectant wafted up.

"Down you go. Most of my work requires a constant low temperature; having the facilities underground helps."

Domino groaned, stirred on his shoulder, then became a dead weight again. Every instinct told Jude not to go down there. Confined spaces and locked doors left little room for maneuvering.

Horace's eyes seemed far older than his tender years. "Mr. Moreno, Judah, just like you, I haven't got a lot of family left. Domino is important, and the means to give him another chance at life is down there." He paused, reached out a hand to Domino's face.

Jude had to grit his teeth to stop from pulling away, but the touch was fleeting, a mere stroke of Domino's arm.

"He's weak, hasn't got long before his soul breaks free. The magic can do a lot, but it can't bring back the dead."

The light got brighter as Jude descended the narrow staircase. The white-tiled empty area looked like a high-end hospital foyer, only without a desk. Six doors led from the room. All were wide enough to push a hospital trolley through; two had double swing doors like those in an operating theater. The only object in the room was a metal coat stand that held a white coat. Horace stopped to put it on.

"I know it's daft, but the right attire helps produce the right mind-set." He grinned.

Jude wasn't in the mood for pointless banter. "Where do you want him?"

Horace indicated the door to the left, one with swinging doors.

Inside, he found a treatment room, complete with two hydraulic couches. A wall of glass-fronted cabinets contained an equal proportion of mundane medical equipment and jars of things Jude didn't want to identify. Many looked organic, including one that had to be eyeballs.

Jude lay his burden on the nearest padded couch, but he didn't step back.

"What exactly do you do here?" Jude asked.

"Patience, Mr. Moreno." Horace turned to the cabinets and began assembling items on a metal tray. The man clearly wasn't as comfortable in his new formal clothes as he made out as he adjusted his collar. Jude didn't blame him; he hated wearing ties too.

Domino groaned, opened his eyes. Jude immediately cupped his face. "It's ok; you're safe. We're in your grandfather's workroom; he's going to help you."

Domino blinked, his eyes glassy, confused.

"Domino, tell him not to move."

Jude's gaze shot up to where Horace stood. He held his palm flat out; on it lay a small bone with a silver clasp that could be attached to a chain.

"Don't... don't move." Domino's scratchy voice didn't sound anything like the frantic intense order he'd given by the roadside, but molasses still settled in Jude's limbs.

Horace dangled the piece of bone between two fingers. "Looks like the others, doesn't it? Well, it should in a way as I created all of them, but there is one subtle difference. The others came from his half-sister, Lark. Do you remember her? Domino? The sister you killed?"

Domino nodded, his eyes glassy.

Gritting his teeth, Jude fought against the thrall. "Salty, release me, I can–"

"You, Mr. Moreno, can't do a damn thing, not while I've got this. The other amulets protected the wearer from his abilities, but this one, part of his own body, means I control him and through his ability, I can control you, and anyone else I choose."

Horace smiled. "Penny dropped yet, Mr. Moreno? I have to say I have nothing against you personally. But you do fit my purposes far better than those odious dogs. In fact, you, Mr. Moreno, are the proverbial two birds with one stone, just like Domino here.

"Unfortunately, I have told you a partial untruth. Domino's body is dying, and there is nothing anyone can do to stop that. However, I can put him in a new body, like I do for myself and my clients. And now that he is here, I have no more use for you. The call for cat shifter bodies is understandably low. Keeping you alive for the improbable circumstance that one of your relatives wishes to avail themselves of my services is impractical, even if my assistants could keep their hands off you.

"Mr. Scibetta, you can now collect your bonus."

Jude's mind screamed in fury as the musky rodent scent got stronger.

CHAPTER TWENTY-ONE

Jude was here, and now he wasn't. Domino knew he had something to do with that, but he couldn't grasp the elusive memory. It flittered away and then hovered just out of reach like a shoal of tiny silver fish. He grabbed again, and again, only to fail each time. They'd both been in Orcus' living room and then...

"Domino, pay attention." The shoal vanished, and the room came back into focus. Antique dining table. Longcase clock. Rain against the window. A man dressed in a dark grey three-piece suit.

"You know, I'm not sorry things turned out this way." The mage looked down at himself as he finished his breakfast of smoked salmon croissant in the large dining room. His hair was no longer spiked, despite his youthful appearance, an air of age hung around him. His movements were precise as if he expected discomfort from merely shifting position.

"This body really is quite perfect, and thoroughly wasted on that boy. You should have seen the way he abused it, risked it with daredevil stunts and a poor diet.

Unfortunately, I doubt procuring another as attractive for you will be as easy even if new souls are ten a penny these days. It was to be yours, but my previous host deteriorated. I couldn't risk it failing while I was in residence."

Oh, sweet Poseidon, he transfers souls to other bodies; that's how he's going to save me, by killing someone else.

The polished man sitting opposite him at the dining table frowned.

"It really would be easier if you stop fighting. You and I are bound for as long as I hold the amulet, so you might as well get used to it. Not that you have the option of deciding, but would you rather have a body who looks like you do now, or something a little different? I have my team hunting down a few leads as we speak."

A finger caressed the small knob of bone that lay against a tanned throat. "Answer me."

Domino swallowed, fought the compulsion, lost. "Jude. I want Jude."

Bottle green eyes widened, then the man laughed. "My dear boy, that is quite an idea. A cat shifter body with an ancient siren's soul. I wonder if your purring would make everyone around you feel content. Unfortunately, even if Mr. Moreno is a match, he is..." A smile twitched his lips. "Currently, and by now probably forever, unavailable."

WHAT DID YOU DO TO HIM?

Domino screamed, banged against the walls of his flesh prison, didn't move or speak.

"But we need to move things along; the sirens want the body you currently inhabit before it expires, which I estimate will occur within the week. Unfortunately, not even my magic can do anything about that.

"It'll be interesting to see if the power marks appear on your new body or vanish from this one when you are no longer in residence. The sirens assume power comes from the flesh, but I know it's all up here." He tapped his temple.

"Old souls, that's where power comes from, and you and I, even if you don't know it, have been on this Earth from almost the beginning. Newsflash, the Buddhists, and Hindus got it right about reincarnation.

"Unfortunately, memories are lost if you transmigrate to a host without the capacity to retain them, such as an animal or a newly conceived baby. But the way I do it, everything is maintained. The package we inhabit is considered to be the person, but that's all it is, a flesh shell to house the essence, or soul as most call it. Personally, I dislike the religious connotation of the word "soul".

"Still, your family don't want your memories or your siren ability, just that body's ability to fertilize, and that's all they are going to get."

All last night, Domino lay in bed in the room he'd shared so briefly with Jude, unable to move, mind whirling. He'd tried everything he could think of, even calling Jude's elemental with his mind, but either the words needed to be spoken aloud or they only worked for Jude.

This morning, the mage had ordered him to strip and climb into the bath. During the night, two sour-faced, silent men, wearing damp coats filled it bucket by bucket, with fresh seawater. The third time, one had mud on his knees. They didn't come again.

Now they were in the dining room, where the mage savored a breakfast of smoked salmon and scrambled eggs topped with caviar. Domino hadn't been offered anything, not even a glass of water.

A tap on the door took the mage's attention. "Come."

"Master, Prince Adnan has arrived an hour early for his appointment," the elderly butler announced.

"Addy always was champing at the bit to get things done." He got to his feet. "Has my new will come back yet? I'd rather the legal transfer goes as smoothly as the physical."

"It has, sir. I have also prepared the documents for the legal name change. They are on your desk."

"Excellent. Horace is such an old man's name with nowhere near the gravitas of Orcus." He stepped away from the table, then stopped, sighed, but didn't turn.

"I can see this becoming tedious, but once the transfer is complete, you'll settle. There'll be no going back then. Come on, Domino, follow me, eyes open, mouth shut. You're going to learn about the family business so I can finally remove those damn rats from my basement."

Domino's body obeyed smoothly, even as his mind fought inside his flesh prison.

The butler was finishing his painful shuffling turn to leave the room as they got to the door.

"For heaven's sake, Dawkins, you don't have to put it on, I know your body's failing. You're already next on the list after Domino and Prince Adnan."

The man's eyes lit up, his hand shaking as it went to his mouth. "You're going to free me, after all these years?"

"Did you doubt my word, Dawkins? I said I'd provide you with a new body after a lifetime of service, and I will. I'll look into a gene match for you. Acquiring your host can be Domino's first project. The international stem cell donor register certainly speeds up the process, and it provides a better class of body compared to law enforcement DNA databases."

The man's eyes became even more glassy. "Thank you, Master. Thank you so much."

Horace wrinkled his nose in disgust. "Do stop dribbling,

Dawkins, and can you please see if you can get rid of that stink? The whole place smells like mothballs, piss, and rodents. My previous host's senses really deteriorated in the last few years."

"Yes, Master, of course. Prince Adnan is waiting in the library."

Drawn by the invisible thread of his thumb bone around the mage's neck. Domino followed silently.

"When we get in there, Domino, tell them to ignore you unless you speak. You are to observe, nothing more."

They entered the library. An elderly Middle Eastern man sat in one of the easy chairs. A younger man, perhaps in his early thirties, stood behind the chair. Domino recited the mage's instructions. The gaze of both men slid away from him like oil on water.

"It's been a long time, Addy. I would say you're looking well, but we both know I'd be lying."

The old man frowned. "Don't insult me, boy. Send for Orcus."

The mage smiled. "Domino, ensure Faheem does not recall this conversation."

Domino locked gazes with the younger man. "Faheem, this conversation is so boring you immediately forget it."

The mage smiled at the Prince. "I am Orcus, my old friend, or at least I am up here." He tapped his temple.

"If you're Orcus, what was the name of my lead polo pony the last time we played?"

"I don't recall, ponies never really interested me. But I remember you covering for me when your father almost caught me seducing your sister's maid, Zaria."

Adnan's face blanked for a second, then he burst into a wheezy laugh that ended in a coughing fit. Faheem proffered a handkerchief. The prince wiped his mouth, leaving a bloody mark, then he handed the cloth back. Faheem resumed his stance and blank expression.

"I remember," Adnan wheezed. "That's got to be... sixty-five years ago. I also remember she disappeared around four months later."

Orcus spread his hands. "Where do you think this body came from? I think the skin tone is far more attractive than my previous pasty skin. Its last occupant thought he was my long-lost nephew, rather than my grandson. When I have a young body, I do my best to give myself as many future options as possible, and I advise you to do the same. Attending university and traveling always helps to maximize future options. Wars and famines can devastate your options if you keep them all in one basket."

"We were so young back then," Adnan said. His eyes narrowed. "And you are young again now."

"I am, and you can be too. Vitality is buzzing in my veins; can you remember what that was like? Believe me, you'll appreciate it far more the second time around. Come and meet your candidates. Luckily for you, your family is well represented all over the world. Shall we proceed?"

The young man helped the prince to his feet. "Thank you, Faheem, you are a good boy. That you are not of my blood will always be a deep regret of mine. I won't forget your assistance in this delicate matter."

The young man bowed, his hand fisted over his heart "As always, my Prince."

Adnan patted his assistant's arm. "Wait here."

Domino followed Orcus and Adnan out of the room. The front door was only feet away. Pulling with all his might, he strained to change direction. All he managed was a slight stumble that went unnoticed before he followed the mage meekly.

Orcus waited until they were in his office before speaking again. "Are you sure you want it to be Faheem?"

The old man pursed his lips. "Let me see where you keep them before I make my final decision. Faheem has been more of a son to me than those I've claimed. I feel like I've betrayed him all his life by not acknowledging the blood we share. And now I'm going to take his very life from him?"

"I understand, believe me. It is always difficult when you are emotionally close to the soul currently inhabiting your new host. But a close family member makes everything far less complicated, both for the magic and legally.

"Consider this if you are still wavering. You protected an illegitimate daughter, and then her offspring, even though you couldn't claim them. You've given them far more than they would ever have had without you, and this way, you can carry on caring for Faheem's family for at least another lifetime. He's your valued assistant, and your blood relationship will come out. People will accept you leaving everything to him, given your estrangement from your legitimate son."

"This body's end will not be considered suspicious by that greedy waste of space? Any hint of a loophole and Mohammed will exploit it."

Orcus patted the old man's shoulder. "He might object when the will is read and seek further examinations, but you are elderly, my friend. There will be nothing to find. Trust me; this isn't the first time, or the hundredth, that I've done this." The mage flexed his hand as if marveling at the strength and easy movement.

"So, how does this black magic work?" the prince asked. "You've only spoken in vague terms up to now."

The mage chuckled. "Black magic? Magic is neither

black nor white. What I do is merely skewing fate a little. Everyone has an eternal soul, but where that soul ends up after its body dies is usually random and results in the loss of memories. Without my help, you could end up as a cesspit cleaner, a leper, or a servant of your son, Mohammed."

The prince visibly shuddered. Domino did too, but not for the same reason. *Yes, living forever sounded like a dream come true, but at the expense of someone else's life?* The poor loyal man waiting in the other room had no idea about what was to happen to him.

"Just think of all the knowledge that could have been retained," Orcus continued, "if certain souls, certain memories, were not wiped by fate but were left to gather more than one lifetime of insight, of research? Think of savants, do you think their skills are natural? They are the result of a more complete metempsychosis, transmigration of the soul, than usually happens, but a child's brain can never hold the experiences of an adult. They learn more quickly, but they are not the person they were before.

"In contrast, I will enable your soul to transfer to Faheem's body without any loss of memory. My magic loosens the ties between body and soul, guides the transfer, but it is your will to live that clinches the process. Do you want to live, my old friend? Do you want to carry on caring for your people?" Orcus offered his firm young hand, and Adnan clasped it between his liver-spotted wrinkled ones.

"I do."

Orcus nodded. "Then that is what will be, once my fee and your paperwork is in order."

"What will happen to Faheem, his soul I mean?"

"I commend you for caring, my friend. So few of my clients ever spare a thought for the other soul. When you settle in your chosen body, Faheem's far younger, weaker, soul will be fully displaced. He will be drawn to the nearest unoccupied body, which should be your old one unless my ancient cook happens to have just conceived." The pair laughed. Domino wanted to run as far from this horror as he could, once he located Jude.

When the laughter died, the mage continued. "Unfortunately, the stress of transfer often leaves the old body badly damaged. A natural, serene death usually follows within a month, and the soul is set free to ride the lottery of reincarnation again." He smiled. "I certainly haven't had any complaints from those souls. Of course, I make their passing as easy as possible. Come. I will show you."

Domino found himself following the mage and the slow, painful movements of his elderly guest down the stone steps.

They emerged into a brightly lit, white-tiled empty room that itched at Domino's memory.

Orcus directed them to the left. The room they entered was beautifully appointed, clean, and comfortable. An elderly man lay in the bed, attached to monitors and IV drips. A half-full catheter bag hung from a rail at the foot of the bed.

The man's eyes fluttered open, then focused on the mage. "You, you evil son of a bitch." He lurched, trying to sit up, but didn't manage it. "Give me my body back, I–"

Orcus moved swiftly to the man's side, turned a small wheel on the IV. The patient, the owner of the body standing next to Domino, subsided, mumbling.

Orcus ushered them out of the room. "Sorry about that. I was unable to prepare him for his sacrifice, but with my new assistant on board, the process will be far easier on everyone."

That's what he wants me for? To make people accept this evil? Never, I'll never–

The mage walked a few steps away, and Domino followed.

"I prepare the prospective host body fully before the procedure starts, so the soul only has a tenuous hold and is easy to displace by a determined, focused older soul."

"And the old body, it always survives?" Prince Adnan asked. "Your old self seemed very distressed, surely it would be easier if the soul just..." he made starbursts with his hand.

"It seems a little cruel, doesn't it? But I assure you it's critical. If the old body dies, the newly displaced soul is freed, and it attempts to regain its former place. A battle of wills ensues. It comes down to who wants to live more. Physical distance only matters in the initial transfer. The displaced soul knows its former home and will do everything it can to return.

"It takes up to ten days to fully integrate a soul with a new body, so I always do everything possible to keep the previous body functioning for at least that long.

"I'll not sugarcoat it; the procedure isn't always successful. Having the link between body and soul severed while conscious is quite painful and shocking for the client, but they need to be aware to make the transfer. Sometimes the displaced soul is stronger than expected and manages to fight off my client despite every effort. But I do everything to select hosts that currently hold young, inexperienced souls. It doesn't matter much if they lose their memories, but for us old, experienced souls? It's a tragedy that I can't save more. What if I'd been able to save da Vinci or Einstein?"

"Your failure rate?" Adnan hung on every ghoulish word.

"Ten to fifteen percent, and that's usually due to the client leaving it too long or the new host having a far stronger soul than anticipated. There are currently over six hundred people walking the earth in bodies they were not born into. Some of my clients are on their tenth host, and I can feel every one of them. The magic creates an unbreakable link, which is another reason why I limit clients. The burden is immense, and I need to change hosts with greater regularity than most people."

"So I would be connected to you for life?" Adnan didn't sound happy. Domino wished him excruciating pain for even considering doing this to the considerate man upstairs.

"For all your lives, my friend, until either of us dies without a suitable host ready and waiting."

"I'd have to find another practitioner if you meet with an accident. How many of you are there?"

"I'm the only one, to my knowledge. The last was my own master, and when he tried to transfer his soul to me, I won."

The prince's head shot up. "Are you telling me that if you die, I die?"

"Makes the part of your fee I spend on protection wards for myself seem more cost-effective, doesn't it?"

The prince frowned, clearly not pleased by what he'd learned.

"It's your choice, Adnan; you could always go home and die. I assure you, I have an extremely long waiting list of wealthy, elderly customers who would dearly like to be bumped up my work order before it's too late."

The mage directed his client to the right. "I'll let you view your other two candidates while you consider the consequences of not continuing. Both are young and without significant ties. Neither will be missed. More importantly, their souls have never occupied a human before and their age means they have nothing like the experience of yours. Transference will not be an issue."

"You can tell the age of a soul by looking at someone?"

"I'd be a pretty poor soul dealer if I couldn't tell the worth of my merchandise, wouldn't I? I can sense the age and strength of souls when they inhabit a body, but that fades rapidly when they are released. I imagine that's because they move on. I'll certainly let you know when I can't feel Faheem any longer; it always gives me a sense of completion, knowing they are living again. You might want to look for him in the eyes of his body's children."

The mage waved his hand over a door then opened it to reveal a corridor with one-way glass on both sides. Four small rooms lay on each side; three were occupied. Two were young men with olive skin. The third, on the opposite side, was an overweight, red-haired Caucasian in his late twenties.

"You use the ruse of bone marrow transplants to get them here?" the prince asked.

"I market it as a rejuvenation technique for the rich. Most prospective hosts jump at the fat fee."

Orcus stopped by the first man, who lay on the single bed, reading a supercar magazine. "This is Carlo Mendes. His great grandmother was a maid in your father's home before you were born. She returned to the Philippines, pregnant, and her son came to the US to study and never left. His parents were drug addicts, and he was taken in by the state at the age of five."

The distaste on the Prince's face must have given the mage his answer as they moved to the next cell.

"This is Lionel Matin." The man's forearms were covered in dark tattoos that disappeared under his shirt. "A similar story to Carlo's, except his mother was a Cuban stripper, who your son, Jaleel, bedded in Las Vegas, twenty years ago."

"You want me to leave my fortune to the infidel son of a stripper?" He shook his head. "No. It will be Faheem. An honorable Muslim man. Who is this other one?"

"He is a prospective match for Domino. Not what I wanted, but we are pressed for time. Domino might look young and healthy, but he probably has a shorter life expectancy than your current body. The body I'm in was my first choice for him, but circumstances changed; my previous host had a minor heart attack. I wasn't going to risk my life as well as those of all my clients."

"You two are related?" the Prince glanced between them as if seeing Domino for the first time.

"We are. My last body produced a particularly troublesome son. I donated him to Domino's mother, in return for an exclusive contract for their magical needs. If it wasn't for Domino's poor life expectancy, I might have attempted a transfer to him if only to see if supernatural abilities pass with the soul or are retained by the body like genes, but I guess I'll find out soon enough."

Domino stared at the red-haired man, *my brother*.

"Come along, Domino. Don't worry; I'm looking at other options. I don't think I could stand looking at that every day either."

As they re-entered the foyer, Domino stumbled again, but this time, he hadn't been fighting, merely trying to stay upright.

CHAPTER TWENTY-TWO

Domino played his pipe, a lilting, soft refrain; a boat becalmed on a vast ocean. *Nothing to see, nothing to do, just floating.*

The almost overpowering scent of jasmine and frankincense from the dozen or so incense burners around the treatment room didn't make sinking into his fantasy easy.

"That's it, ignore the body; feel his essence, wrap around it, lift, ease it away, never jerk or pull." Orcus stood behind him as he sat between the two treatment couches. One of the mage's hands lay on Domino's nape.

One treatment couch held the naked, unconscious body of Faheem, the other, a wide-awake Adnan. Both had undergone the initial cleansing funeral rites of their religion, although Adnan had bathed himself. The prince vibrated with nervous energy but had been warned to keep quiet by Orcus.

Every fiber of Domino's mind cringed away from what he was doing, but with the amulet around the mage's neck, he couldn't resist. Its power wrapped around him as he, in turn, enfolded the soul he was drawing from its body.

Domino concentrated on his playing and the scene in his mind. He refused to look at the face of either man who lay only inches from Domino's bare shoulders as he sat in a plastic padded wheelchair.

How many vibrant young souls have spent their last few hours trapped in ancient bodies in this chair? He cringed at the touch of his bare skin on the plastic. At least Orcus let him keep his underwear. Faheem and Adnan had to be as naked as when their souls had entered the world the first time.

"Lift him, my boy; gentle, always gentle. Don't wake him."

Every instinct screamed at Domino to make Faheem run for his life. Barring accidents, Faheem's body would naturally live at least another five or six decades. After this process, his mind might survive a matter of days, maybe weeks, trapped in Adnan's failing husk. *Wrong, it's so fucking wrong.*

Domino's future was the exact opposite of Faheem's if Orcus got his way. Death already lurked at his shoulder, a sense of growing disconnection from his body. It felt as if everything that made him Domino, was pulling into his mind. If he believed Orcus, his soul was naturally preparing itself to leave this body behind. A process he was forcing on Faheem.

"This will be the most serene transfer of all time," Orcus whispered, pride and restrained excitement in his tone. "No conflict, no pain. Marvelous, just perfect."

Adnan believed the old host bodies were always treated with respect, but Domino's wouldn't be. It would be sold to the sirens, forced to perform again and again, and if it survived, his Aunt would use the silver sacrificial knife to cut out his heart and quicken the pregnancies.

The prince had pretended to care about Faheem's fate, but he didn't. After the ten-day risk period of Faheem reclaiming his body passed, what possible use would Orcus have for the old bodies, complete with angry new souls? He'd seen a single past host on their tour. It was damn convenient that the previous hosts seemed to pass "peacefully and naturally" a few days after the risk period ended. Orcus was a soul mage; it wouldn't be tricky for him to rip a soul free from a frail body.

Orcus and the sirens needed to be stopped, like Jude stopped the Karnaks. Quick and final, job done, move on, don't look back. Jude had dedicated his existence to getting revenge, justice, for those who couldn't do it for themselves, and he loved doing it. Domino couldn't change the world, but he damn well wouldn't roll over and play dead, Jude wouldn't.

A lax hand brushed his bicep, Domino flinched.

"I explain this, nothing to worry about." Orcus' voice was low, soothing, as he bound Faheem's hand to Domino's bicep with a spelled cloth.

"Now, Addy, hold Domino's arm. Think of your new body; it's yours, not his. You deserve it more, need it more, claim it.

"Now play, Domino, draw them in, be the path, the route, nothing but a conduit."

Domino's body itched, buzzed; every cell swelled, stretched, was going to burst, the souls, the magic... too full, too much.

His playing faltered. Orcus squeezed his neck. "Stay with it, boy. I know it's difficult, I can feel how tired you are, but it won't last. Remember what I told you? Open the gate, yes, yes, that's good." Domino kept on playing.

"Nearly... nearly... Addy, push harder. Now, Domino, sever the ties."

Domino blew a discordant note. Energy blasted through him, terror that he'd explode flared then vanished along with the souls. He dropped the pipe to his lap, gasping as if oxygen would replace what had been taken.

Adnan and Faheem both moaned; the Prince's hand left his arm. Orcus cut the cloth, severing Domino's physical connection to Faheem's body.

"Beautiful, just beautiful," Orcus mumbled to himself as he fussed around his client and donor.

Using one of the syringes he'd prepared earlier, Orcus injected the older body, murmuring, "Sleep Faheem, rest now; you've done your master proud."

He moved to the younger body, injected him too. The man groaned. "Orcus? Did it work?" It was Faheem's voice, but it sounded so different.

"Up now, Addy, you did it. Come, feel your new young self."

Great joy from one man, satisfaction from another, horror from the third. *So wrong.* He had to stop this, had to return the souls to where fate had placed them.

He'd lifted Faheem's soul from his body, maybe he could do it with Horace's soul too. The vibrant young soul had to be able to reclaim its place. With the mage occupied, and with his body still lax, Domino twisted, strained against the cage Orcus had created.

"Hmm, you're stronger than you look, or at least your soul is." Orcus crouched in front of him; Adnan and Faheem were gone. "You really are a naughty boy, trying to upset all my plans." A hand cupped his face, stroked over the power mark on his cheek.

"Hmm, your soul is hanging by the tiniest thread. It's

like a spider, strong and sticky, beautiful. Anyone else and it would have broken. But with just a little more stretching or a snip..."

Orcus' lips pressed together. "What to do.... Send you like this and lose any chance of retaining your irreplaceable ability to ease transfers, or risk you passing during your own...

He stood up, movements fluid, those of a young man, not an ancient one.

Stolen, you stole that body. You evil son of a bitch.

Orcus smiled. "Such hate for someone who can extend your life."

Domino reached for every ounce of strength he possessed and whispered, "Won't be my life though will it?"

The mage's eyes widened a little. "Impressive. But you really shouldn't be talking. The sirens won't pay for a dead body, although it would save time. I already have orders for spells only you, or rather only your body can fulfill. Whether I send it to the sirens or not, your body will end up in my work room in pieces, helping to pay for my, and now our, work."

CHAPTER TWENTY-THREE

THE NIGHT BEFORE

The windowless room, carved out of living rock, centered around a firepit. Wide couches that also functioned as beds lay around the room. The residual aroma of roasted meat reminded him how long it'd been since he'd eaten, but he wouldn't accept anything from the rats, even if they offered it. After a single glance at the walls in the flickering firelight, Jude refused to look again.

Domino's compulsion lasted barely three minutes, but it was long enough for the rats to strip Jude and shove him into a cage made of metal strips. One of the four male rat shifters who had half-carried, half-dragged him here, turned a crank. The cage rose in the air, swinging on a chain. By the look of it, the cage could be moved around six feet so it hung over the... Jude swallowed bile down as he saw soot marking his skin.

He pictured himself swinging the cage, trying to keep it out of the flames. Eventually, he'd become exhausted, wouldn't be able to swing it anymore, and he'd slowly cook.

He vowed never to beg, never to ask for anything from these murdering fuckers. He'd fight, would at least return some of the pain he received, but Domino...

Against Orcus' magic, Domino didn't stand a chance. The youngster was already failing. The brief thought that he should have let Domino die in the ocean he loved swept through Jude's mind before it broke against his determination. Where there's life, there's hope, and Jude would fight to the bitter end for Domino. He'd gotten him into this, and he'd get him out, somehow.

The residents, some human, some rat shifters, emerged from the makeshift beds, and doors that led off the main room. Twitching, whispering, grinning, they closed in around him holding sticks and pokers.

"Well, Moreno, this is a day that's been coming for a damn long time. I hope you enjoy our little 'get to know you' party." Jude didn't have time to identify the speaker before the first poker jabbed his back. He twisted towards his attacker, only for someone on the other side to do the same.

A female squealed in excitement. Jude hissed at her; she stepped back eyes wide and grabbed for the male next to her. Jude's victory lasted only a second before two more strikes hit, bicep and thigh.

"Go on, show us your fur, kitty." Jude twisted, identifying the hated figure of the man who had molested Delilah.

"Morris," he growled.

"The one and only, Moreno. Ready to die?"

Jude didn't know how many hours he'd spent in the cage suspended in the center of the Scibettas den. In human form, he couldn't stand, only crouch on all fours or sit.

The cage didn't look strong enough to hold his fur form, but Jude didn't dare shift, even through the almost constant torment. The rats came and went, going off to get drinks, food. Occasionally, one came or went through the door that led into the complex under the mansion. He could almost smell the strong magical wards around him.

Dealing with the pain was easier than looking beyond the sea of bodies. Apart from hiding behind Orcus' magic wards and protection amulets, it appeared the Scibetta pack enjoyed trophy hunting. The various trophy heads and skins could all have belonged to non-sentient animals, but the three black-spotted, golden pelts with attached heads spread on the wall opposite proved otherwise.

He'd counted twelve different individuals during the night. Five weren't even rats, but some humans, like Rory, got drawn in by the thrill of being with supernaturals.

Every person here was a Scibetta now, and guilty in his book; they'd all got a genuine thrill from hurting him. He'd remember these faces until the day he died, which unfortunately didn't seem far off. Between them, the Scibetta kept a constant watch on him. There were always at least six in the room, one holding a gun, two or three others tormenting him.

The females were worse than the males. They kept going for his junk, cackling as he hissed, tried to protect himself from the hot pokers prodding through the bars at all angles.

The last five times the mouthy female poked him, he hadn't reacted. Bored, she'd wandered off. Jude slumped down, exhaustion dragging at his mind and body.

This was why he'd never found them; they'd been living under the protection of a powerful mage all this time. His only hope was that someone, maybe Milo or Oroshi, would track him down before it was too late for him.

For Domino... From what Orcus said, Domino was doomed anyway. The siren certainly believed it.

He's a bounty, just a bounty. The lie didn't work. Even if Jude couldn't save him, hell, he couldn't save himself right now; he vowed to make Domino's end as serene as possible. He'd take him to the beach at the resort where Milo lived, hold him on his lap in the water, tell him he was loved, appreciated for himself, not for what he could do, that Jude would miss–

"Wake up." The command came with fleeting white-hot pain across his hip. He hardly hissed, just another burn to add to all the rest.

"Shit, Morris, will you stop burning the new rug? It'll look like moths have gotten at it."

"Yeah, Morris, behave like Junior tells you," Jude growled. The brief rest had returned a little energy.

This time the poker stabbed rather than touched. He flinched, his face mashing against the bars. Licking the blood from his split lip, he stared back at the four rat shifters who moved around him.

"You should think about being more careful about how you talk to my family, cat," Morris said. The oldest Scibetta he'd seen so far.

Jude didn't recognize 'Junior' but his enthusiasm for Jude's skin to join the others on the wall added him to Jude's death list. If he ever got out of here, which right now seemed unlikely. Oroshi certainly couldn't hear him with the wards.

"You know, I remember him being far more upset the last time we met. Then again, we were killing people he loved," the rat he'd nicknamed Junior replied.

"You weren't there. I would've remembered your ugly face." Jude hoped on Del's memory that he was right, but given what the owner of this mansion did, he couldn't be sure. His surroundings vanished as reality hit far harder than anything the rats had done.

I could've killed four innocent people locked inside Scibetta bodies.

Not my fault; it's their fault, they knew, tricked me. They killed them, not me. Thoughts rebounded in his head, split and multiplied.

What if it was more than four? His mind recoiled as if it'd been burned. *I don't talk to bounties on the dead or alive list; I just put them down. If the body swap strategy worked for the Scibetta, how many more? Orcus would do it, give him enough money, and he'd–*

Jude met the young rat's gaze. *Say you were watching. Go on, you bastard, say you were hiding behind the others. That's why I didn't see you. You weren't involved, you were just a kid along for the ride.*

Junior grinned. "That's because I didn't have this face then. Your bitch of a mother took my eye, so I took my son's body."

Jude latched on the far easier idea of an evil Scibetta rather than having killed innocents himself. "You killed your son?"

The shifter Jude now knew was Eugene Scibetta, the leader on the night Jude's mother and sister died, shrugged.

"Mage says it's easier if you're closely related. Little fucker tried to claim the bounty on me. He deserved it. And he's not dead; he's right here." The rat held his hands out, did a slow twirl.

"A walking, talking trophy," Morris laughed.

"And Orcus' magic let us breed with humans," the vicious young woman who'd been torturing Jude the most said. "Means, I got this." She looked barely out of her teens.

"And very nice you look too, Ma." Junior's smile

dropped from his face, "This body aside, I prefer trophies to be on the wall or the floor. How about it, Moreno? Wanna join Mom and Pops on my wall? All you gotta do is shift. I'll make it quick; like you did for Boris and Carl, I promise." Eugene's smile got broader. "You think you got more? Bad luck, pussy cat."

Two. I only killed two innocents. Jude's teeth itched to sink into the throat of the man responsible, to feel him struggling as his lifeblood drained away.

"The package doesn't change what you are inside, Eugene; you're a coward. Picking on women and children, using magic and spells?" He shook his head. "That's low, even for a rat. If you want to redeem yourself, let me out, fight like the man you pretend to be."

"Yeah, right. Like an adolescent rat against a two-hundred-pound adult leopard is fair?" The other Scibetta laughed at their leader's joke.

"Didn't seem exactly fair when six grown men attacked a pregnant woman and two thirteen-year-olds. And you still didn't fucking get me, did you?"

For all his bravado, Jude couldn't bring himself to look at the three skins nailed to the walls. He couldn't tell which of the two larger skins had been his father or his uncle, But the smaller one, the fine spots and the snarling muzzle... He retched.

"Something bothering you, cat?"

Jude swallowed down bile. "Yeah, you stink, or maybe it's a hairball. Come closer; I'll see if I can throw up on you."

"Abner talked shit too, he always did, until I started skinning his little brother in front of him. Then all he did was cry and beg. Are you going to beg like your daddy? Wanna know which one is him?"

Jude stared at the top of the cage. He refused to give them his emotions. Eugene had to be lying. Cats didn't beg.

"Do you even know which one is your father?" Morris asked. He walked over, stood in front of the pelt of Jude's mother, and stroked down the skins on either side.

"Abner," Morris said, ruffling the golden fur on the right. "And this is Bernard, or was it the other way around? Not that is matters. I've fucked on them both, used your Ma to wipe my shitty ass."

Jude turned, sat up, knowing his eyes had shifted to the golden of a great cat. "I will end you, rat."

Morris wrinkled his long nose. "Correct me if I'm wrong, because isn't that what you spent the last twenty years trying to do, and yet... Still here."

"Yeah, hiding in a hole in the ground surrounded by walking corpses while I walk free."

Morris stalked over, peered into the cage, holding onto the bars. "Not so free now, are you kitty? And most of us do go out. We collect the new host bodies that don't fall for the medical donation spiel."

Jude lunged, but he wasn't quick enough. Even with a partially shifted hand, he only managed to catch the side of the rat's thumb. Morris fell back on his ass, making the other rats laugh.

"Getting slow, old man, better get your name down on the transfer list. Orcus says it'll be a lot quicker and less painful with the siren."

"Fuck off; I'm not living in a fucking human."

The comment sparked an argument between the rats in human bodies and those who could still shift. Jude took the opportunity to rest as the Scibetta shouted around him.

Eugene didn't join in the name-calling. He approached

the cage, fingering a well-worn broad-bladed knife he'd taken from the mantlepiece.

"In case you were wondering, this is the knife I used to skin them; the knife that'll skin you too. I think continuity is important, don't you?"

Jude had no doubt this would only end in the deaths of either the rats or himself, but he still didn't know what had started the feud. Abner had been a cop, and Jude had always envisioned he'd gotten too close to the Scibettas' crime organization.

"I think you talk a lot of shi–"

Every one of Jude's muscles lit up for three agonizing seconds; then it was gone. He lay there gasping, heart thundering in his ears, trying to work out what had happened.

"You like this, honey?" a female voice said.

"Better than a burn; good thinking, Ma. Hit him again."

Jude threw himself against the bars on the other side of the cage, it swung with his movements, but the cattle prod still reached him. Fire raced along every nerve. Jude hissed, felt his canines growing, his talons extending. He ruthlessly suppressed the shift.

"You nearly got him that time; hit him–"

Jude held up his hand, needing to buy time before facing that again. Eugene was right; he'd been too damn close to shifting. "Just... just tell me why."

The fire popped in the silence. Eugene spun around, one hand going to his head before one word exploded out of him. "Why? You've been hunting, killing, my family for twenty years, and you don't even know why?" Eugene folded in demented laughter. "This... this is too damn rich."

"Laugh it up, rat. The jokes on you. How good is revenge when the subject doesn't even know why you're doing it? I never met Abner or Bernard; I didn't even know their first names until that night on the road, I still don't know their family name, where they lived, or anything else.

"All my gran told me was that Abner was a cop. I hunted you for what you did to my mother, my sister. But I would have done it if they were strangers, just like all the other bounties I've brought in. They deserved justice."

"Justice?" The woman shrieked and grabbed for the knife in her son's hand. Eugene wrapped his arms around her. "It's alright, Ma, don't let him upset you; he can't hurt us anymore."

When she'd calmed a little, Eugene handed her off to one of the other women.

"I bet you think your alley cat of a father was a pillar of the community?" Eugene said. "Well, here's news for you. Abner Cullen was worse than any criminal because he pretended to be something he wasn't. My Pa paid him protection money for a decade in downtown Chicago, but Abner couldn't even be an honorable dirty cop.

"He took a bribe to look the other way while a rival outfit raided my family's clubhouse. They killed Pa, three of his brothers, and then burned it to the fucking ground, with my three little sisters still upstairs. They were eight months old.

"Morris and I only managed to pull Ma out, but she got burned to fuck trying to save her babies." Eugene came in close. "So, who do you think deserves justice now, you sanctimonious piece of shit?

"We killed the humans and their families, killed your shit of a father, his clueless brother, and their bitch. That only leaves your hide between us and finishing what Cullen started."

Jude met his gaze, but only because he couldn't back down, but feeling that knife in his gut would've been less painful. He'd met a hell of a lot of liars in his time, but Eugene's bitterness, his hatred, screamed genuine. Whatever had happened, Eugene Scibetta believed what he said.

My death will end it.

No more innocents would die in a pointless feud that could carry on for generations if it didn't end here. Jude had never understood Domino's death wish before, but now.... Yeah, he got it.

If he shifted now, it'd be quick, and the revenge killings would end. If he didn't, the chances were that they'd get him to shift anyway, in the end. Even if he got out of this cage, there was no way all the rats would survive. The feud would continue. His cousins, their kids...

A woman came in, whispered in Eugene's ear.

"No. Tell him to bring them in here. If he argues, tell him I want the cat to see it. Hopefully, it'll push him into shifting. I want my full set of wall hangings; the Scibetta are done hiding."

CHAPTER TWENTY-FOUR

"Is this the guy I'm here to help?"

"Yes, Mr. Brown, and with your help, his life expectancy will be increased by many decades."

"Call me Tommy." The man smiled. "Mr. Brown sounds like my Grandpa."

Domino hadn't said a word, but it appeared that Tommy thought physical weakness also meant he had a brain deficit. Domino could walk, or at least he thought he could, but Orcus seemed frustrated by constantly having to order him to move.

The instructions Orcus gave waned in power in two or three minutes if Domino concentrated. They faded even faster if Orcus wasn't touching the amulet with his fingers when he gave the order. Fighting them steadily sapped Domino's remaining strength, but he'd be damned if he just rolled over and gave up. The last instruction had been almost five minutes ago.

Catching the red-haired man's gaze, he poured everything into his words. "Leave. You don't–"

Orcus' hand slapped over Domino's mouth. A blank-faced Tommy got to his feet.

"Nice try. Now, tell him to sleep." Like barbed wire around his heart, the compulsion took hold. Domino gave the order that would end this innocent's life. Tommy sat back down, fell sideways, closed eyes that Domino might be looking out of the next time they opened.

Orcus spun the wheelchair around so Domino faced him. Jasmine wafted in his face. Tweed tailored trousers confronted him; they didn't belong on the man wearing them. Ace should be dancing in jeans, laughing, enjoying his youth. Instead, he was stuck in a crumbling old man, wearing a diaper with a tube up his cock to collect his piss.

"You'll feel different when you transfer, I promise. The first time is always the hardest, but this needs to happen. I don't know how to impress it upon you any more than I have already. You are so much more than him, my boy, you are unique; he–" Orcus sighed, "–is cannon fodder. You have no idea how many like him are on the planet. He's utterly forgettable and pointless. Left alone, he will drift through life, maybe father a few equally unremarkable brats with some floozy, and die of overindulgence in his fifties. An utter waste of a life."

Apart from the floozy and dying in his fifties, Domino thought Tommy's life plan sounded bloody brilliant. Loving and being loved, working hard with people he knew well and who appreciated each other. A home, making a difference to a few rather than the world. *Fucking awesome.*

"The best contribution Thomas Brown can make to the world," Orcus carried on, "is enabling you to continue being your remarkable self. Think of the things you'll be able to do if you have the time to learn. The sirens have it wrong; it's not your offspring who will rule the world, it's you, Domino, but only if you strive to live. Understand?"

As Orcus had asked a question, rather than given an instruction, Domino could answer.

"If I do retain my abilities, I'll make you, and every client that you've transferred, end up in battery chickens for eternity."

Orcus let out a bark of laughter. "See? You've proved my point yet again. Tommy here would probably only imagine a little red guy with a pitchfork. But as you'll soon be joining us, I guess that opinion will change.

"Now, be quiet and listen. Unfortunately, as you won't help with your own transfer, it'll be a little, no, more than a little, rough. We'll need to make this body intolerable to occupy so your soul flies free. Tommy's body will be ready and waiting, and I will draw you into it when you escape this one.

"Unfortunately, the only consistent, successful stimulus I've discovered is pain. However, I'm all for being economical, and your pain will have several purposes. What's the phrase, 'buy one, get one free'? Or, in your case, two free."

Domino silently vowed to devote the rest of his existence to stopping Orcus. The mage would slip at some point. He didn't know when or where, but even if it took several lifetimes, Orcus would pay for the lives he'd destroyed.

Two men appeared over the mage's shoulder. One chewed gum as if his life depended on the rate his jaw moved. The other shifted from foot to foot, eyes darting around.

"Eugene thinks this guy will get Moreno to shift? Is the cat fucking him or something?"

Orcus whipped around. The crack of hand on flesh echoed off the tiles.

"You will treat him with respect, understood?"

Gum guy held the other's arm. "Sorry, my Lord, we meant no disrespect."

"I'm sick of toadying up to this bastard, no matter what body he's in. We work like dogs for him, and all he does is–"

"Gives us sanctuary and immortality? You've got a new body; I haven't." Gum guy's eyes widened as he looked back at Orcus. "And that is not the only reason for my loyalty, my lord; I fully appreciate how–"

"Stop groveling, Edward. I don't let you stay because I like any of you. You're useful, nothing more." He glared at the man he'd hit. "And when you stop being useful, I can always take back what I've given. Remember, most of you are related. A host for one soul can easily become the host for another."

Both men bowed their heads, mumbling apologies.

"Hubert, carry the human. Edward, bring the board and equipment in the metal tray on the side in the treatment room."

Orcus pushed Domino through a door at the end of another white corridor. Heat, woodsmoke, the musk of many bodies, hit Domino.

A few spotlights illuminated various pieces of taxidermy mounted on the walls. Domino only had eyes for the bruised, burned, naked figure in the cage suspended near the firepit in the center of the cave-like room.

"No, take him out of here; he's done nothing to any of–" Jude blurted.

A woman wearing denim shorts that barely covered her butt cheeks thrust a rod through the bars of the cage. Jude jerked, causing the cage to swing.

"So that's where it went. Next time you wish to borrow my equipment, Lucille, please ask."

The woman sashayed over to Orcus, her eyes running over him as if he was a side of meat.

"I am really liking the new look, Orcus. Fancy working on some options for our next transfers? I bet we can make beautiful kids together."

"Ma, please," a man who looked the same age as the woman exclaimed.

"Anyone got a bucket?" Jude's voice was rough, but at least he could still talk.

"Not yet, but it could be a useful precaution. We wouldn't want to spoil any of these lovely furnishings. Thank you, for your suggestion, Mr. Moreno.

"Eugene, perhaps you have something we can use to cover your floor?"

The young man frowned, and Orcus indicated the opposite wall.

Eugene's eyes lit up. "Orcus, you're a fucking genius. Ma, bring the tickling stick."

Jude groaned, rested his head on his forearm. *He looks... defeated.* That, more than anything else Domino had seen, pissed him off. Nothing fazed Jude.

Two of the rats went to the spotted pelts on the wall, took two down, and laid them next to each other in front of Jude's cage.

"No, we won't need the prod, not this time. It was brought to my attention earlier that our little siren needs almost constant control. Even with this rather magnificent body, I have lapsed once or twice when I've been concentrating on other things. Therefore, I think a safe contingency plan would be to have more than one control amulet."

The rats blinked, but Domino understood. He fisted

both hands as if that would stop Orcus from taking his fingers.

"Hubert, put the host on the bigger pelt. Domino, lay on the smaller. Your mother, I believe, Mr. Moreno? I hope her spirit will be able to guide Domino to his new residence."

Domino stood up, took a step towards Jude. His bare toes brushed the pelt, and he cringed.

"Salty..."

Domino looked up, met Jude's gaze. The pain in the cat shifter's eyes mirrored his own.

"I'm sorry, I'm so damn sorry; if I hadn't taken your case, if I–"

"Don't fret, Mr. Moreno, Domino will thank you, eventually. Although, maybe not in the next few minutes; I imagine he'll be cursing you to hell then. I hope that having his fingers severed without anesthesia will push him through his reticence about changing bodies.

"I've had difficult hosts before, but never a client this bolshie. If you don't want to watch, I suggest shifting, and one of the rats will put you out of your misery. However, that will not change what happens to Domino. Time to lay down, Domino."

His body jerked, complying as he screamed inside at the soft dead fur underneath his naked back and the skull that brushed the top of his head.

Orcus joined Domino and Tommy on the furs, sitting between them. He placed a cool hand on each of their foreheads.

"Now, I require two volunteers. One to cut, the other to cauterize. The body does need to function for the next week or so, although the sirens do not require fingers."

I can do this. It hurt with the Karnaks; I can do it again. I'll hang on, I'll–

Orcus leaned closer. "You think you can stand it, right? You were sedated when the dogs took your thumb. It's going to hurt more than you've ever experienced before. I know; I've done it myself many times. But the sooner you reach for your new body, the sooner it stops. Now rest, think about your new body, think about feeling energetic again."

"Orcus, you can do anything you like to me, just leave him alone, please, he hasn't done anything, he–"

"And that's the point, Mr. Moreno. Domino hasn't been able to live his life yet, thanks to his physiology, and I'm going to give him that chance. I'm not sure if we'll have to do this every decade, but we will if we have to. Eugene?"

Domino hadn't noticed the man sitting down beside him.

"I'm ready."

Domino's heart stuttered as the blade Eugene held caught the light.

"Arioch, I was wrong, I need your hel–" Jude's frantic voice morphed into a grunt of pain. Domino pushed against the compulsion to stay still; his arm moved, but Eugene pinned his wrist down. The back of his hand hit...

Wood. *That's... a fucking chopping board.*

He twisted, wrenching away. A hand came down on his shoulder. "You sure we shouldn't be tying him down?"

Fingers on his jaw. Hazel eyes bored into his. Orcus held the bone amulet an inch from Domino's nose.

"Stay still, do not make a sound, and use the pain to break free from this dying shell."

Domino's eyes closed, and this time, he didn't physically flinch when the back of his hand touched the chopping board. It felt like his soul was rolling up, cringing away from the flesh about to be abused.

"Please, don't hurt him. I'll shift, I'll–"

"Just like his fucking father," Eugene said. "Begging as soon as things get tough."

Domino braced his mind. *Which one is he going to–*

The microsecond of time between the decisive cut and the pain hitting his brain hung like a lifetime. His mind screamed; his body stayed still.

Cold air against his flesh where his little finger should be. Blood warming the rest of his hand.

His hand rose. Foggy, he registered heat against his skin before pain hit him again, along with a hiss and the scent of burning flesh.

"Reach for the tie, Domino. This stops when you sever it. Again, Eugene."

Metal clanged, the screech of a furious big cat blasted his ears, pain rode over him like a tsunami.

Unable to move, Domino pulled away with his mind. Something stretched, spider silk thin. The red-hot poker touched the new stump, and he broke free. The pain vanished.

Floating free, he looked down at the scene. The cage swung wildly as a great black cat threw itself around in the confined space.

A man, the oldest Domino had seen so far, tried to track Jude's movements with a gun while a woman shrieked about ricochet.

An identical woman stood just behind the screaming one, but she was... insubstantial. Domino looked down at his body, but it was Orcus that took his attention.

A line of shadowy figures stretched behind him into the distance. Each had a crowd of indistinct bodies pressing against them so closely that Domino couldn't distinguish individuals.

The souls, the severed souls, don't return to the wheel of life. They're trapped forever, following the soul who stole their flesh. Tommy's body pulled at him like a whirlpool, but Domino could see the man's soul, attached by a thin thread, floating just above it.

Domino fought the current Orcus's magic produced with all his strength. *No, I can't doom Tommy to that; I can't–*

"Come on, Domino, don't fail now," Orcus growled to himself as he leaned over Domino's body, performing chest compressions.

Ghostly female arms appeared around his body. "No, no more; he's suffered enough. Go, Domino, I'll make sure Judah finds you."

The scene froze, no sound, no movement.

CHAPTER TWENTY-FIVE

"Shocking, isn't it?"

Domino had no idea where the voice came from until a man wearing a black suit and a red tie pushed away from the wall where the last pelt hung. Two small red horns rose from his jet-black hair.

"Come down from there; you're giving me a crick in the neck."

As if the newcomer possessed a control amulet of his own, Domino floated back to the floor, a foot away from the body Orcus had been trying to revive.

"Name's Arioch. I'm your friendly neighborhood vengeance demon."

"You're the one–" Domino stopped, shocked that his voice worked.

"Amulets don't work so well on spirits. But yes, Jude called me, something I've been trying to get him to do since the night Bella and Delilah died." He nodded at the frozen drama on the floor. "Bella seems to have taken a shine to you."

Domino blinked, trying to focus. "You can help? Save me and Jude?"

The demon wrinkled his nose, wobbled his hand from side to side. "Depends what you mean by "save". I'm a vengeance demon, not an angel. Causing justified suffering is my bag not saving-" he held up a finger, "–unless survival means more suffering for the revengee." Arioch's brow wrinkled. "You would have thought that after several thousand years, I would have come up with a better term, but victim implies a certain innocence. None of the people here are innocent, except maybe Tommy, and that includes you and Jude."

"Sean." Domino hadn't intended to voice the name, but it still echoed in the silence.

"Precisely. I have to say, I was very impressed with the amount of guilt you produced all on your own without a single prompt. Not that Sean ever thought about revenge anyway. He was too busy being guilty about denying he was bisexual and the pain he caused you. And that faggot comment?" Arioch grinned. "Shit tons of regret. But you don't need to feel bad anymore; he moved on almost immediately. Sean's soul is..." Arioch's face blanked for a moment before a smirk curled his lips. "–currently terrorizing a little girl with a spider in the gardens of the Hollywood mansion of his sports promoter father. Way to go, Sean. I love naughty kids, don't you?

"I don't think he'd go back to his previous life if it were offered. Don't think I can do that, because I can't. Time travel is impossible." Arioch wrinkled his nose. "Mostly. Although I have to admit to never putting serious effort into that direction."

Domino couldn't link the conversation with the bloody,

painful scene around him, so he stopped trying. If this was a death dream, he intended to enjoy it.

"Right, shall we get back to this delicious tangle?" Arioch rubbed his hands together.

"Would be nice. By the look of it, I'm about to kick the bucket."

Arioch stared at him, then chuckled. "I knew I liked you from the moment you made the severed cock up your ass comment."

"You were watching?"

Arioch rolled his eyes. "Obviously. The Karnaks provided me with a nice snack, bit 'fast food' for my liking though. Jude is a little too efficient at killing. Rory was much better, until you made him all happy and relaxed. Anyway, I know having your soul forcibly extracted is probably a little distracting, so I'll explain in simple words.

"I am a vengeance demon. I feed on the suffering of those who have wronged others, or revengees." He shook his head, pursed his lips. "Got to think of a better word for them. Sinners? No, too biblical. Anyhow, and here's the kicker, I can only exact revenge if I'm invoked. Souls, living or free, can call on me to exact justifiable revenge on their behalf, or in really juicy cases, I pop up and ask in person.

"I asked Jude the night his mother and sister died. He decided to handle it himself which still strikes me as a trifle rude. Even demons have to eat, and the angst that night..." Arioch smacked his lips.

"Wait, you were already there?"

Arioch wagged his finger, grinning at Domino. "Clever boy. Yes, I was already there, on behalf of Eugene's father."

Domino's jaw clenched. "You organized the deaths of his mother and sister?"

"Nope, that was all Eugene, and it moved him from

revenger to revengee. He cocked his head. "Inciter to receiver? Eh... maybe. Family vendettas can provide food for decades, sometimes centuries. And I'm digressing again. Intelligent conversation is so hard to come by in my business. All my clients are so... focused on themselves."

"I can see why, what with the painful violent death and everything." Domino indicated the scene around them.

"Right, sorry. Here are the short notes. You can perform revenge on a person who has greatly wronged you, but taking it to innocent parties? Not good form. I organized Abner Cullen falling into the hands of the Scibetta, but the moment they laid hands on Bernard, Jude's biological father, all bets were off. Bernard is, was, a genuine nice guy. Not too bright though. His hero worship of his big brother was damn stupid.

"But it's clear cut now. Jude, Bella, Bernard, and Del, she hates being called Delilah, all have the right of vengeance on the souls of the Scibetta involved in their deaths. They can't rest or move on until the issue is resolved, and Del is an epic nag, which is why I'm happy to move this along.

"And that's not even considering the shit Orcus has done. I must admit to being impressed with your battery hen idea. Subtle and inventive. Not quite what most of the souls queuing up for him have in mind though. Ace is particularly impatient, then again, he does have a chance at getting his body and life back, so he has a point."

Domino blinked, concentrated on the scene. A skinny, translucent, teenaged girl had her hands on the lock of Jude's cage. *Has the cage moved a little?*

"Time's nearly up, Domino. What do you want to do?"

His attention shot back to the demon. "What are my options?"

Arioch chuckled. "So damn bright. Your options are: One, invoking me to deal with it. Two, trying to handle it yourself like Jude did, which will leave you in Tommy's body, Jude as a rug, Tommy on his way to visit with your wonderful family, and all these poor souls still doomed to hang around until someone with more sense than balls comes along."

"What would you do?"

"Interrupting is rude. But on the spur of the moment, I'd... Put Orcus in a chicken, Ace and Faheem back in their bodies, Tommy still in his, and Jude released. "But–" He held up a finger. "That still leaves you dead and Jude a loose cannon even if he gets out of here with all these rats about. If he does escape them, one day, he'll kill the wrong person, and he'll end up on my list, and not in a good way."

"Or?" Domino prompted.

"I like you, Domino, and your reaction under epic pressure tonight has persuaded me to offer you an interview task to be my apprentice. If you pass that and the trial period, you get your horns." Perfect manicured fingers stroked the red horns poking out of dark hair.

"I'd become a vengeance demon?"

Arioch stroked his horns again and shuddered. "Hmm, that never gets old. Sorry, what?"

"Me becoming a vengeance demon?"

"Oh, yes. If you pass, you'll become a junior vengeance demon, an imp, feeding off the suffering of naughty souls. Orcus and all his clients would be fair game as would most of your family. But I might keep Orcus for myself. I'm a demon; being selfish comes with the fetching and remarkably sensitive horns. How are you with paperwork and dealing with nagging souls? I recently fired my prospective assistant, literally."

Domino blinked. This was an incredibly fucked up hallucination, but he decided to go with it anyway.

"Um yeah, I can do paperwork, but can we get on with this, I'm definitely dying down there."

"Right, right. Ok, the perks of the job include immortality, at least until I decide otherwise. That's why I have a vacancy. Alastor was such a disappointment. The ability to translocate, and of course shape-shifting."

Domino stumbled back as Arioch expanded into a classic devil; eight feet tall, complete with red skin and a forked tail.

"Well?" Arioch sounded like rocks grinding together.

Domino swallowed. Aunt Tethys scared him more, but he wasn't going to tell the demon that.

"Inventive wins?" Domino confirmed.

"Yes, but only for revenge you're not directly involved with; this is work, not pleasure."

Anger flared. "I can't hurt Orcus?"

Arioch shrank back down, brushed at his suit. "Not directly, no, not if you want to join the ranks of vengeance demons. Remember, fear, pain, suffering, and making them regret what they did is the name of the game. Oh, and because of that most disrespectful flash of anger you have to be alive to win the prize. A special little twist just for you." A bright smile lit his face. "Ready? Because it starts in three, two, one–"

Sounds and movement increased around him, but slowly, as if in molasses.

"Pipe, I need my pipe."

The familiar chrome whistle appeared in the demon's still red hand. "Impress me, Domino, and we could have a very long, fruitful relationship. I don't make this offer often and even fewer pass the test."

Domino almost snatched the instrument from his hand.

"Bella, Bernard, Del, do you agree to come back just to settle this?" Domino called out.

An insubstantial man and woman rose from the pelts on the floor, looked at each other and nodded.

The girl next to Jude's cage called out, "Hell, yeah."

Putting his pipe to his lips, Domino played a lilting discordant melody as time sped up.

"What? What the hell's happening?" Hubert said as he walked stiffly over to where Orcus still performed chest compressions on Domino's unresponsive body. The rat stood staring down at himself in disbelief that he'd become a passenger in the body he'd stolen. The other spirits displaced by the Scibetta were also shoving their former bodies to where Hubert stood.

Eugene swore, made for the door, only to fall flat on his butt. The living in the room couldn't see him, but the soul of Eugene's son had clotheslined his former body.

"You're not getting away that easily," he snarled at his murderous parent, then turned to Jude's family who had gathered near the cage. "Make it hurt."

Bernard, who had Jude's build and dark hair, nodded. "I promise," he said, then looked over at Domino. "They killed us in cat form, used us as trophies, I think–"

Domino interrupted. "Already on it."

He was about to play again when he was jerked down toward his body.

"I won't have disobedience," Orcus ground out. "You will not escape me by dying."

Domino opened his eyes, looked up into Ace's stolen face. Pain flared again. *Too late, I wasn't quick enough.*

The amulet hung away from the mage's skin. Domino's body felt like lead as if rigor mortis had already set in.

"Switch, damn you," Orcus growled out. A wrench, a final tearing. Domino opened his eyes. Orcus no longer kneeled above him, he was... Domino pulled his hand up, stared at his arm. *No marks, no marks at all.*

"At last," Orcus swiveled around, looming over him, over Tommy.

"Breathe, relax Domino, you did it. Now I know the first few moments can be–"

The amulet dangled from its chain, tantalizing, teasing. Domino reached up, pulled. Orcus grabbed for his hand and Domino put Tommy's bulk to good use, catching Orcus across the jaw with his fist. The mage fell back sprawling across Domino's lax body.

He struggled to his feet, staggered. Came face to face with Tommy's translucent soul. The guy looked utterly bewildered.

Domino couldn't do it, couldn't take this man's life. He held up the amulet. "Take this and run. Run as far as you fucking can and never come back. Got it?"

"Yeah, what the fuck is going–"

Domino found the small thread that connected his soul to Tommy's body and ripped it free.

"No, no, you can't," Orcus' frantic voice came from above him.

Domino had so much to say, so much to do, but his time was up. He managed a smile as darkness closed around him.

"Someone grab that damn host before he gets away," Orcus shouted and began pumping on Domino's chest again.

"I can't fucking move," Hubert called out.

Domino rose out of his body, reaching for the pipe his corporeal self could never play again. Before he'd been on the cusp between life and death, now, his body didn't feel right, didn't feel like *him*. It was a thing, nothing more.

Even though he'd failed Arioch's test by dying, Domino would see this thing through. Jude's family and Orcus' victims deserved justice. Now that the chance of becoming a vengeance demon had vanished, he was free to do whatever the hell he wanted. Top of his list was pain, terror, and death for those who had wronged innocents, who had ripped their futures away.

Thanks to the displaced spirits, a dozen people, a mixture of rat shifters and humans, bunched together a step away from Domino's physical head. But the spirits were fading, becoming insubstantial without his magic to keep them here. Hanging above his corpse, Domino played again, bolstering the displaced spirits. When he could barely see through them, he changed the tune. His physical body tilted; a woman screamed.

Flat pelts plumped, moved. Slowly, the two leopard furs got to their feet. Domino's body flopped to the bare rock floor. It didn't matter, it wasn't him anymore. Orcus scrabbled backward on his butt, eyes wide.

The cats' heads turned towards their victims, still in the rictus the taxidermist created. Then, as one, their faces animated, eyes lit up, and they hissed.

The Scibetta, both males and females, broke from the spirits holding them and ran for the exits, screaming and fighting each other to get in front.

High above them, Domino kept on playing as the biggest cat pounced on Eugene, mauled his shoulder. The rat shrieked, twisted, but Jude's father didn't seem inclined to deliver a killing bite, not yet. The female cat was on her third victim, blood dripping from her fangs. Domino blinked; another female cat, almost identical to Bella except more insubstantial, efficiently dispatched the last running rat.

A third, smaller leopard cornered Morris, hissed.

The three adult cats stalked up behind Del.

Morris whimpered as urine stained the front of his jeans. Domino found the stink of blood and feces revolting, but the sharp tang of ozone in the room was surprisingly good. If this was how revenge smelled, Domino liked it.

The second adult female cat morphed into her human form, an old woman.

"Don't mess with my family," she said.

"Gran?" Domino's playing almost faltered at Jude's choked voice. "They killed you too?"

The woman turned, smiled. Domino's heart nearly broke at the look of love she gave the bruised, battered, and burned, shaking figure in the cage.

"No, Judah, my sweet boy, they didn't do it. I felt the tug from young Domino. I was near to passing anyway. Another day, perhaps a week? No, this was worth it, and I got to see you again."

The smallest cat pounced. The crack of bone reverberated in the deathly silence. A door slammed.

Damn, Orcus. Domino didn't stop playing; it was the only thing holding the leopard spirits here. The others had already departed, moved on.

Bernard and Bella shifted, and Jude's father retrieved the key to the cage from Eugene's ravaged body. The four members of Jude's family congregated around the cage as Bernard opened it and helped his son out.

The two stared into each other's eyes. Same height, same build, one alive, one dead.

"Dad."

The man stiffened. "Never thought I'd hear that. I'm proud of you, son; I wish I could've known you."

Bella snorted. "I'm glad you didn't. You were good in the sack, but you didn't have a responsible bone in your body. Fun was all that interested you. Thanks to Mom and me, Jude grew up in peace, without the crap that idiot brother of yours caused, but you always stood by him, didn't you? And look where that ended."

Jude's lopsided smile glistened with the cut on his lip. "Ma, nothing changes, right?" Then his face crumbled. "I miss you so damn much." The two fell into each other's arms, and Jude's gran hugged them both from the side.

Domino kept on playing despite tearing up. He felt like an intruder on the touching scene. This last goodbye should be somewhere else than in this slaughterhouse. As he watched, Bernard pressed his lips together and walked away. A second male figure joined him, slung his arm around Bernard's shoulder, just before they both faded to nothing.

Sniffing, mother and grandmother stepped back from Jude. "Look after yourself, son," his mother said, and like his father and uncle, they faded away.

Jude was left standing with his sister.

"Hey, Titch."

"DeliLAH." The pair grinned at each other. Domino could see what Jude had looked like as a kid. Cheeky, annoying. Nothing much had changed. Jude's smile dropped, and Domino revised his assessment. Plenty had changed, but Jude's base personality still tried to break through the bonds the stress of adulthood produced. Domino wished he could snap those smothering chains and let Jude experience real joy again. He carried on playing, wanting to allow the twins all the time they needed to say goodbye, to let them both move on.

"You good, where you are?"

She looked around. "Damn sight better than here. But now this is done and dusted, it's time to move on, for us anyway. You look after yourself, and if a bratty kid kicks you in the shin in the next few years, look a little closer."

Tears welled in Jude's eyes. "Will, will you watch out for Domino? He's with you now, right?"

Delilah looked right at where Domino hovered over his body. "He is, and he isn't. I think he's walking a different path to either of us now." She went up on her tiptoes, pecked Jude on the cheek, whispered, "Try to be happy, Titch," and vanished.

Loud, slow clapping came from behind him. Arioch leaned up against the wall, next to the scattered remains of two shifters Bella had dispatched.

Jude didn't appear to hear Arioch as he walked slowly over to Domino's body.

"Now that was spectacular. All the screaming, the running and blood? Most of them pissed themselves too. Always a good sign of terror. I lied about the being alive thing. You get a definite pass. Sometimes slow revenge is better, but there is certainly something to be said for tying everything up in a nice neat bow and moving on. Especially when it rids me of a pesky nagging soul." He pushed off the wall.

"Speaking of tying things up and moving on, Orcus is currently poised over his old body with a knife. He's got some odd idea that–"

Domino pictured the decrepit figure in the bed and found himself next to it.

"Switch back," he blurted.

Both men's eyes widened. Ace stumbled back, dropping the knife as his hand went to his chest. The spirits that had been crowding around the younger body, now surrounded the one in the bed.

"Ace, wait," Domino said.

Wide eyes turned to him. "Who, who are you? What happened? I... I was in that."

Waves of anger, of fear, spread from the man in the bed. No regret, no guilt. It wasn't right.

"You were, and you would have died there. He planned it all. This is what he does, steals the bodies of the young so those with money can live longer."

"That's... that's fucking evil. I'm... I'm his nephew, and he–"

"Grandson, actually. Just like me, but I'm..." Domino couldn't bring himself to say dead, even though it was true. "He's already signed everything over to you. You own all this now."

Ace looked at Orcus, whose mouth moved, trying to form words as saliva dripped down his chin.

"Everything fucking hurt," Ace said, "–just lying still. I even crapped myself, and that was all his doing?"

Domino nodded. "He was about to kill you, this body anyway."

Horace bent down, picked up the knife.

A whimper came from the bed. "Please, if you kill me, hundreds will die, all the people I've helped, all–"

"And they deserve it and more. Thanks to what you did to me," Domino said, "I can see every single soul whose body you stole. They stretch for miles, and they are not happy."

"No, you're lying. They move on, get reincarnated," Orcus croaked.

"News for you, Orcus, they don't pass on. They're stuck trailing around after you and your clients, watching and waiting. You like to go for strong bodies, don't you? Criminals? Inmates of asylums? Vicious people who had little to lose in life, and nothing at all now they're dead. Would you like to chat with them? Try the bullshit arguments you used on me?"

A hulking tattooed man pushed to the front of the spirits. "Tell him something for me."

Domino looked over, listened. "I agree, totally unnecessary. I hear it's a damn painful way to go."

"Who, who are you talking to?" Orcus's voice wavered.

Domino repeated the name the spirit gave him. "Frank Ardizzone. He's a little pissed about the strychnine and about you and his uncle stealing his body to avoid a death sentence."

Orcus' gaze shot around the room, as a warm sensation filled Domino's mind and body. It felt like... seawater infusing into him.

"That's regret; tasty, isn't it?" Arioch sat on the end of the bed, but from Ace's lack of reaction, the human couldn't see the demon.

It felt good, right, but Domino couldn't stay here forever; he needed to find Jude, tell him he was still here.

"But they can't interact with Orcus without me to interpret, can they?"

"Are you sure about that? Do you know how many people residing in padded cells are actually recipients of ongoing justified revenge?"

Domino raised his pipe.

"You don't need that," Arioch said. "The females need instruments, but it's always been just a prop for you. A thought will do it, as long as you mean it."

A second later, Orcus scrabbled up the bed, trying to escape the spirits surrounding him. The wave of terror from the mage, the satisfaction from the spirits, made Domino groan in pleasure, but there was one more thing he had to do before finding Jude. He concentrated on Faheem.

Domino found him looking down at the body of Prince Adnan up in one of the bedrooms.

"He was a good man," Faheem said, not looking at Domino. "One moment I was looking out of his eyes, then there was pain, and I was back in my body."

"He used you, tried to steal your life."

"And I gave it gladly."

"What? You knew?" Domino couldn't work out why someone would willingly sacrifice themselves.

"I did. I've known he was my grandfather for many years. Its why I took service with him. And now, now it'll all go to that devil of a son."

"No, no it won't. He changed his will, you inherit, you can–."

For the first time, Faheem turned to him. "You are a spirit now. Move on. You have no business interfering in the business of the living."

The thought wrapped around him, pulled him away.

CHAPTER TWENTY-SIX

Jude crouched beside Domino, no pulse, no breathing, trying to work out what Del had meant by "a different path." *She didn't say he's dead. Water, he needs seawater.*

Jude scooped up Domino's body, trying to ignore the way his own ached and the sluggish blood dripping from Domino's mutilated hand.

Moans and cries of fear came from one of the doors in the white-tiled foyer, but Jude carried on up the stairs, smashing open the door of Orcus' study.

"Sir, can I help–" Dawkins started.

Jude hissed, putting every ounce of cat fury into the sound. The elderly man fell back, clutching at his chest. Moving as fast as he could with his scarily lax burden, Jude wrenched the front door open, not caring that snow billowed in weak sunshine or that he and Domino were both naked.

As soon as his feet hit the sharp gravel of the driveway, he threw back his head and bellowed, "Oroshi, you're awesome."

"Crap, could you be... Oh fuck. Where to?"

"Water, he needs seawater and medical help, he–"

Moonlight, warmth, a drifting calypso rhythm. Jude stumbled the few feet to the ocean, waded up to his knees then fell on his butt.

Domino didn't move. Jude scooped frantic handfuls of water, splashing it over him. "Come on, come on, this is all you need; I saw it before. Fight, damn it."

The marks on Domino's face and chest looked so dark against the pale skin.

But deep down, Jude knew Domino didn't want to fight, didn't want to live in this world with him. In the end, Domino hadn't trusted Jude to keep him safe, and he'd been right.

Shouts came from further up the beach. Jude cradled Domino's body against him, rocking him in the surf as the waves broke against them. "I'm sorry I couldn't save you; I'm so damn–"

"Jude, let me have him; Amtai might be able to help," Milo's voice came from beside him.

Jude held on tighter, shook his head, the salt of his tears joining the ocean. Domino didn't want to live, didn't want–

A slender female hand snaked through his hold, pressed against Domino's throat.

"He's gone. I'm so sorry."

An hour later, Jude paced the medical room where Domino's body lay.

"No, it needs to happen now. They'll come for him; they'll send people like they did before. I promised, damn it, Milo, I promised they wouldn't get him."

"Jude, there are no sirens here. Give us time to organize things. We don't have the facilities for a cremation and the guests–"

He rounded on the short, slim blond canine shifter. "Fuck the guests and fuck you too. All he wanted," Jude swiped at a traitorous tear. "All that poor fuck wanted was to be left alone, and if they get him–" Jude grabbed Domino's mutilated hand. "See what they did? They'll use every bit of him like a fucking spare part inventory if–"

"I have an old wooden rowboat; you can use that," the white-haired selkie said. "I know what sirens are like, and Jude is right; they treat their dead as commodities. I thought it was voluntary, but–" she gave a sad smile, "–it seems not. We'll fill it with wood and kerosene, tow it out far enough that the guests won't be disturbed. There will be nothing left but dust in the ocean." She patted Jude's arm. "I'm sure he'll rest in peace."

Jude hoped with all his heart that she was right, but if Domino wasn't with Del, where was he? Although what did it matter? Jude couldn't change anything, and wherever Domino was, he wasn't coming back.

An hour later, Jude silently watched Domino's body burn in a Viking funeral a mile from the shore.

When they got back to the beach, Jude let Amtai treat his wounds. She prescribed at least a month of rest and relaxation. Milo gave him the key to a vacation hut on the edge of the development, telling him he could stay as long as he wanted.

Jude nodded, walked away. Jude's fellow male leopards had it right. No attachments, no pain, because even after only knowing Domino for a matter of days, this hurt so damn much.

He'd been right before, do the job, don't get involved, don't get hurt. He'd stay until he was fit again, then he'd go back to work. The money didn't matter, not anymore, but maybe he could prevent some poor innocent fuck suffering like Domino had done or, at least, get justice for them.

CHAPTER TWENTY-SEVEN

"I wouldn't advise it," Arioch said. "I've got more than enough work involving only humans on other continents. You'd never have to encounter him again."

Domino rolled his eyes. "What don't you get? I want to see him. The longer I leave it, the more of a shock it'll be. As far as he's concerned, I'm dead."

They sat in Arioch's office, a pleasant modernist sanctuary from the red, glowing walls and the suspiciously familiar screams of terror. If he broached the subject with Arioch, the guy would posture, growl, and then probably reveal a hidden entertainment system that provided "atmosphere". The longer he stayed here, the more Domino suspected that this wasn't some alternate reality underworld but somewhere far more mundane, maybe below the supernatural prison which was also Arioch's responsibility.

Arioch sighed. Put his fat cigar down. "You are dead, or at least the body Jude knew is. Plus... it's been two months for him."

Domino stiffened. "What? It was two days ago; it can't–"

"It can, and it is. I left you in limbo for a while." He scowled. "What? I've been busy. I didn't have time for pesky questions. As for Jude, he is getting on with life. He's teamed up with Milo and those other misfits. And now that Orcus is dead, he–"

The sucker punches were coming thick and fast today. "Dead?"

"Yep. Although he doesn't know that yet. He still thinks he's in a geriatric ward filled with dementia patients and soiling himself." Arioch chuckled, sucked on the cigar, then blew out a ring of smoke. "I'll wait until he's been wishing he was dead for a century or so before I let him go. And then I'm putting him in a chicken. Or a pig. Haven't decided yet."

A phone dinged. Arioch reached for the handset that appeared. "Oh good, I've been waiting for this one. A sleazy Hollywood producer is about to get a bit of a shock."

The black-suited male demon stood up. Color expanded from his scarlet tie to cover a now curvy female body.

"And do think about leaving Jude to get on with his life. You're immortal now, he isn't. Think how cut up you'll be if you spend a century together before he dies. It's up to you, though; I'm only a damn paper pusher most of the time."

"And I've said I'm happy to help with that, after I've seen him. How do I get to him?"

Arioch frowned. "If I have to tell you that I made a mistake. But before play, you have a little work to do."

Domino frowned.

Arioch raised her gaze to the ceiling. "Give me strength. Your dear mother, aunts, and cousins? They did kill your father, among many others, and not all of them deserved it.

Although, I have to say I've put several worthy candidates their way.

"And don't forget about your cousin Melody. A greedy, scheming girl, but not evil in the broad sense. Although you not dying, not entirely anyway, would please her spirit, if she wasn't already in another body. Now get going and remember," she gave a bright smile, "be inventive. Boring vengeance demons get dissipated. Keep a tally of vengeance achieved too. After the Alastor disaster, I'm instigating a points-based reward system. Number of jobs completed and thoroughness count."

Domino blinked at the dissipating smoke ring in Arioch's now empty office.

Taking a breath, he concentrated, putting a detailed image incorporating all his senses in his mind. The loft room that had been his bedroom hadn't changed much. A new wardrobe stood in the corner, and a second bed was pushed against the far wall. It smelled mustier than he remembered. This had been his whole damn world for so long, because of his kin.

Wrapping the memory of the tearful, loving interaction between Jude and his family around himself, he let the anger rise. He'd been worthy of being loved by more than Melody, but he hadn't been. For years he'd let them rule his thoughts for every minute of every day. Even when he'd been lost in a moment of sex or dancing, they were there, lurking, whispering that he should enjoy it as much as he could as it couldn't last.

They can't hurt me anymore, not physically, and if I give them more of my emotions, that's on me.

He took a deep breath. This was his job now, his existence, and he wouldn't do a good job if he didn't enjoy it. They deserve to be frightened like they frightened so many men over the years, including his father —a man whose son didn't even know his name.

Enough guilt to rock Arioch rolled through him. *I never asked, not once.* That's what the sirens do to men, belittle them so much not even their names matter.

A gull squawked outside, breaking him from his thoughts. Despite it being early evening, he couldn't hear anything else. The sorority should be practicing their harmonies at this time. With a thought, he stood in the deserted living room of his old home.

There could be only one reason why the whole sorority was absent. Not knowing how many people were in the rock chamber, or if he could possibly land "in" someone, Domino relocated into the water outside the cave, without his clothes. He didn't have time to wonder how he'd done it, as the poor bastard his family had captured could have seconds, or minutes left, or he could already be dead because Domino had been wallowing in the past.

Domino ducked under the cold water. Energy rushed into him as it'd always done. He grinned in relief; he'd been worried that losing his physical body would change his siren response. Apart from the translocation thing, he looked the same, but he had more energy and all of his digits. He'd been ashamed of his marks before, had hidden them. Now he considered them a sign of strength, of defiance.

Domino pulled himself down to the cave entrance with long, powerful strokes. A glow of light and close harmonies distorted by the water proved he'd been right. His head broke the surface without a ripple.

The naked man chained, spread-eagled on the sloping rock didn't move, thralled by the dozen naked women around him. Most would have taken his seed in the last few days. A month ago, the sight of his aunt, his mother and the rest would have had Domino turning tail and swimming for his life, but now he held all the cards.

It looked as though the climax of the ceremony had arrived. Aunt Tethys, still singing, reached for the rock that hid the ceremonial knife.

Domino walked up the slope. The first one to see him, his half-sister, Sonata, screamed and pointed.

Her fear warmed him. Yes, he could do this, enjoy this, but he'd put his own stamp on revenge rather than copying Arioch's, big, bold style. Ace must have had a terrible time cleaning up the mess in the Scibetta den.

"Keep singing; there's strength in numbers," Tethys blurted before increasing her volume.

Domino winced as he carried on wading out of the water. "You really do need to practice more; that's terrible. Please stop."

The sound cut off. He smiled as many of the women grabbed their throats.

Holding the knife, Tethys turned, brandished it.

"I heard you were dead."

"Oh, I am. Well, my body is anyway. The legend that male sirens who use their voices die young is quite true."

His mother lifted a shaking hand, then put it down as if frightened to touch him. She'd never bothered before. "You're a... a... zombie?"

"Mother, dearest, did you think that Orcus had branched out into necromancy? Does the thought make you happy or sad?" He turned to the other sirens present. "Would you all still ride a dead cock if you thought it'd help you become the mother of the ruler of the world? Because that's pretty revolting even for you lot."

His mother glanced at her sister. "Would it still work? I

thought it was releasing the sire's soul that quickened pregnancies? His soul looks like it's pretty much–"

Domino tutted. "Mother, mother, mother. And here was me thinking you were merely a beaten down follower, someone too scared to stand up to her overbearing sibling, but you're just as black as the others."

One of his mother's cousins spoke up, head held high. "We're sirens; we are what we've always been."

Domino gave a dramatic sigh, thoroughly enjoying himself. "Have any of you heard of the new supernatural council guidelines? Is this guy sanctioned by them?"

Tethys snorted in disgust. "There is a waiting list and we wouldn't get a choice. Have you any idea of the average intelligence and attractiveness of condemned prisoners? If we just used whatever the council graciously deemed to give us, sirens would degenerate into ugly imbeciles in a few generations."

"So this poor bastard is?" he asked.

"An Icelandic fisherman. Took me and Sonata a day to tow him back after we tipped him off his boat." The pride in her voice made his determination grow.

"Cousin Sharell, nice to know you're getting enough exercise. Pre-pregnancy plan I take it?"

"With the rumors of your demise, we thought it was time to get on with life, but if you're back, we can let him go and you can take his place."

"What's his name?"

The women looked at each other in bewilderment.

"Hey, what's your name?"

The man's eyes flickered open. "Johann. What the fuck is–"

"Sleep, forget," Domino ordered, then he wobbled his head from side to side as if considering. "How about if I just send Johann home," he waved his hand and the naked man vanished. "and we discuss it?"

"What are you?" Tethys growled, brandishing the knife.

"I'm still Domino, Auntie, but I've had a bit of a tune-up."

The urge to frighten, to make these cocky women regret what they'd done, surged through him. His head itched, then stung.

Sonata cried out, "Demon!" pointing at him.

He lifted his hands. Sure enough, horns poked through his hair. He brushed his fingers up them, wondering how big they were. They were sensitive, not what he'd expected. When he touched the tip of the right hand one, a thrill shot straight to his cock. He closed his eyes, stroked it again. *Oh fuck, that felt–*

A splash was all the warning he got that Tethys was lunging for him.

"Stop!" he called out, and she did the most fantastic inelegant belly flop. Floating face down, bubbles broke on either side of her face. He bet her belly glowed scarlet from the impact with the water.

"Mother, actually I'm going to stop calling you that. Mothers care about their children. Aria, come fish your sister out before she drowns. I haven't finished with her yet."

Tethys remained as stiff as a surfboard as Aria pulled her from the water. She'd probably be more useful like that than in her normal form.

"Now, what to do..." Domino tapped his finger against his lip. "Perhaps you can help me out. You see, just as I expired at the hands of Orcus, —thanks for that by the way, it wasn't pleasant— I was offered a deal by a vengeance demon. As you can see, I grabbed it with both horns." He grinned, pointing at his head. "Do you get it? Horns?"

Stony faces met his eyes. "Huh. Tough audience. Well, the boss likes inventive revenge." He looked around. "Anyone? Well, there's the old 'pillars of salt' thing, but that's been done to death, as has the seafoam option. It needs to be apt, unpleasant, and frankly fucking funny. Which kinda cuts out killing you all on the spot, although that would be neat. Surfboards? Auntie inspired that idea. Lobsters in a restaurant? I hear they get boiled alive. I can just picture you all trying to hide behind each other while humans pick out dinner." His kin grabbed at each other, but there was no begging, not yet. He clearly wasn't hitting the mark.

An idea popped into his head. He grinned. Perfect.

"Now, before we get on with it, can anyone tell me my father's name?" The women stared back, most with fear, all with hate. "First one to tell me gets to pass the suffering she's about to receive onto the woman next to her."

All of them, except Tethys, blurted out a name, every one different.

He tutted. "Naughty girls. Didn't anyone ever tell you not to lie?" He made a spanking motion with his hand and all of them grabbed for their backsides. "The next liar gets transported to the Sahara."

"Joel Rankin," a voice at the back said. Domino crooked a finger and a siren who was surprisingly showing her advancing age a little stepped forward.

"Gran, how not nice to see you again. How are you so sure that was his name?"

"I keep the genetic register for the sorority. Every sorority has one, and we share information."

A brief thought produced a hard drive in his hand. Technology was a wonderful thing.

"I choose Tethys."

"What?" Domino frowned.

"I chose Tethys to receive my pain," the elderly woman ground out.

Domino grinned. "Oh, I lied about that. Demon now, remember? Now, who would like to go first?"

Twenty naked women all trying to get in a tunnel only wide enough for two was a fitting start.

CHAPTER TWENTY-EIGHT

With his family dealt with, Domino concentrated, pictured Jude, his easy smile, the way his eyes twinkled with mischief when he called him Salty. What he hadn't imagined was drifting calypso music, warmth, the scent of the sea, and laughter. Somehow, he'd pictured him on some grimy city street hunting down some evil bounty.

Domino stood at the edge of a beautiful white sand beach, beneath waving palm trees. A group of fit men and dogs played in the surf. But he only had eyes for the figure sitting on the beach a good twenty feet from anyone else.

The scene was serene, dreamlike. Domino didn't belong. Putting his hand on the tree trunk next to him, it felt soft, like spongy fabric. The bark was visible through his hand. *So this is how invisibility works; you just don't want to be seen.*

Smooth tanned skin. Nothing remained on Jude's back to tell of his ordeal, no burns, no bruises. It didn't mean his mind wasn't scarred, then again, it didn't mean it was either.

What right do I have to disturb him? Yes, he looks sad, but he could just be recovering from a heavy night of having fun. He survived the loss of his family, twice; he'll survive losing me. I don't even know what or who I am yet, not really. I've got no right to impose on him.

Domino knew he should leave, and yet he lingered, unable to form the thought that would take him back to the cell-like room where he'd woken up. He didn't want to be there, he wanted to be here, in this wonderful, fantasy-like place. But vengeance demons brought pain; at best a sense of completion for those wronged; if they even knew the revenge had happened. The purpose of his existence was to hurt the perpetrator, not make the victim happy.

People came and went, but Jude still sat on the beach, staring out to sea, resisting every interaction with people who approached him. Most tried to engage him in conversation, but after a few non-committal answers, they left him to brood or nurse his hangover.

The sun was sinking into the sea by the time a small blond man wearing baggy board shorts sat beside Jude without saying a word. The urge to rip the guy away, throw him far out to sea filled Domino as Jude's hand absently played with the guy's collar-length, sun-bleached hair. The blond head leaned against Jude's tanned, muscled shoulder.

Domino knew he should leave Jude to his new life, his new lover. *Fuck, who am I kidding? A one-way blow job does not a lover make, and that's all we had.*

"They're not together if that's what you're wondering."

Domino spun around, nearly losing his footing.

A tall, elegantly dressed man leaned up against a tree a few feet away. "Judging from the mark on your face and the way you're making cow eyes at the cat, you must be Domino. I do hope you haven't come to cheer him up. Your funeral was very touching. His regret and guilt have been feeding me for the last two months."

"You can see me?"

The corner of his mouth twitched. "Dad's slipping if he's recruiting idiots."

"Arioch's your father?" Domino said, even though he knew it sounded stupid.

"Give the shiny new demon a prize. I'm Silas. Dad performed some very naughty revenge on a vampire. I'm the resulting cuckoo in the nest. Unfortunately, I didn't get any of the perks you clearly have."

"I'm sorry?"

Silas snorted. "No, you're not. I got that bit at least." He indicated Jude. "He is though. I'm surprised you can't feel it even at this distance. Guy's damn good at wallowing."

Domino swallowed, dying to ask the question but this was a complete stranger.

"I can't stand the suspense, so spit it out," Silas drawled. "I was getting bored with cat for dinner every night anyway. If it lasts much longer, I'll be getting hairballs, and in this suit?" He waved a hand down his body.

Domino tilted his head so he could look up at the taller man through his hair. It'd always worked with Jude.

"Cute. I think you could give Ezra a run for his money."

"So... I can, you know, with someone who isn't... like me?"

An eyebrow rose. "Like you?"

"You're really going to make me say it, aren't you? Jude's alive. I'm not. Funeral, remember?"

Silas tried to hide his smirk by looking down; he didn't succeed. "He's really taken on too much this time. How long has it been for you since you died?"

"Two days."

This time, Silas didn't bother hiding his deep, rolling chuckle. "He's had you sitting in limbo for two months?

That's fucking rich, but I guess I can give dear old Dad a hand with a quick induction. He did give me Ezra after all.

"One, you're only non-corporeal when you want to be. Two, you can live anywhere you want, be with anyone you want as long as you don't piss off the boss. Three, if he gives you a job, do it. Doing extra will make him happy, and you'll get a ping when you're near someone who ticks the 'justified revenge' box. You don't always have to go big and spectacular, although those ones get the highest of high fives. But if that isn't your thing, many small acts of revenge make the world go around. Think of it as snacking rather than banquets. Oh, and don't forget to log your work. You do not want to find out what Arioch does to slackers."

There were a lot of people in the world, a lot of reasons for revenge. So far, he knew of one failed vengeance demon, Alastor, plus Arioch and himself. The task was daunting.

"How many of us are there?"

"I'm not part of the 'us,' remember? You lot aren't like blood or sex demons; you aren't born, you're created by an agreement, literally selling your soul to the devil, or dear old dad in my case. The base soul can be anything, another demon, human, shifter, elemental, or... you, whatever pigeonhole you fit into. Although why you, I have no idea."

"He thinks I'm inventive."

"And why does he think that?"

Domino shrugged. "I just came from my mother's place. I erm–" He leaned in and whispered in Silas' ear.

The slap on his shoulder sent Domino stumbling. "I think I like you after all. Now go give that cat something different to brood about."

Domino looked back at Jude, swallowed.

"Well, go on. What's he going to do, hiss at you? Just conjure up a ball of string; he'll be eating out of your hand in no time." Still chuckling, Silas turned, took a few steps, stuck his fingers in his mouth, and whistled so loudly Domino winced.

The blond man leaning on Jude's shoulder transformed into a blond terrier and shot past Domino after Silas.

The beach looked so exposed, just walking out there, for anyone to see, sent old anxiety bubbling that people would stare at his marks. *I could make them vanish.* Jude had said that the marks didn't bother him, that he even liked them, so who would Domino be changing them for? The sensibilities of bigots?

He remembered the idiot on the road. Revenge on him had been fun, until his conscience kicked in, and Domino hadn't even been a revenge demon back then. He searched his feelings for the concern, the regret he'd felt, didn't find it. That guy had deserved everything he'd gotten. Bigotry was a choice in this day and age, and Domino could do a lot to bring the die-hard idiots down one by one.

I could exact immediate revenge on anyone who stares or comments. Giving them a damn big wart on their nose, or somewhere more embarrassing would be very satisfying.

The steel band music drifting from further down the beach turned into Bob Marley's 'Three Little Birds,' the song he'd sung to settle Jude's nightmare.

The music and the man called to him as it had that night in the van, and Domino found himself walking towards Jude, singing the gentle refrain. Even when he sat beside him, Jude didn't look sideways until the track ended.

As if preparing himself for a horrible surprise, Jude screwed up his eyes, turned his head a fraction, then opened one eye. The other swiftly followed.

"You're not Del."

Domino fought not to get lost in those dark eyes. "No, should I be?"

"The last time you sang that song, it brought me here, and I made my peace with Del. She was sitting right where you are."

"It's a lovely spot. I can see why you love it."

"So, I guess my fucked-up subconscious is telling me to do the same with you."

"Do what?"

"Move on, look forward not back."

Domino stayed silent, letting Jude work through his thoughts. If the shifter was over him there was nothing he could do.

"I can see through you."

"That's because I'm here for you, not anyone else."

Jude nodded; lips pressed together. "I wanted to bring you here, you know, at the end. I couldn't think of any other view you'd like more than this to be your last."

Jude rubbed the back of his neck. "Crap, this is hard, even though I'm talking to myself. Just get on with it, Moreno." Jude blew out a breath then turned to Domino again.

"I knew you were dying, you told me enough times, but I just... I couldn't let go without taking that one stupid chance even though that fucker had every alarm bell possible ringing in my head." Eyes now glassy, Jude carried on. "I'm sorry for that, sorrier than you'll ever know but I did bring you here, afterwards. I sat in the sea splashing you like I was fucking demented. I didn't let you go for hours, just in case you were doing some special siren reset thing." He chuckled, wiping at his eye. "Funeral was pretty fucking fantastic though. We did a burning Viking longboat thing just in case your family ever..." he trailed off.

"I wish I'd seen it." The regret rolling off Jude buzzed in his veins, but it was a sweet and sour meal. Domino had never been loved this much before, but it also hurt that Jude was in pain. He bet Silas was lapping this up.

They sat, Jude staring out at the sea, Domino committing every inch of Jude to memory.

Domino knew he should leave, let Jude continue thinking he was nothing but a figment of his imagination. The shifter was moving on, coming to terms with what had happened. Domino didn't move.

Jude sighed, turned to him again. "So, are things ok where you are? Del said you weren't with her."

"I'm not, but it's looking pretty damn good from where I'm sitting." Domino couldn't take his eyes off Jude's lips as he spoke.

Jude snorted. "You haven't changed, Salty, still trying to get in my shorts."

Domino closed his eyes, willed a coin into his hand, flipped it. As it'd done by the freezing river, it came up heads.

Stay.

"I've changed a bit," he said, willed his horns into being and tapped his head.

Jude's gaze rose to his head, his mouth opened and closed again.

"They're a present from Arioch. He, erm–"

Jude's hand shook as it rose. The featherlight touch on his horn sent a shot of pleasure straight down Domino's spine to his cock. He groaned, and Jude pulled his hand back as if burned.

"Fuck, did I hurt–"

Domino pushed Jude down on his back, straddled him.

"Don't touch the horns if you don't intend to follow

through. Believe me, you don't want to leave me hanging. I'll go all demony on you."

Jude gaped, swallowed. Domino itched to lick, to nibble his throat.

"You're really here."

Domino ground his butt against Jude's groin. "If I'm not, you've got a hell of a dirty imagination."

"You were dead."

"Yep, as a doornail. I'm not exactly sure what I am now, but I've got these back." He spread his hands, displaying his intact fingers and thumb. "Seawater still gives me a buzz, my voice works as good as ever, plus I have these seriously cute horns. Might even be able to manage a forked tail if I really try."

A smile crept over Jude's face. "You sound like a real handful."

"Do you want to find out?" *Say yes, fuck, say yes.*

"Well, I do seem to remember saying that after you were all better I'd fuck your brains out. Do you feel all better, Salty?"

"Where are you staying?"

Domino pulled the image from Jude's head, and they bounced onto the bed.

Jude didn't twitch. "That... That could be useful. Are you going to make me call you awesome before you take me anywhere?"

Domino leaned down, caged Jude's head with his arms. He wanted this perfect moment to last forever.

"Tell me you're sure because dumping a vengeance demon would probably be a bad idea."

Fingers and thumbs closed around both his horns, massaged.

"Oh fuck, that's–" he groaned before Jude used his horns to pull Domino down.

The kiss was slow, like an unstoppable rising tide. Everything vanished, past, future, in the wake of the need to get as close to Jude as possible. Jude abandoned Domino's lips to mouth at his jaw. Tilting his chin up, Domino got exactly what he wanted, Jude's rough tongue and lips on his throat, his pulse point. A palm pressed against his cock, he groaned, tilting up.

Flipping Domino to his back, Jude sat on his heels, pulling at Domino's stubborn jeans. With a thought, Domino was naked.

"Show off." Jude grinned. "Gonna do me too?"

Domino's gaze dropped to the cock outlined by the fabric of Jude's tight swim shorts. Small bumps decorated the area behind the head and at the base. The last time he'd seen it, he'd chickened out, now, anticipation prickled as he wondered how much it would hurt.

"The spines won't do any real damage, but most guys, hell everyone except incubi and a few extreme masochists, run a mile. You could always top." Jude radiated resignation, disappointment.

Domino traced his fingers just inside the waistband of Jude's shorts. "I'm not most guys; I don't think I ever was," he said and pulled Jude's underwear down, letting his cock free.

He'd felt Jude's cock in the shower at Orcus', the roughness near the head and base, but it hadn't prepared him for how beautiful it was. Thick, not overly long, and dark with blood. The spines were no more than three or four millimeters long. He couldn't help imagining them inside him, scratching, stimulating, like Jude's rough tongue. *Fuck, what would that feel like against my prostate?*

Reaching out a finger, he flinched as the cock twitched, then laughed. "Fuck, I feel like a damn virgin."

"Well, you are unless you've been a naughty demon, and even if you have, I bet you've never had anything like this."

"No, there's been no one else. You?" Domino immediately regretted asking the question as Jude winced.

"Angry fuck with Ezra, and I think he thralled me into it. Felt good though, I don't regret it. No revenge, ok? He is what he is."

Domino wondered if everyone would assume he was constantly "on duty" from now on. Thinking about it, a little respect would be fucking wonderful.

His gaze flicked up to Jude's face, and he smirked. "No promises. You fed him, so it's only right I get a snack too."

Wanting to see his expression, Domino reached out blindly and closed his thumb and forefinger around Jude's erection under the head. Stroking down, it felt similar to running over three- or four-day stubble. He reversed direction; the spines scraped, folded back. Jude gasped, shuddered. His eyes closed, basking.

Domino smiled. "Good?"

"You have no idea," Jude murmured.

Hard muscle, a scattering of dark hair, breathing hard with lust, *lust for me.* Domino felt like he'd been underwater for too long, breathless, desperate for air but not wanting to leave the encompassing water.

"Holy Poseidon, you're beautiful."

Jude laughed. "Right back at you, Salty." The pads of his fingers tickled over Domino's ribs making him shiver.

The smile dropped from Jude's face as he grasped his cock. Pushing it down, he rubbed the head against Domino's shaft. They moaned at the same time. The scrape against his tender skin was like nothing else, and his hole clenched at the thought of that inside him.

With a thought, he removed Jude's shorts. Rising up, he positioned Jude's cock at his entrance, took a deep breath, tried to think "relaxed" even though he was so horny he almost vibrated with it.

A palm landed on his thigh, rubbing, reassuring. "You ready?"

Letting out a little of his power, Domino replied, "Yeah."

Jude chuckled. "Not trying to influence me, are you?"

"Fuck yeah, I am."

Jude grabbed Domino's cock, squeezed to the point of pain. His breath hitched at the pressure.

"Who's in charge here?" Jude's voice shone with amusement.

"I hate you." Domino's comment produced a chuckle.

"You're going to hate me a hell of a lot more by the time I'm finished with you. Shuffle forward, I want to feel your hole."

Jude seemed determined to do things at his pace, no matter what Domino said or did. It was perfect.

The cat licked his finger, wiggled his eyebrows.

"And I thought I was meant to be the one who–" Domino forgot what he was going to say as Jude's finger tapped on his hole then pushed inside. In, out, in, out, a little deeper each time. Then Jude pressed against his prostate.

He ground down, then gasped, jerked, as the touch sharpened, causing an electric spark of sensation.

Jude froze. "Not good? Because that's what–"

"No, no, I'm sorry; it was almost too good," Domino

blurted, words falling over each other as they fought to escape before Jude backed off.

Jude's broad grin had Domino scowling.

"I like hearing your voice, love making you lose control."

Domino returned the smile. "Then you'd better let me get on with it, hadn't you?" He pushed back onto Jude's finger. "I'm not as delicate as you think I am, not anymore."

"Your wish is my command."

Domino wasn't quite sure about Jude's tone; he sounded positively evil, but this was an experience he wouldn't miss for the world.

Jude pushed in another finger. It burned, but it felt so good to have this physical connection, to be able to do something for Jude, with Jude.

"Still good?"

Domino gritted his teeth. "Stop asking that. Believe me, I'll let you know if I don't like something. If you find yourself naked on top of Everest, you'll know you've pissed me off."

"If that's meant to frighten me, forget it. I've still got my pet air elemental."

With a thought, he fastened Jude's wrists above his head in handcuffs.

Jude frowned, pulled. The cuffs rattled, and Jude looked up. "And this is ok, how?"

Domino grinned. "Revenge for teasing me in that diner, Daddy."

"That was funny," Jude deadpanned.

"That was humiliating, and you know it. And now I'm going to use your unwilling body to my heart's content."

"Oh no. Someone save me." Jude cocked his head as if listening. "I don't think anyone heard me. Such a shame."

Domino stayed still.

Jude rattled the cuffs. "Well, on with the revenge then. I haven't got–"

Rising up, Domino positioned Jude's shaft at his entrance. Holding Jude's gaze, he sank down until his butt rested on Jude's balls. Closing his eyes, he concentrated on the sensation as he lifted back up. With other people he'd felt full, stretched, but with Jude, he could feel the contact, the rough sensation deep inside. He stopped moving when only the head remained inside.

"If that doesn't feel good, I can always stop," Domino said.

Jude thrust up, burying himself inside again and again.

The cuffs clanked and Domino removed them with a thought. Domino's back hit the bed. He looked up into a wicked smirk.

"My turn." Jude balanced himself on his forearm beside Domino's bicep.

Thrust in, tilt, drag out over his prostate. Domino groaned at the delicious torture that pushed him higher.

Jude's free hand closed around Domino's cock, twisted at the same slow, torturous pace.

He took up all of Domino's senses, every part of his mind, his body, nothing else existed. Each drag across his prostate, each twist on his cock, sent him a little nearer to ending this.

"Ready to come?" Jude's raw voice showed how near he was to exploding himself.

"No, don't stop; don't ever stop," Domino gasped.

Jude closed the few inches of space between their mouths, gave him a hard, possessive kiss. Cock scraping in his hole, hand jerking his dick, then Jude's fingers found one of Domino's horns and twisted.

Domino's vision whited out, nothing but almost painfully intense pleasure.

Hanging in a serene sea of nothingness, a voice drifting closer, pulled him upwards.

"Hey, Salty, you still with me? Come on, open those eyes for me."

A smile curved his lips. "No."

Fingers brushed a strand of hair from his forehead. "Open or I tickle."

Domino cracked his eyes open. Jude stared down at him, a soft smile on his face.

"You're evil."

"I think you'll find you're the demon, not me."

Domino twitched as a tingle ran through him.

"What? Someone walked over your grave, or in your case, swam over it?"

"No, I think–" he fell silent as he searched and followed the sensation to its source.

His eyes flicked open.

"What?" Jude radiated concern.

Domino grinned. "Aunt Tethys just got a bit of a shock."

"And she is?"

"The evil bitch who ruled my sorority."

Jude's eyes narrowed. "What did you do?"

"I turned every one of them into guys–" he held up a finger, "–sterile guys, and implanted them with GPS trackers. Then I sent the app to every other siren sorority. I told them that the last one to be caught could have her body back. I might have lied, just a bit."

Jude's mouth snapped shut, then he laughed out loud and his lips came down on Domino's.

EPILOGUE

It'd been eight months since he'd died, and they were sitting with Ezra's group outside the house they all lived in. Domino still wasn't sure who owned the sprawling property on the rocky "tail" of the island, but it didn't seem to matter. Several of them could afford to buy it outright, and if push came to shove, Domino could probably magic an extra bit of land and put a house on it.

Jude and Domino had their own room, but living with the group suited them both. When one was busy with work, they knew the other wouldn't be lonely. The on-going prank war with the shifter twins made it even better.

Yesterday, they'd found a huge empty cardboard box in their room with "Enjoy, Kitty. Love, Jericho," written on it. The writing was suspiciously ragged for the stoic bear shifter. Jude scowled. Domino had to sit on the bed he was laughing so hard. Jude's revenge sex left Domino gasping and beautifully sore.

It was eight p.m. and the sun had set a few hours ago. Those who needed to eat mundane food had finished their evening meal. Domino ate with Jude, not from any real need, but because it pleased the cat shifter.

Finn, being human, and Jude, whose dislike of the cold had become a running joke, both wore long-sleeved shirts. Domino wasn't cold, and the canine shifters and the two other demons didn't seem to mind the cool winter sea breeze.

"Hey, Finn," Ezra called and twitched his chin up. Finn got up, walked over, and settled on the demon's lap. Ezra wrapped his arms around the slight human, keeping him warm. The canine shifter twins, Gethin and Glyn, shared an indulgent smile.

The love between all the members of the group, the family by choice, warmed Domino's heart. The urge to climb onto Jude's lap in a similar way itched, but he didn't think it'd go down well with Silas, who, as usual, sat at a distance, observing. Domino didn't know how much contact the hybrid demon had with his father. Having Silas report less than demonic behavior to Arioch was always a possibility. As he was still on probation, Domino didn't want to risk losing his horns, and not only because of their place in his and Jude's sexual relationship. One of the cat shifter's favorite techniques was to stroke and suck on Domino's horns until he came, hands-free.

Out of the group, Silas was his least favorite person. Yes, Domino was a full revenge demon to Silas' hybrid ancestry, but Domino spread the pain he caused around, and always to those who deserved it. Silas only seemed to want Ezra's angst. Although the incubus was no angel, he'd suffered more than enough in his life to make up for it.

"So, what's everyone been up to today?" Pixie, the tiny pink-haired fae asked. Information, particularly secrets, provided her energy. This nightly get-together was as much for her sustenance as it was for group bonding. Domino felt included, valued, and apart from being in bed with Jude, he'd find it tough to rank this in his top three activities against swimming and singing.

"I visited my dear stepfather," Silas announced.

Ezra stiffened. Any mention of the vampire incarcerated in the supernatural prison always got this reaction, and Silas loved it. *Bastard.*

Domino got up and plonked himself on Jude's lap. He smiled sweetly at the now scowling hybrid demon.

Finn's lips twitched with a brief smirk. Out of all of them, the surprise had been how well he got on with the young human. Although, the huge changes in both their lives did produce a bond the others couldn't possibly understand.

"He still isn't sorry about what he did to you, but he does regret getting caught." Silas' relaxed statement had everyone tensing, ruining the atmosphere Domino had been enjoying so much.

"Milo and I tracked down two more procurers today," Jude announced, clearly feeling the need for a little revenge too. "They were from your old clan, Silas. And surprisingly happy to see me when I turned up to collect them. No idea why." As he spoke, Jude gently ran a talon down Domino's back. He took the not so subtle hint.

"I know because I got there before you."

The shifter twins sat forward, eyes bright. "What did you do to them?" Gethin, the more impulsive of the dark-haired, dark-eyed, muscled pair said. Domino pictured him in his fur form, ears pricked, tail wagging, eager for juicy details.

Domino's work wasn't an entertainment for others. Perhaps he could do something about that, as well as the hybrid demon's unnecessary torture of Ezra.

Looking right at Silas, he said, "I had them gnaw the other's balls off. Slowly. There was surprisingly little blood, but they did gag quite a–"

Gethin bolted from his seat. The sound of him noisily throwing up rent the air.

"So many tears. The begging was particularly impressive mainly because the second one had a lot of trouble. The other guys' balls had almost crawled right back up inside. He had to pop his fangs out, hunt around, bit like a walrus."

"I'll erm..." Glyn got up, headed in his brother's direction.

"Inventive," Jude commented. "They did look a little pale."

"Then I made them fry their own balls and eat them." That provided the breaking point for Milo, Silas, and Finn.

With his lap now empty, Ezra looked at Domino. "I'm glad they suffered, but next time, please leave the details out if you're ripping off balls. It's going to be damn difficult for me to get a meal tonight." The incubus stood up.

"Sorry?" Domino offered.

Ezra shook his head. "No, you're not. Demon too, remember?" He wandered off in search of his bedmates.

Domino turned his attention to the only remaining member of the group apart from Jude. "And after that I–"

"I was around for the Christians versus the lions," Pixie said. "I don't shock easy, even if I believe what you said, which I'm not sure I do. I don't think anyone cruel enough to do that would be as soppy as you too are together."

"It's rude to interrupt, even if you are thousands of years older than me. Ever heard of compartmentalization? But to answer your question, anyone can love. Good, bad, and ugly people all love.

"Those two procurers were as bad as they come, but they loved each other deeply, which made the revenge even sweeter. But all this talk of unusual love reminds me of what I was about to say before you interrupted. After I got home, I put hair removal cream in Jericho's body wash. He should be getting up right about–"

Pixie swore and left the patio at a run.

Jude's rich chuckle rang out and Domino joined in. The cat shifter's laughter died, and he traced the power mark on Domino's face with a finger. It didn't bother Domino in the least, another thing that had changed in the last year.

"You know, I used to dream about hearing you laugh. It's better than I ever imagined."

Domino snuggled down against him, listening to the regular thump of his heart. It was better than any music Domino could play. "Getting soppy in your old age, Moreno?"

Jude tightened his grip.

At first, Domino thought he was imagining things, but no, the vibration under his ear grew. Jude purred every now and again in his fur form. It only happened when Jude shifted after sex and Domino petted him, played with his fur until they both fell asleep. Jude had never made that noise in human form.

Without moving, he asked, "You purring, Judah?"

A kiss pressed to his hair. "Yeah, Salty, I guess I am."

"Does it mean anything?"

The arms tightened around him and another kiss pressed to his hair. Domino smiled. Actions always did speak louder than words.

Concentrating, Domino started to purr too.

The End

If you need more of Ezra and friends, dive into the Incubus series!

THE GRIM AND SINISTER DELIGHTS SERIES

mybook.to/GrimSinDelights

Naked Ambition by Lisa Henry
With A Twist by Kate Sherwood
Bound by Sean Azinsalt
True Mate's Kiss by Rorie Kage
The Elves and the Bondage Daddy by JP Sayle
Pied Piper by Emma Jaye
The Devil Told You by Alexis Jane
Crimson Painted Snow by Brea Alepou
Shards of Ice by R. Phoenix
Beauty Bound by Megs Pritchard
False Feathers by Adara Wolf
The Reijorling by Leona Windwalker
Consequences of Crying by Abigail Kade
A Merman's Tail by M.D. Gregory
The Black Sea by Dora Esquivel

ABOUT THE AUTHOR

Emma was destined to be a little quirky after being born as an unexpected twin in Hungry Bottom (Yes, it's a real place).

Known as the Queen of Angst because she loves putting damaged, often sweet and funny characters through hell before letting them have a HFN or HEA ending.

She blames her rebellious muse (who looks like Chris from the Paint Series) for the erotic aspects tickling the angst and the humour climbing into bed with the erotic.

When not writing or reading in leafy Sussex, England, she herds Birman cats and sons; both groups argue that there are too many of the other sort.

For free books and special offers, join my newsletter http://bit.ly/EmmaJayeNews

To stalk me everywhere linktr.ee/EmmaJaye

ALSO BY EMMA JAYE

DeMMonica

Raw, emotional angst-ridden m/m stories set in the same paranormal world

Piped Piper (Grim and Sinister Delights collection)

IMPrisoned

Incubus series

Lust is Life for an Incubus

Series includes scorching man-on-man scenes, including dubious consent, torture, orgies, plus broken and healed hearts

Incubus Seduction

Incubus Possession

Incubus Pain

Incubus Trial

Incubus Freedom

Incubus Revived

Incubus box set (I to VI)

Vascellum Revenge

Lies

If contemporary m/m dark romance, with slavery, kidnap,

dubcon, noncon, mental health issues, and packing angst like never before is your thing, you'll love the Lies Series.

Sweating Lies

Splitting Lies

Tooth fairy Lies

Paint

Contemporary m/m dark romance

Contemporary m/m dark romance. Hurt/Comfort with mental health issues. Angst with a capital A, plus heart and irrepressible damaged snarky characters who go through hell.

Some violence, but not between couples.

Paint 1: Optical Illusion

Paint 2: Blank Canvas

Paint 3: Invisible Ink

Paint 3.5 Doctor's Orders

Malthusia

Queer science fiction/genetic engineering

Fate

Family

Printed in Great Britain
by Amazon

13877345R00178